ALSO BY DAN FREY

The Retreat

THE FUTURE IS YOURS

THE
FUTURE
IS
YOURS

A NOVEL

DAN FREY

NEW YORK

Copyright © 2021 by Moon Media, Inc.

Published in the United States by Del Rey, an imprint of Random House, a division of Penguin Random House LLC, New York.

DEL REY is a registered trademark and the CIRCLE colophon is a trademark of Penguin Random House LLC.

Library of Congress Cataloging-in-Publication Data
Names: Frey, Dan, author.
Title: The future is yours / Dan Frey.
Description: New York : Del Rey, [2021]
Identifiers: LCCN 2020024418 (print) | LCCN 2020024419 (ebook) | ISBN 9780593158210 (hardcover ; acid-free paper) | ISBN 9780593158227 (ebook)
Subjects: GSAFD: Science fiction. | Suspense fiction.
Classification: LCC PS3606.R4864 F88 2021 (print) | LCC PS3606.R4864 (ebook) | DDC 813/.6—dc23
LC record available at https://lccn.loc.gov/2020024418
LC ebook record available at https://lccn.loc.gov/2020024419

Printed in the United States of America on acid-free paper

randomhousebooks.com

9 8 7 6 5 4 3 2 1

First Edition

Book design by Elizabeth A. D. Eno

For Casey.
My future is yours.

THE FUTURE IS YOURS

CHAPTER 1

EMAIL

From: Ben Boyce
To: Ben Boyce, Adhvan Chaudry

My Dudes,

IT WORKS! Seriously. You did it.

This is so weird—I'm sending this on Feb 28, 2022, knowing that I'll receive it (already DID receive it) on Feb 28, 2021. Pretty trippy, right?

So listen up, Past Ben . . . First of all, high-five! You were right to believe this whole time—in yourself, in Adhi, in all of it. Your dream of becoming the first Black CEO to launch a billion-dollar company is gonna come true . . . and I can say that with certainty, because for me, IT ALREADY DID.

And Adhi. Bro. You're the brilliance that makes it possible. I always said you'd do something to change the world and I was right. It's crazy—you're sitting across the room as I write this, but I still remember your face the day you read it. Pick up your jaw and keep reading.

Now, I know you're both about to flip out and start using the Prototype to look up everything you can, so lemme just save you a little suspense.

1: Stanford's season is gonna be terrible, so just detach

yourselves from that shitshow right away and save yourselves the heartache.

2: Stock tips–wise, yeah, of course, you COULD get
into some foolproof investments today. But I promise
you'll be better off not mucking around with all that,
cause the main thing you gotta do is invest in your motherfuckin SELVES.

I just wanna take this moment to say: everything is
gonna be fine. The Prototype works (obviously). And
whatever happens, don't trip. Not about money or respect
or prestige, any of it. Just pop that cork and enjoy the best
shitty champagne of your life, I remember it well. From
here on out—trust the process, enjoy the ride, and most
of all, stick together.

Sincerely and eternally your friend,
Ben from the future

EXCERPT FROM TRANSCRIPT OF CONGRESSIONAL HEARING — DECEMBER 1, 2021

SEN. GREG WALDEN (D-OR): The Committees on the Judiciary and
Commerce, Science, and Technology will come to order. We welcome
everyone to today's hearing on the new commercial venture known as
"The Future," and the potential legal, ethical, and policy ramifications
of its technology.

Though not unprecedented, this hearing is a unique opportunity to
anticipate and address serious social consequences of a new consumer
technology. This legislative body has a history of playing distant catch-
up to new innovation, as evidenced by last year's hearings about social
media and privacy issues. The hope is that we can be ahead of the
curve—especially in light of the recent whistleblower leak, which seems
to suggest that this technology may pose an existential threat to our
nation and our people.

BOYCE: Mr. Chairman, I object to characterizing it as—

SEN. GREG WALDEN (D-OR): You have not been invited to speak yet, Mr. Boyce. And regardless of your objections, we have seen data, from your own company, which many reputable scientists interpret to mean that we are on a course toward the obliteration of civilization as we know it, on a time horizon of less than two years. Now if that's not an existential threat—

BOYCE: I just think it's irresponsible to call it that, without proper consideration of all the factors.

SEN. GREG WALDEN (D-OR): Do not lecture me on *irresponsible*, Mr. Boyce. And if you will not adhere to parliamentary rules of decorum, you will be charged with Contempt. Understood?

BOYCE: . . . Understood.

SEN. GREG WALDEN (D-OR): Good. Now, the members of this body have called two witnesses, the founders of the company called The Future: Mr. Benjamin Boyce and Mr. Adhvan Chaudry. However, let the record show, at the time of this hearing, only Mr. Boyce has appeared before the committee. Mr. Boyce, can you answer for the absence of your colleague?

BOYCE: No, I cannot. And I'm worried. If Adhi's not here, clearly something is wrong, and it would be best if we can adjourn for now.

SEN. GREG WALDEN (D-OR): This is not a meeting held at your convenience. You are answering a subpoena before forty-four members of Congress. Since one of you has failed to appear, a warrant will be issued for the arrest of Mr. Chaudry, and he will be charged with Contempt of Congress. Now, if you wish to avoid similar charges, are you prepared to proceed with the hearing?

BOYCE: . . . Yes, sir. I would just like the record to reflect my request for postponement.

SEN. GREG WALDEN (D-OR): Duly noted, and we can all hope that at some point today, your co-founder will deign to join us. He is certainly earning his reputation for intellectual hubris.

BOYCE: I just want to point out, it's not really hubris if it's earned, is it? No offense or anything, but Adhi is smarter than anyone in this room.

SEN. GREG WALDEN (D-OR): That may be the case, Mr. Boyce. But this body is convened because trusting people who are ostensibly "smarter" has gotten us in quite a bit of trouble in the past. No doubt the data scientists at Cambridge Analytica were very proud of their intelligence, as were the eugenicists of a century ago.

BOYCE: Come on, is that really a fair comparison?

SEN. GREG WALDEN (D-OR): We are dealing with a technology that apparently has the potential to end the world as we know it. So excuse me if my comparisons offend, but it is well worth discussing how Mr. Chaudry's intelligence has created problems in the past.

ADHVAN CHAUDRY'S COLLEGE ADMISSIONS ESSAY

Submitted January 12, 2012, to Stanford University

Education is bullshit.

I know it may be ill advised to say so in this particular forum, but I hope that Stanford recognizes rigor and rewards honesty. Allow me to explain how I reached this particular conclusion.

My parents came to this country shortly before I was born. They were seeking to escape the caste system of India. It had been formally abolished in 1950, but was, for practical purposes, still firmly in place twenty years ago. Since my parents were Shudras (poor laborers), they never had any hope of becoming Rajanyas (rich merchants). But they believed in America they could.

When they arrived in San Francisco, they tried their best. But they were frustrated to discover it is just as impossible to move up in the world here. Not only that, they learned that the Indian system had been preferable in a way—because no Shudra is ever made to feel *guilty* about being poor. It is their lot in life. But in America, poverty equates to failure. It is a source of deep and abiding shame.

So they pinned their hopes on me. They sacrificed and worked long hours. They instilled the value of hard work in the hope that I would go to a great college and win for myself a job better than either of them had the privilege of having. They saw education as the way out.

However, from my experience in the academic world so far, I have seen that it is all a facade. A rigged game. A system of smoke and mirrors, to separate the wheat from the chaff, and perpetuate an oligarchic system that rewards privilege generation after generation, just as much as the caste system did. At the "prestigious" prep school that I attend (on a full academic scholarship), the vast majority of my fellow students are from wealthy families. And cheating is rampant among my peers. Most parents are complicit in a system that values perfect grades, test scores, and a robust résumé of activities . . . but does not give a damn about integrity.

We are admonished to be scholars and gentlemen "at all times," and students are threatened with expulsion for their conduct on the weekend. Of course, when our school president's son (one of my classmates) got so drunk at a school basketball game that he stumbled onto the court and vomited on the foul line, he was merely given detention, and the incident was swept under the rug.

With all this said, you are probably wondering—does this kid even want to attend Stanford? And the answer for me is unequivocally yes.

I know that my low opinion of education will always sound like an excuse, unless it is backed up with experience. I know my earning potential will be bolstered by the diplomas, even if they don't mean a thing. I intend to get the best schooling I can get, all the way through a PhD, so I can assert with utter confidence that education, top to bottom, is total fucking bullshit.

EXCERPT FROM CONGRESSIONAL HEARING—DECEMBER 1, 2021

REP. CORINNE SOTHEBY (R-NE): Mr. Boyce, I'd like to discuss the origins of your connection to Mr. Chaudry. I understand that you met in college.

BOYCE: Yeah, that's right. Freshman year. Well, Adhi was actually a year older than everyone, but he still had to come in as a freshman. He'd been rejected by Stanford his first time applying, believe it or not. Even though he had perfect grades, SATs, all of it, they turned him down. Because of his essay, supposedly. Which really just means, he didn't know how to play the game, how to tell people what they want to hear.

So he did a year at a junior college, somewhere in the East Bay, and then he applied again. And since he was out there publishing math papers as a freshman at a JC, Stanford saw they'd missed out on something, and they let him in the next fall. He was not happy about having to take all his core requirements again, or being a year older than everyone else. But under all the bitching, I could tell, he was happy to be at Stanford. And so was I.

That's when we met. Randomly assigned to the same dorm. And right away, first day, we hit it off.

REP. CORINNE SOTHEBY (R-NE): Were you immediately interested in a professional partnership with Mr. Chaudry?

BOYCE: When I was eighteen? I wasn't interested in professional *anything*.

REP. CORINNE SOTHEBY (R-NE): It's just, the two of you seem like rather unlikely friends.

BOYCE: You've never been friends with anyone different than you? Personally, I liked that Adhi was quiet. These days we'd probably say "on the spectrum." Which is why he'd never really connected with anyone before.

But I liked him right away. Even though not everybody saw it, I thought he was funny as hell. Since he wasn't really the talkative type, we'd be at our computers, same dorm room, chatting over IM for *hours* while we were supposed to be studying, and I would just lose my shit cracking up.

What I'm trying to say is, we might've been different on the surface, but we were in the same boat at Stanford. Neither of us fit in. I wasn't as smart as all the other superachievers around us . . . and Adhi, to be honest, he was *smarter*. Smarter than the other students, smarter than the professors. Too smart for his own good, sometimes.

It was us against the world. I helped him meet people, he helped me with my homework. Six months in, we were best friends.

REP. CORINNE SOTHEBY (R-NE): That's very sweet. But it's also when the trouble started, isn't it? Even early on in your college career, you two seem to have developed an attitude that the rules did not apply to you. Would you care to elaborate on that?

BOYCE: You're bringing up, what, the library thing? I don't see what that's got to do with any of this.

GCHAT CONVERSATION

MAY 4, 2014, 8:16 PM

Benjamin Boyce:
YO! Where r u bro?

Adhvan Chaudry:
Library
Art history final tmrw

Benjamin Boyce:
Laaaaame. Come back.
Picked up Nattys.
U gonna make me drink n Halo by myself?

Adhvan Chaudry:
I'm srsly gonna fail this class if I don't learn all of it tonite
So annoying.
I took art history last year
But these snobs won't count any of my transfer credits
Which, lets be honest, is bc I didn't pay a Stanford premium for them

Benjamin Boyce:
Dude lets be honest, neither of us actually payin tuition here

Adhvan Chaudry:
It's the principle that counts.

Benjamin Boyce:
Come on back bro
I have world myth final tmrw, don't see me stressin

Adhvan Chaudry:
Not all of us can get by on charm

Benjamin Boyce:
Hey I bet we could both get out of our finals if the library floods

Adhvan Chaudry:
Haven't checked the weather but seems highly unlikely

Benjamin Boyce:
Dr. Dark could make it flood tho
I bet Dr. Dark controls the weather

Adhvan Chaudry:
Hahaha yes.
And there's nothing his nemesis Benny-Boy could do to stop it.

Benjamin Boyce:
Benny-Boy would join forces w him for that one

Adhvan Chaudry:
Actually . . . I think I could manage a flood in the library.
Or at least, a storm.
If called upon.

Benjamin Boyce:
Uh, consider yourself called upon then.
U serious? That would be so fuckin sick.

Adhvan Chaudry:
Worth a shot.
Meet me up on the 2nd floor

Benjamin Boyce:
Bro if this gonna work I'm gonna get the word out . . .

SOURCED FROM STANFORD UNIVERSITY STUDENT RECORDS

INCIDENT REPORT
Student Disciplinary Board

> Student: Adhvan Chaudry
> Major: Computer Science
> Standing: Freshman (Transfer)
> Time: May 4, 2014. 11:20 PM.
> Location: Wilkes Library, 2nd floor stacks.
>
> Nature of Offense: Student unlawfully gained computer access
> to building's system controls and set off fire-control sprinkler
> systems in the library.

Actions were clearly premeditated, and plans had been publicly shared, as students were present in the library with bathing suits and water guns.

Damage to property is estimated in excess of $50,000 due to water damage to facilities and books.

Action also resulted in two students being treated at the Health Center as a result of falls sustained due to water present on tile floor.

University also incurred liability damage due to arrival of the Fire Department. Damage to systems and necessary investigation and patching of online systems vulnerabilities estimated at $12,000.

Actions were also disruptive to other students who were studying in the library during Finals Week.

Damage also incurred to University's reputation and good public standing, due to news coverage and Internet circulation of "Library Water Party" videos.

Student Disciplinary History: This is the second time Student has been caught illegally breaching University computer protocol. First offense involved the projection of lewd messages on stadium scoreboard during Stanford–UCLA football game in Fall 2013.

Recommended Action: Due to the severity of the damage, the repeat nature of the offense, and the brazenly illegal nature of the crime, SSDB unanimously recommends expulsion, effective end of this semester.

LETTER — SENT MAY 13, 2014

Esteemed Members of the Student Disciplinary Board,

I am writing to you in regard to Adhvan Chaudry, or as I have come to know him, Adhi. Adhi was brought before the Disciplinary Board for his role in the prank that took place in the library last week, and he's looking at potentially getting expelled from this University.

First, I want a chance to speak to Adhi's character. I have first-hand knowledge of it due to the fact that I share a dorm room with him—and as you all may hopefully remember, there are few secrets between two guys living in a 10 by 20 foot room.

Adhi is a man of great moral principle. He is totally uncompromising in living by values he believes in. Everybody on our dorm floor recognizes that while he might not be the most outgoing guy around, he's helpful to almost all of us. People even call him "IT" because he's been so generous in troubleshooting technical problems for everyone.

Even more than that, Adhi is a great friend. The transition to college has been exciting for me; I honestly never wanted anything more than to come to Stanford. Adhi has helped me keep some perspective. He and I took philosophy together this semester for one of our core reqs, and he helped me study. I have ADHD and dyslexia, so it's not easy for me academically here. Adhi has been a patient tutor, but also never helped me in any way that might possibly verge on cheating, because he is a man of integrity. I will have to find some new person to proofread this letter, because Adhi has always been the one to do it for me, and never asked anything in return.

Now, with regard to the prank Adhi is being disciplined for, I know it was a mistake. He never anticipated the level of damage it would cause. And I can say that with total certainty because I was part of it too. To be honest, the whole thing was my idea. I pretty much talked Adhi into it.

Now I'm aware that by disclosing this, I am setting myself up to be punished along with Adhi, and yes, even potentially be expelled with him from this school that I love so much. As the first member of my family to attend a university, I do not take that lightly, and I know that my mother (who passed away last year) would be immensely saddened to see me go.

But she would also be proud of me for doing what is right in this situation. And it is only fair that I be treated in the same way as Adhi. So I would like to leave you with this quote by Aristotle from the *Nicomachean Ethics:*

Between friends there is no need for justice, but people who are just still need the quality of friendship; and indeed friendliness is considered to be justice in the fullest sense.

I hope you will find it in your hearts to do what is just and allow me and Adhi to stay on at this beautiful University.

Sincerely,

Benjamin Boyce

EMAIL—MAY 22, 2014

From: Stanford Disciplinary Board
To: Adhvan Chaudry

Mr. Chaudry,

On behalf of the Stanford Disciplinary Board, I am writing to inform you of the outcome of the Hearing regarding your conduct on 5/4/14, with regard to the damages incurred to Wilkes Library.

The SDB has determined that you will be placed on Disciplinary Probation for a period of at least 1 year. That means that if you are involved in any other disciplinary incident, you will be expelled from the University.

Additionally, you will be assigned a Behavioral Counselor, whom you will meet with a minimum of sixteen
times per semester. Your continued enrollment will be
contingent on clearance from your Behavioral Counselor.

Thank you,
Mary Kleeman
Vice President of Student Affairs

EMAIL (DRAFT)

From: Adhvan Chaudry
To: Ben Boyce

B—
Just got word from the bigwigs . . .
No expulsion. Fuck yeah.
See ya in the fall after all.
I can't really express how
The way that you stuck your neck out
Dude that was above and beyond, I

The foregoing draft was composed May 22, 2014, but never sent.

EMAIL—MAY 23, 2014

From: Tumblr Admin
To: Adhvan Chaudry

Welcome to the Tumblr community! Thank you for reg-
istering your new page: *The Black Hole: Musings of an
Anonymous Sci-Fi Superfan*

As a member, you are expected to abide by all terms
and conditions of our User Agreement. All material that
you post to your new blog is represented to be your own

intellectual property, and is subject to takedown in the event that it violates any of our community standards or guidelines surrounding IP.

Happy blogging!

TUMBLR BLOG POST—MAY 23, 2014

THE BLACK HOLE: MUSINGS OF AN ANONYMOUS SCI-FI SUPERFAN

"The Head and the Heart"

The greatest love story of our time is not between a man and a woman or even between two people at all.

It is between a human and a Vulcan.

The brash, emotional Kirk, and the stoic, logical Spock.

"I have been, and always shall be... your friend."

Kirk has always been seen as the main character, of course.

The swashbuckling captain, the fearless leader.

But Spock is the more compelling character.

For Spock, it is initially painful to find himself on the *Enterprise*.

He doesn't fit in.

His logic and intelligence make him anomalous. Even threatening.

Kirk recognizes his value but cannot understand him.

Yet over time, Kirk sees that Spock's way of being is not a *lack* of feeling.

It is merely a necessary compartmentalization.

The Vulcan feels deeply . . .

but his feelings are not allowed to make his decisions.

They balance each other out.

They get each other's backs and save each other's lives, time and again.

Gene Roddenberry sought to make a show about ideas,

but it is the emotional bond between those two that has made it last.

When it comes to the films, *Wrath of Khan* is undeniably the best.

The martyrdom of Spock, when he dies for Kirk and crew, is touching.

But *Search for Spock* is the one that cuts the deepest.

When Kirk risks his captainship to rescue his first officer—

when we see that the love between them transcends rank and duty—

when even death cannot break their bond,

and the reborn Spock, cleansed of his memory,

nevertheless recognizes his old friend and says, "You are . . . Jim,"

even the most hardened Vulcan heart swells with joy.

EXCERPT FROM CONGRESSIONAL HEARING — DECEMBER 1, 2021

SEN. BOB HOLDER (R-AZ): I'm sure it felt very noble, to stick up for him like that. But the incident with the "library party" was brought up to help paint a picture, for the committee, of the nature of your relationship.

BOYCE: We were friends. Adhi would've done the same for me.

SEN. BOB HOLDER (R-AZ): That is certainly one way to view it. Another is that Mr. Chaudry carried out a publicly damaging use of technology, while you sheltered him from the consequences. That pattern of behavior seems to be very much in line with what has happened with your company.

BOYCE: Is there a question in there that I'm missing?

SEN. BOB HOLDER (R-AZ): I'm trying to illuminate the nature of your partnership—especially in light of the fact that you were both lawfully summoned before this committee, yet you are the only one who appeared.

BOYCE: I wish Adhi were here too. But he's not. And I honestly don't know why. I haven't heard from him in a couple days.

SEN. BOB HOLDER (R-AZ): You're saying, Mr. Chaudry has . . . what, disappeared? Should we be alarmed?

BOYCE: Look, he does stuff like this sometimes. He gets in his head, and . . . Adhi's just not really made for the real world, you know? People like him thrive in a controlled environment, like school. By the time we graduated, I was eager to get out, but Adhi went straight into the grad program. And that's where he started cooking up the ideas that led us here.

SEN. BOB HOLDER (R-AZ): So an antisocial introvert doing everything in his power to avoid the world . . . may have created a technology that will end up destroying it? Interesting. I have no further questions.

CHAPTER 2

GRADUATE STUDENT DISSERTATION

Submitted to University Faculty on September 7, 2020

THE FEASIBILITY OF QUANTUM-STATE DATA TRANSFER ACROSS TEMPORAL GAPS

Adhvan Chaudry
Computer Science Department, Stanford University
Stanford, CA 94305

Abstract

In this paper, I explore the feasibility of constructing a data-processing device which combines quantum-state computing with a relay mechanism that would enable the transmission of information 4th-dimensionally—that is, from a fixed "present" point in time, to an earlier "past" point in time.

Quantum computing is a field in its relative infancy, but the fundamental underlying principles are well understood. Quantum processors use quantum states as the medium for data storage, and employ an interference mechanism whereby those states are altered in such a way that they can serve as a data medium. Instead of the "1" and "0" of an electrical transistor, quantum spin states are the medium for data, and by altering those states, it is possible to perform calculations and informational transfer.

These well-understood foundations can be combined with two underlying principles of quantum mechanics, namely:

i. Quantum entanglement: Two quantum particles can be paired, such that the "spin" state of each particle (positive or negative) will always be opposite the "spin" state of the other.

ii. Bell's theorem: Which postulates that when two quantum particles are entangled, changing the spin of one will *instantaneously* change the spin of the other, regardless of the distance between them.

The fact that the spin state changes instantaneously means that information is transmitted between the particles, across any distance, over a time interval of 0. This is in violation of Einsteinian General Relativity, defying our assumption of light speed as an absolute limit.

Consequently, information could be relayed to an earlier relative moment in time than the one in which the transmission was initiated.

By extending this relay process—i.e., by "pinging" data back and forth within a quantum-computational framework—it should be theoretically possible to build a stable structure which could transmit data to an earlier moment in time than the one from which a given operation was commenced.

In layman's terms, this means that, in the given present, you could receive data directly from the future.

(Note: The body of the paper, detailing the theoretical workings of the proposed device, has herein been REDACTED.)

Conclusions

According to these explorations, the device in question is theoretically feasible. However, it faces existential obstacles in three major areas:

1) Scalability

In order to create a stable relay protocol that could transmit data across a sufficiently meaningful timeline, the processor would need to be created from a large-scale array, with fast enough read/write capability to monitor a vast number of quantum states (approx. 3.8×10^{22}).

Current quantum-computing systems are several orders of magnitude removed from this threshold, which means the technology is out of reach until a significant breakthrough alters the QC landscape.

2) Commercial Viability

The development of the product would most likely need to take place at a commercial enterprise with the resources to invest in building and testing the requisite technology. However, it is unlikely that any commercially minded enterprise would undertake the expense, which may prove to be on the relative level of the space program.

3) Ethical Hazards

The construction of such a technology poses significant dilemmas in terms of the regulation of its usage, which would likely prohibit serious investigation of the technical feasibility.

EXCERPT FROM CONGRESSIONAL HEARING — DECEMBER 1, 2021

REP. WANDA MOONEY (D-AR): Mr. Boyce, I trust that you are familiar with the particulars of Mr. Chaudry's graduate-school thesis paper that formed the basis for your technology. But I'll be honest, it's Greek to me.

BOYCE: No reason to feel embarrassed, ma'am, it's pretty complicated.

REP. WANDA MOONEY (D-AR): I suspect that it's equally confusing to more of the members of the committee than would be willing to admit it. But we have in the submitted evidence a series of slides as well, from a presentation that you often gave on the technology.

THE FUTURE

A LAYMAN'S GUIDE TO THE THEORETICAL FRAMEWORK
OF TRANS-TEMPORAL INFORMATION TECHNOLOGY

BOYCE: Right. That's from a presentation that we gave investors.

REP. WANDA MOONEY (D-AR): Mr. Chairman, for the benefit of this hearing, I would prefer to use the remainder of my time to invite Mr. Boyce to explain the technology in his own words.

SEN. GREG WALDEN (D-OR): Are you prepared to make such a presentation, Mr. Boyce?

BOYCE: Uh, yes, sir. I usually present this with my co-founder, but . . . I could do my best, sure. Is somebody . . . ? OK. Well, if you want to bring up the first slide, we can . . . there we go.

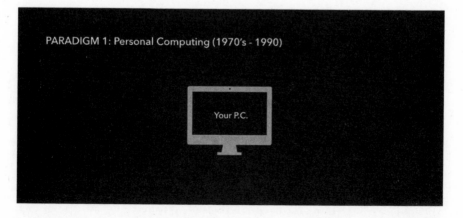

BOYCE: So, this first image, this is meant to just establish what we're all used to. The computer we all know, the machine that changed the world. This little box of transistors that could perform the calculations needed to fly to the moon, and store more information than you could read in a lifetime, and play some pretty fun games. But the potential of what computers could do, it changed to a whole other level starting sometime in the '90s. Next slide, please.

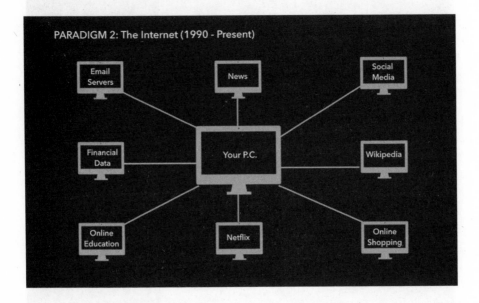

BOYCE: When the Internet came along, that was a different ball game. The underlying technology for the modem dates back to the '70s, actually, but in terms of consumer usage, 1990 is really when the PC stopped being a device of isolation, and instead became a means of *connection*.

All of a sudden, your machine could link up and exchange data with another machine. That's how you access your email, news articles, your Instagram account, most of your entertainment. One machine talking to another, like all the little lines on this grid. And that paradigm is powerful, no doubt. It gets more powerful every year.

But let's be honest—we're running out of things for the Internet to do. Because really, the paradigm hasn't changed. Web 2.0, 3.0, whatever you call it, what's new? From the AOL dial-up tone you grew up with to the broadband in your pocket today, the Internet has transformed our world . . . but it's not changing anymore. Not in a fundamental way. Next slide, please.

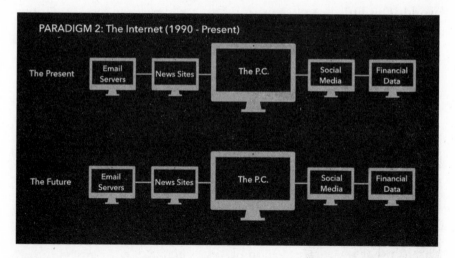

BOYCE: So it's time to think about the Internet in a new way. Because as much as it grows every year, you have to ask yourself, is it really *evolving*? This top line represents where we are today. You've got your device, linked to all these others. And in the future, the lower row—you have the same machine, the same connections. And how do we take the paradigm to a whole new level? Next slide . . .

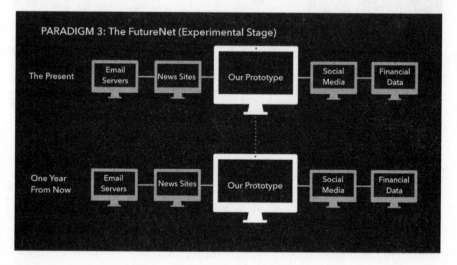

BOYCE: This is how. Our technology connects a machine to its future self. Internet connections today let you access data from other machines in your same timeframe—that's what the horizontal lines represent. But the vertical line here represents *our* technology, connecting the *present* to the *future*, for the first time in human history. It's a way to access data from the future.

And how do we do that? I mean, that's what Adhi's paper gets into, but the short answer is: through the magic of quantum computing. The technical specifics are a trade secret, of course. But the underlying principle is a weird little quirk of quantum entanglement, which enables data transfer faster than light speed. That means data can effectively be sent *back in time*. Or, from our vantage point . . . data from the future can be accessed today.

Imagine that. Your laptop, or eventually your phone, linking up with the future version of itself. You could see all the pictures you're going to take in the next year. Read all the files on your future hard drive. But that's just the tip of the iceberg. The true game-changer here comes in the fact that the future version of your computer is connected to the Internet. So . . . next slide.

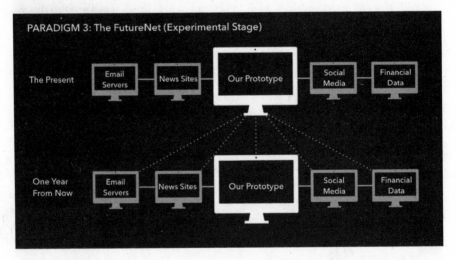

BOYCE: That means, by extension, that our Prototype is connected to the Internet of the future. You can log on today, and read all the email you're going to receive one year in the future. Watch the news, one year before it happens. Check out your Facebook page from next year, and see every status and photo you're going to post. Check how much money is in your bank account, or track stock prices in real time. A *year* in advance. Talk about sound financial planning, right?

Now, obviously, that paradigm is going to change everything. That's why we're moving to sell this technology to the masses. So—next slide, please—we can eventually live in a word like *this* . . .

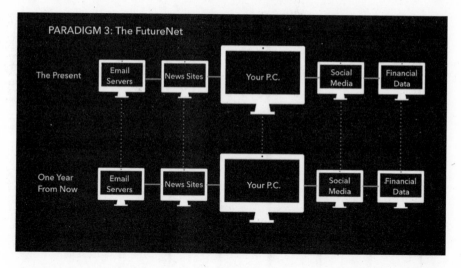

BOYCE: A world where *everyone* has access to this technology. Where every computer is connected to its future self. Where your email is seamlessly linked—past, present, and future. Where you'll read a news story today, written by a reporter who's gathering information from the future. Where people on your Instagram feed are not only posting the trip they just took but the one they're about to take. A world where companies are not only able, but compelled, to give accurate predictions of their future revenue. And at every turn, the consumer is empowered with the best information.

That's our vision. That's the world we believe in. And we're going to get there. We've already seen it. Now is your chance to get on board . . .

At this point, when we're presenting to investors, we typically transition into talking about the business plan and the financials of the company. Which, obviously, are rock-solid, since we have a direct line on what's coming next. And we've elected to keep our funding private and rolling, so even now, as people learn about it, there's an opportunity to get in on a sure thing.

REP. WANDA MOONEY (D-AR): Thank you, Mr. Boyce, we don't need you to court investment in the midst of a congressional hearing.

BOYCE: Of course not, ma'am, I am merely cooperating to the best of my ability. If my cooperation has the unintended consequence of eliciting investment interest in our company, I have no control over that.

REP. WANDA MOONEY (D-AR): No one here will be investing, I assure you. And I find your presentation, like your personality, to be heavy on hype, light on substance.

BOYCE: Hey, sometimes hype is what you need. It's definitely what Adhi needed. I mean, the paper you referred to earlier, he had trouble getting people to take it seriously even in grad school.

EMAIL—SEPTEMBER 28, 2020

From: Dr. Jenelle Emory
To: Adhvan Chaudry

Adhvan,

The formal letter is being drafted and mailed, but as you requested, I'm writing to let you know the outcome of the committee meeting to discuss your thesis and defense.

The committee has ultimately decided, at this time, to recommend that your thesis should not proceed to defense. The other professors are collating their feedback, which will be submitted to you throughout the next week. The feeling is that much of this work, in its present form, falls outside the purview of Computer Science, and that the thesis cannot be represented as academically rigorous by the CS Department.

Hopefully, this outcome is not a surprise. I want you to know that I put your work forward with no caveat regarding my own feeling, and that the responses of my colleagues were independent and uncolored, but nonetheless in line with my own intuitions.

Your intelligence is universally recognized by our department, and I hope that you will consider narrowing the focus of your paper as we discussed, and reworking your paper for submission next semester.

Sincerely,

Dr. Emory

REPLY

Dr. E—

Firstly, thanks for the heads-up.

Secondly, no I don't blame you. But come on.

The work is strong.

I'm not saying it's undeniable or speaks for itself.

I know that people are likely to have some questions.

But is that not what the defense is for?

Am I really to be kicked back a year and asked to work on some comp-matrix problem no one cares about, simply because they can't wrap their heads around what I'm trying to do?

Nikolai graduated last year with a similarly experimental thesis.

I'm not asking them to blindly green-stamp my work.

I'm asking for a chance to proceed to defense so I can defend it.

—A

REPLY

Adhvan,

To be clear, the criticisms raised by my colleagues were both technical and fundamental/theoretical. The most common reaction was, quite simply, "Is he genuinely talking about how to build a time machine?" And while I'm aware that is an oversimplification, I'm sure that you are aware of where it comes from, based on the topic you selected.

Regarding the defense, the best I can say is, that's not how it works. In my entire tenure here, I have never chaired on a project that failed its defense. Works proceed to defense when, and only when, they have the support of the entire committee. You do not have that support.

It's not simply a formality. It is intended to be a collegial challenge, one that deepens the thought and work of the presenting academic and enriches all who are present. Nikolai Guriev's work on quantum transistors was experimental in a much more tangible way, and he has now proceeded to actually building prototypes.

I don't think it is beneath you to work on a project that might actually have tangible benefits to people working in our field, as opposed to a theoretical "moonshot" that feels, frankly, more like a thought experiment than a meaningful attempt to build something. CS is not the Philosophy Department.

Sincerely,
Dr. Emory

FORWARD

From: Adhvan Chaudry
To: Nikolai Guriev

N—
Am I being unreasonable here?
Or are they?

—A

REPLY

From: Nikolai Guriev
To: Adhvan Chaudry

Hahahaha, ho-ly fucknuts, you got some huevos pushing back like that.

Thing is, if you want to do academic anything, you gotta learn to roll with these punches. I think your paper is dope but that's not the point. They passed my quantum transistor paper through the system because they saw potential for a big article, which means money. Your time machine? Not so much. More reputational hazard for them. It's all optics. That's the game you gotta play in the academic world.

Nikolai Guriev
Stanford Dept. of Computer Science
Post-Doc Research Fellow
Quantum Analytics Lab

TEXT MESSAGE EXCHANGE

BEN BOYCE
October 4, 2020 5:16 PM

Hey A!
How you been?

ADHVAN CHAUDRY
Hey man.
Same ol same ol.

Your mom hit me up, she's worried bout you.

Oof sorry about that.
I just couldn't handle talking to her last week.
I'll call her back soon.

Yeah she thought maybe some girl broke up w you?
LOL you gotta keep me in the loop!
I didn't even realize there was some girl to do so

Me neither.
I told her I went on one date, big mistake.
Now she's wondering when the baby's due.

Aw man your mom just wants you to be happy
And one date's a step in the right direction!

> Her profile said she was into physics.
> Turns out she meant metaphysics.
> Like chakras and crystals.
> I deleted the app after that.

Hahaha well if you want to get back out there, lmk
Leila's got some seriously nerdy friends
D&D-playing chicks

> Thanks but dating is not a priority right now.
> After everything last year, better to focus on myself.

WORD.
So everything's good?
Just ignoring your moms for the heck of it?

> My thesis was rejected.
> If I want to continue, it will be at least another year.

Aw fuck man, sorry to hear
I'm sure your shit is just over their heads

> Yeah. So.
> I haven't been leaving home much.

Dude you know you can't hole up like that.

> I'll be fine.
> How bout you, how's Freewerx?
> You a millionaire yet?

No Freewerx is fucked.
I got the full Series A round and the founders blew
through it without getting to a working prototype
Two months of runway then we're toast

> Well, since we're both failures . . .
> Want to come over, get drunk, and play Halo?

Always.
But don't give up so easy on grad school.
Even if it's another year.
I mean, how you gonna fulfill your dream of
being a supervillain if you don't get that
doctorate?

Haha I haven't thought about that in years.
Benny-Boy vs. Doctor Dark.

I still got half an issue waiting to finish.

Too bad we both suck at art.
And writing, probably.

Even more reason to finish that degree.

I'm getting sick of the academic grind.
It's pretentious and disconnected from reality.
Thinking I might jump early.

You wouldn't be the first.
Zuck didn't even get thru undergrad
You getting out and applying?

Not much.
Clarification: not at all.

I've met a couple recruiters, could put a word in?

Thanks but I don't need you looking out for me.
I'll be fine.

Alright dude.
Well I gotta get goin
But I'll let you know about Halo, maybe Friday.
Keep your head on straight.

You too.

EMAIL

From: Ben Boyce
To: Dina Vargese

Hi Dina,

Ben Boyce here, I got your card at the LinkedIn mixer last month in the Castro. The guy with the fly bow tie, if that helps! I'm always on the hunt for a good opportunity, but currently reaching out to toot a horn other than my own.

My good friend Adhvan Chaudry is doing his Comp Sci PhD at Stanford right now and has gotten bogged down in the bureaucracy over there, so he's open to leaving his program early. I can't really overstate how genius this guy is. If people were startups, I would put every penny I have into the Adhi Seed Round. If Google is serious at all about wanting top-level tech talent, there is an incredible opportunity here. This is the moment where you have a chance to draft LeBron straight out of high school, don't miss out.

Sending along his contact info. If you don't mind though, maybe don't tell him I put him forward. Just keep me in mind down the road if anything opens up over there on the management side!

Best,
Ben Boyce

EMAIL

From: Adhvan Chaudry
To: Prisha Chaudry

Mom—
Sorry I haven't called you back.

Sometimes it's hard for me to talk on the phone.
Meaning, always.
I'm considering leaving my program.
But I don't want you to worry about me.
I just need to figure some things out.

—A

REPLY

Hello Adhvan thank you to write me email. Easier to phone but when you can you can call. Maybe this wekend you are able to coming over I can make saag. You must be staying in the school program, educating is the key to sucseed. You do not want to be working the dry cleners with me. When you come too you can bring a girl would be nice!

EMAIL

From: Adhvan Chaudry
To: Dr. Emory

Dr. E—
I should make you aware, I am being recruited for a position at Google.
Even with All-But-Dissertation status, they invited me for an interview.
I had hoped, given the fact that I finished an intellectually rigorous thesis, that I would be leaving with the blessing of the university.
But many hopes attached to this endeavor have been dashed.

—A

REPLY

Adhvan,

I understand that the current Valley culture places limited value on a completed degree. Zuckerberg certainly wears the dropout label proudly, as do many others. There is, no doubt, a certain appeal to the starting salary that they've offered. However, before you jump into that deep end, I would urge you to consider a couple things.

First, the fad for degreelessness will subside, as it ebbs and flows every few decades, and your long-term career will be served by the PhD suffix to your name.

Second, the private sector, for all its appeal, can be unfriendly to individuals like you (and me). I'm aware of your qualms with the academic world, but I can assure you, the world of billionaires is far more dark, unstable, and duplicitous. If you wish to avoid unpleasantness like last year, I would proceed with great caution.

Third, the university will support you staying on for another year. You can continue through next year, with full funding in place, maintaining your same position as my TA and lab assistant. This community will be happy to keep you.

I share these warnings not only as your adviser, not only as a mentor, but truly, as a friend.

Sincerely,
Dr. Emory

REPLY

Dr. E—
OK I don't want to burn bridges but it has to be said—
Community?? Ha.

The over-privileged undergrads I taught C++ to?

No, I will not miss them.

You might be right.

I might hate private as much as I hate academic.

But I cannot imagine staying here one more year.

I don't want to be ungrateful.

You made it bearable. You saved my life last year.

But I'm out.

—A

EXCERPT FROM CONGRESSIONAL HEARING — DECEMBER 1, 2021

SEN. ALONZO MARQUEZ (R-CA): So to be clear, this technology was developed by Mr. Chaudry as part of pursuing a graduate degree, which he never even completed. And during that period, you were . . . what, exactly?

BOYCE: Well, I took on a couple entrepreneurial roles out of college, put together some other startups with VC backing. Promising and innovative stuff, but turned out they were both a little ahead of their time, so—

SEN. ALONZO MARQUEZ (R-CA): To be clear—you started two companies, and they both failed.

BOYCE: Look, 90 percent of tech startups don't last two years. Innovation is about placing bets. "Fail Fast," that's the motto. But after Freewerx went belly-up, I decided to make a move; I didn't want to get a rep as a wantrepreneur.

SEN. ALONZO MARQUEZ (R-CA): As a what?

BOYCE: A wannabe entrepreneur. Somebody who's all talk. So I decided to take a corporate position with a major comm-tech company. Getting some big-corporate fundamentals while I cooked up my next move.

INTERNAL DOCUMENT FROM VERIZON PERSONNEL DATABASE— OCTOBER 2020

QUARTERLY EMPLOYEE REVIEW

Employee: Benjamin Boyce
Position: Corporate Account Sales Associate
Time: 6 months (2nd quarter of employment)
Manager: Tabitha Poole—Director of Corporate Account Sales

Strengths: Benjamin has demonstrated strong commitment to growing and expanding his role within the company. He has been highly proactive in sourcing new clients, and has actively recruited contacts at a variety of businesses outside the normal sphere of our department's client base. His ambition to rise to a senior position is apparent, and he has proven himself proficient in forging positive social relationships with senior managers.

Growth Areas: In the future, Benjamin would do well to focus on managing his assigned workload, which he has a tendency to neglect in favor of pursuing new opportunities. He could be more of a team player by investing his time and energy in our own department, rather than constantly exploring possibilities outside of it.

Salary: Benjamin has requested placement into the performance-based bonus system early, but has not yet demonstrated reliability with his assigned workload. Recommendation to maintain salary at least through 4th Quarter of employment, then re-evaluate.

TEXT MESSAGE EXCHANGE

BEN BOYCE
December 25, 2020 10:08 PM

Merry Christmas motherfucker.

ADHVAN CHAUDRY
Thanks man, you too.

I got you a present.
It's a joke.
How many computer scientists does it take to
change a lightbulb?

> Oh boy.
> Dunno.

None. That's a hardware problem.

> Hilarious.

How bout: Did you try turning it off and back
on again?

> Slightly better.
> OK here's my gift to you
> How many Ben Boyces does it take?

You tell me

> Only one.
> He holds it in place and the world revolves
> around him.

Clap . . . clap . . . clap . . .

> I'll be here all week.

Hey man congrats again on the gig at Google.
They're lucky to have you.

> Thanks.

If anything ever opens up that sounds like a
good fit . . .
Would be rad if you could put in a good word.
I'm dying at Verizon.
Hungry to get back into tech.

> I'll keep an eye out.
> But honestly, no one is looking to me for HR recs.
> Apparently I'm not considered a "culture fit."

Haha tf does that mean?

Hell if I know.
See if you can translate, forwarding now . . .

FORWARD

From: Adhvan Chaudry
To: Ben Boyce

Original Email—December 18, 2020
From: Matthew Constantine, Senior Manager
To: Adhvan Chaudry

Hey Adhvan,

Hope it's a great Friday my man! We've all been impressed with your work since you came aboard. Definitely a solid start here, and your intelligence is a wow-factor. Which says a lot in a place like this!

However, wanted to make you aware, there have been some concerns about your culture fit. We're a team-based organization, and it's important for everyone here to invest in our community. If social skills are not your forte, the company offers many great opportunities to connect with other people, from Volleyball to Yoga to Ceramics and more!

We'd like to have you in for an informal chat first week back after the holiday. Janice from HR will be joining us, just as a formality. This is totally meant to be a conversation, not dictating anything. It's really just an opportunity to discuss how you're vibing and explore opportunities for growth.

Swing on by my office after the holiday break, say Monday the 4th at 4:00?

Your bud,
Matt

TEXT MESSAGE EXCHANGE

BEN BOYCE
December 25, 2020 10:55 PM

> ADHVAN CHAUDRY
> LMK what you think of that.

Hahahaha it means you're a weirdo.
Even at a company that employs thousands of
computer engineers.

> FML.

Just join a book club or somethin
You like books.

> Ugh it's gonna be some Tony Robbins shit.

Tony's the man.
Don't knock him till ya try him.

> Kill me now.

Hang in there bud, it'll blow over.

> Hey if you're free tomorrow night . . .
> Wanna go meet up at the Dish?
> Old times' sake and all that.
> Drink beers and look at the stars.

Aw man love to but we're doin some big
dinner thing with Leila's fam.
Ham and carols, white people heaven.
You wanna join?
I'm sure it's cool, one of Lei's friends is
comin too
And she's single and smart af;)

> Thanks but that sounds like literal hell for
> a brown dude with social anxiety.

Haha fair nuff, another time
Btw meant to ask you awhile back, you ever
do anything w the dissertation you worked on?
Your thwarted grad school brilliance

> Oh yeah, it's been a game-changer for me.
> Paperweight-wise.
> Hell of a doorstopper too.
> And if you need homemade chinese fans . . .
> It can transform into 117.

Think you could send it my way?

> Sure.
> It's not exactly a page-turner.
> But knock yourself out.

Thanks man.
Take care.

CHAPTER 3

To: Adhvan Chaudry
From: Ben Boyce

Hey man, read through your thesis paper over the break, and. . . . WHAT?! This is insane in all the right ways. Just to be clear what you're talkin about here—it's a mother-fuckin TIME MACHINE. Right?!

Why are you not doing anything with this RIGHT THE FUCK NOW? Why are WE not doin this? Bro is this what you're workin on at Google?

Hit me back ASAP,
Ben

REPLY

B—
Glad you enjoyed the paper. That makes one.
First off, it's a theoretical device.
As I explain in the Conclusion, there are currently numer-ous technical obstacles for which technological solutions do not yet exist.

It is decidedly not what I'm working on at Google.
My work here is tangentially related
(in the sense that it involves Quantum Computing)
but it's for much more prosaic commercial purposes.
Financial models, weather patterns, shoot me now.
Granted, I have gotten to work with technology here that
would actually solve one of the aforementioned technical
obstacles.
Google is much further along on Q processing than any-
one in the academic CS world is even remotely aware.
But I digress.
Calling it a Time Machine is not strictly accurate.
It's more . . . a computer that could talk to its future self.
Nothing worth losing your mind over.

—A

REPLY

Hey man you're massively underselling yourself (as usual)
and the shit you came up with. OK I get it's not some HG
Wells go-back-and-meet-the-dinosaurs type of deal, but
whatever you wanna call it, a computer that talks to the
future is a big deal! You get that shit working, you could
see forward in time, right? You could make that and just
win the lottery overnight, yeah? Who wouldn't want that?
It's gotta be worth exploring. What do you need to make
it happen?

Let's do this,
Ben

REPLY—JANUARY 8, 2021

B—

Sorry for the delay, my plate has been full.

I'm hanging on by a thread here.

My participation in Google book club did not go well.

Mostly bc I did not agree with the author's utterly unscientific claims that we are happier

if we "dare greatly" and "practice vulnerability."

I don't mind being called "confrontational"

but when someone labels me with the word "robotic"

I know that I have, effectively, been exiled from the group.

With regard to the tech—

I'm not sure how it would work.

Building it is not something I could undertake with my own resources.

The coding part, yes, I could manage.

But what we're talking about is hardware not just software.

Conservatively, I would need $50K+ budget for materials, lab space, basic R&D, just to start.

And honestly, hundreds of hours.

My "free time" these days amounts to maybe 10 hrs/week, and my free brain space is at 0.

—A

REPLY

Dude I can solve all those problems. Money, time, R&D, what you're talking about is Seed Funding. And if there's one thing I'm good at, it's raising a seed round. It's all about the right idea at the right time.

As far as that's concerned, this idea is perfect, cause this year, quantum is the new blockchain. It's the magic word, you put that shit in a prospectus tomorrow, you get VCs droppin their panties and shittin out seed rounds. Nobody knows what the fuck quantum processing is (just like nobody knew how blockchain worked) but everybody knows it's the future.

The Future. That's the name of the company. Think about it!

Let's . . . build . . . THE FUTURE!

Hit me back quick or I'm gonna blow up your phone with texts, this shit is too good to sit on,

Ben

REPLY

B—

OK I don't want to dampen your enthusiasm but I have to raise a couple points.

1) Re: funding, you're talking about Freewerx, right? I don't want to pour salt in that wound but it's not exactly a success story.

2) Re: "the new blockchain"—in the wake of the crypto bubble bursting, that hardly seems like a ringing endorsement.

3) Re: The Future . . . No. Just, no. That is literally the dumbest name for a company that I've ever heard.

—A

REPLY

Alright bro, I'm not gonna press you on it. You can stay put and live that nice mediocre Google life, maybe someday make your way up to middle management, build a better widget, whatever . . .

But on some of those shots, I just wanna set the record straight. Freewerx wasn't a bad idea, it just wasn't the right team. If I'd had you in the mix, might've even panned out. And I *did* succeed in doing my part, which was working my ass off to raise $1.5M in less than six months to get that off the ground. Just didn't have legs. Or wings, I guess. For lots of entrepreneurs the first failure is just the price of admission.

Blockchain—OK, point taken. I'm just saying, I got my finger on the pulse, and I know what it takes to get funded.

The Future is a deadass great name, not backin down on that one bit. You think TheFacebook.com was a great name? Hell no. But now it's shortened and ubiquitous and people say it like a verb. I guarantee we get your machine working, people gonna talk about "I'm gonna Future that . . ."

Your boy, now and forever,
Ben

REPLY

B—
What about the ethical hazards I raise in the paper?
We can't just ignore that.
Have you read the original research paper for the Google search algorithm?

It's available online.

In the conclusions, they undercut their own idea.

They say there is probably no widespread application for it bc they identify selling ads as the only potential revenue source,

and then proceed to lay out the ethical challenges of doing so.

Selling ads compromises the integrity of search.

Yet it became their entire business plan.

Do you really want to weave moral compromise into the fabric of a new business, from the moment of its inception?

—A

REPLY

Dude you are actually making MY point! The things that they called ethical challenges in that paper, turns out they were actually just the ingredients in a recipe for printing money. If you get stuck in old-fashioned morality you can't move forward. And now, OK, they're making money selling ads in search, big deal . . . meanwhile their algorithm made the Internet what it is today, and they're funding Google X and doing all kinds of amazing save-the-world research.

Don't you want to be the next Sergey and Larry? Don't you wanna take over the world together?

REPLY

B—

To be clear . . . you want me to quit my job.

Knowing my history, knowing what happened 2 years ago, knowing I need stability . . .

You want me to risk all that for this business.
Based on an idea that is borderline insane.
Just making sure I got this right.

—A

REPLY

Yeah man, I wanna go all in. Both of us. I know what you got, I know what it means, but I promise you, I'll help you keep your feet on the ground. I'm not gonna push for 90-hr weeks. I guarantee I'm gonna get us funded in 6 months, that's all the runway you gotta commit.

And the most important difference from 2 years ago: you're not gonna go through this ALONE. I'm with you, lock-step, equal partners, ride or die. There's gonna be accountability, structure, and SUPPORT. You've gotten good professional help and meds, and if we do this you're gonna have ME, all of me, a friend who's got your back every single day.

Look, I need this, I need an excuse to get out of this job before I lose my mind. But I think you need this too. I know you dgaf about getting rich, but the one thing you gotta ask yourself is . . . don't you wanna KNOW?! If it could WORK?!

REPLY

B—
Of course I want to know.
Jesus, straight for the achilles.
Hmmm.
What does Lei think?

—A

REPLY

Now we're gettin somewhere! Lei thinks it's a great idea, she's all for it, we talked it over and she's excited.

TEXT MESSAGE EXCHANGE

ADHVAN CHAUDRY
January 8, 2021 3:40 PM

Hey Lei.
I know it's been awhile.
Hope you're doing well.

LEILA KEENER-BOYCE

Hey A, great to hear from you!
I'm good, working at my dad's firm these days.
I know I swore I never would, but turns out the
job market is oversaturated with lawyers, soooo
here I am. The hours are nuts, but I'm working
my way up.

Well . . . to thine own self be true.
I'm sure you're doing what's right for you.

Thanks! How are you?

Not bad.
Google. Salary, benefits, yada yada.
2 years I've been stable on my meds.
Just like a canceled TV show . . . No episodes.

Haha glad to hear it. Have you found a nice
girl yet?

Not really.

Still playing the field? Just a few Google Groupies?
Hey you should call them GOOPIES.

No Goopies. Waiting to meet the right person.
Anyway—I was actually reaching out bc of Ben.
Wanted to check, you really think this is a
good idea?
He says that you do.

4:02 PM
Hello?

TEXT MESSAGE EXCHANGE

LEILA KEENER-BOYCE
January 8, 2021 3:57 PM

Hey babe.

BEN BOYCE

Hey Princess!

What is this idea Adhi's asking me about?

Oh it's a business plan.
I was gonna talk to you about that tonight.

Mmm-hmm. I bet you were.

But I can tell you now.
You wanna talk on the phone?

I'm in the office now.

Well, Adhi and I want to launch a startup
together.
Me + him.
It's some tech that he cooked up in grad school.
And I think there's real potential to it.

So would this be a side project, or a full-on
quit-your-job situation?

I mean, you know how it is.

A startup's not a side hustle.

This's why I wanted to talk about it later.

And this was his idea?

Yeah, totally.

He just wanted me to help found and run it.

I can say no, of course.

But I want to support his dream.

And I know you wanna support mine too.

TEXT MESSAGE EXCHANGE

ADHVAN CHAUDRY

Hello?

Lei, you still there?

January 8, 2021 4:15 PM

LEILA KEENER-BOYCE

Hey, sorry, I just had to take a call, but I'm here.
Look, you're the smartest person I know. I believe
in you to change the world. If you want to bring
Ben along for the ride, by all means, go for it.

I know he wants this.

OK then.

Away we go.

Sometimes it just surprises me that you guys are
still friends. You are two very different energies.

Well . . . we both like Star Wars.

Haha is that all it takes for 2 dudes?

Honestly, out of everyone, you should understand best.

Ben is super ADHD.

But when his light shines on you, it shines bright.
And you feel like the center of the universe.
(You do know if you tell him any of this, I legit
will have to kill you)

                              Not to worry, cone of silence.
                    And yes I'm certainly familiar with the feeling.
                      But I'm sure you also know, when his light
                              STOPS shining on you, it's hard.

Yeah. I know.
But I can't live my life waiting for my one real
friend to get sick of me.

                    What about me? I'm not your real friend?

Of course.

                    Listen I just want you to take care of yourself.
                    Ben's not gonna do it. When he gets his eyes
                    on something like this, he's a dog with a bone.
                              And anyone close to him can get bit.

I know.
And hey, take care of yourself too.
You deserve that.

                    Oh believe me, three years being married to
                    that man, I know how to take care of myself.

I'll try not to read into that too much.

                    Haha you can think whatever you want ;-)
                              See ya around, Adhi.

Later Lei.

EXCERPT FROM CONGRESSIONAL HEARING—DECEMBER 1, 2021

REP. AMANDA BLAKELEY (R-AZ): Based on the records we've seen, it appears that, from the very beginning, your company has been intimately connected not only with your so-called best friend, but also with your wife, Leila Keener-Boyce.

BOYCE: Yes, ma'am, that is correct. My wife is a corporate attorney, and has been a great asset.

REP. AMANDA BLAKELEY (R-AZ): And did your wife counsel you in advance of this hearing?

BOYCE: She helped me prepare, if that's what you're asking. I have tremendous professional respect for her. The way her mind works is next-level. And on top of that, she's just really good. You know? Her ethics. She's not only worried about winning, she's got this deep sense of right and wrong that goes into everything she ever does. She is . . . honestly, I don't use this word lightly, she's a hero.

REP. AMANDA BLAKELEY (R-AZ): And yet, whenever you address her, it is as *Princess*.

BOYCE: Yeah, but that's just an inside joke. Her name's Leila, so—like Princess Leia, in *Star Wars*? 'Cause she's tough. In the movie, when they go rescue her, she says, "Aren't you a little short to be a stormtrooper?" And she gives them shit . . . Sorry, she criticizes them . . . for such a poorly planned operation. It was Adhi's joke originally, and believe me, my wife is a strong feminist; it would not fly if it were demeaning in the least.

REP. AMANDA BLAKELEY (R-AZ): And have you ever had concern about her ongoing relationship with your co-founder?

BOYCE: Oh God no. Wow, you guys got this all wrong. Our relationship never would've even happened without him, and he's been the biggest supporter of us since the very start.

BEST-MAN SPEECH

SOURCED FROM CHAUDRY'S PERSONAL COMPUTER
Delivered April 16, 2017

Good evening, everyone. Thank you to the Keeners and the Boyces for hosting this beautiful evening. That ceremony was pretty incredible, right?

For those of you who don't know me, I'm Adhvan. The groom's best friend, best man, and as he once said, his brother from another mother. Which I'm sure he only said because he didn't have any actual siblings, but neither did I, so I guess it's lucky we found each other.

I'm pretty nervous to be speaking in front of this many people, so please forgive me if I keep my head buried in my notes. I would do the picture-them-in-their-underwear thing, but you're just all too good-looking. I'd end up feeling alternately inadequate or turned-on, and all in all, quite uncomfortable. As I've probably just made you feel. Kinda my thing.

Now, I've known both the bride and the groom since they were freshmen at Stanford. Ben and I were roommates. He snored, in case you were wondering. And he gave himself pep talks in the mirror. And there are even more embarrassing things I could say, but knowing what he could say about me, I will stop there.

I'm sure it will shock no one to know that in college, I was too scared to talk to girls. Or, honestly, most humans, regardless of gender. But Ben was so confident, he would ask any girl for her phone number. Seriously, he asked out our RA. And I will not say how that went, but I spent more than a few nights sleeping in the study lounge.

I don't mean to talk out of turn. But it's important for you to know, Ben wasn't afraid to talk to any girl, ever.

Until Leila. Who was the one girl I *did* talk to.

Leila and I were in a bio lab for one of our core electives first semester. We got randomly picked to be lab partners. Somehow, through the process of dissecting a fetal pig, a friendship was born.

She and I would study together and eat Thai food in my dorm room. Which, of course, I shared with Ben. The first time that Ben came in when Leila was over was the first time I ever saw him tongue-tied in my life. I think the first thing he ever said to her was, "Hey. Ben is my name. You like classes?" Hardcore fail. And when he was gone, Leila asked me . . . "What is your roommate's deal?"

So, second semester rolls around, and Leila and I decided to both take Intro to Western Philosophy. Ben had already taken his World Thought core requirement, but knowing Leila was in, he signed up too.

In class, I'm used to sitting by myself in the back. But I somehow end up with the most beautiful girl at Stanford next to me, and the most popular guy in our freshman class on the other side.

Ben was constantly trying to flirt. But if any of you have ever seen Leila in class—and I know some of her law school classmates are here—she does not mess around. She has a whole system with color-coded highlighters. And she had another class right after philosophy, so she could never come have lunch with us. Ben was *dying*.

Luckily, there was a group project at the end of the semester, and you got to pick your own groups and topics, so it ended up being the three of us. And Ben had this brilliant idea that our topic would be the Philosophy of Love. Eye-roll, I know. We were presenting on the four different Loves covered by Aristotle's *Poetics*.

So we spent a lot of time together in the library, and back in our dorm. Through all of it, Ben's looking for a perfect chance to ask Leila out. But the moment never comes. I tell him, just ask for her number, she likes you. But he says no, I want to make it special.

The day of our presentation rolls around, and we're giving our report for the class. It's a big section with seventy students. And we break it down so I'm quoting the text, Leila is doing the lion's share of explaining Aristotle's concepts. Then Ben gives an example for each one. We get through *Agape* (love for everyone, like charity) and *Storge* (which is parental love), and then we get to *Philia,* brotherly love, and that's when Ben goes off-book. He says that it's like what he feels for me, his best friend. It was nice, but also very embarrassing.

Even worse, I can see where this is going. And probably you can too. Because the last love is *Eros*. Romantic and sexual passion. The root of the word "erotic." I introduce it, Leila explains it, and Ben— right in front of the teacher and the whole class, he says, "This is the feeling I am developing for my teammate Leila." And then right there, at the end of our final presentation, he asks her out, in front of the whole class. And she freezes. But from the front row, one of our classmates just yells, "Say yes!" And pretty soon, everybody starts cheering. *Somehow,* no lie, they started up a chant. *"Say yes! Say yes!"* Even our professor got into it. *"Say yes! Say yes!"*

I'm pretty sure Leila was not thrilled to be asked out like that. But she had no choice at that point, with our final grade hanging in the balance.

While Ben and I lived together, I had a front-row seat to watching these two get closer, building the foundation for an amazing life. We had some great times, all three of us.

And then, the two of them decided to move in together. And while it was a delight to see my best friend so happy, it was painful to see him leave me for a girl.

Watching the two of them here today, of course, I know it was for the best. I know that when there is an invitation to love and happiness, you must, in the words of our entire Intro to Western Philosophy class . . . Say yes.

So, ladies and gentlemen, I hope we can all learn from these two. Raise a glass to the new Mr. and Mrs. Boyce, and as you clink glasses—say yes.

EMAIL — JANUARY 8, 2021

From: Adhvan Chaudry
To: Ben Boyce

B—
I'm in.
Let's do this.

—A

REPLY

FUUUUUUCK YEAAAAAHHHHHH BROOOOOO!
You are NOT gonna regret this!

REPLY

B—
Before we get ahead of ourselves, we're gonna need some help.
Materials, lab space, someone who knows the fabrication side.
My buddy Nikolai is still at Stanford on a post-doc.
Cool if I hit him up?

—A

EMAIL

From: Adhvan Chaudry
To: Nikolai Guriev

N—
I'm quitting Google to work on a startup, which is roughly based on the device I proposed in my thesis.
You were always the one who believed in this the most.
You should take a sabbatical and come help us make it work.

—A

REPLY

So you want to build a time machine, eh? Eeeenteresting.
Ummmm lemme know what the comp would look like.

REPLY

N—
Currently we are pre-funding.
Comp at this point would be all equity.
Ben is offering 5 points.
Considering that we're seeking a valuation of $100M . . .
that's potentially a LOT of money.
As soon as we get a prototype working, we'll make that
easy.

—A

REPLY

"As soon as we get a prototype working"? Hahahahahaha.
Of your time machine? Hahahahaha. Greeaaaat opportunity friendo.

    Also, you're doin this with Ben, meaning like your old
roommate from undergrad? Isn't he a bit of a twat? You
sure he's not just using you for the supercomputer btwn
your ears?

REPLY

N—
I know that no venture is a sure thing, but this one is more
likely than you might imagine.

And Ben is not a bad guy.

He's just . . . a business guy.

And—rare among that category—a good person.

He has had my back at some crucial moments in my life.

I would follow him into literal battle.

So yes, I'm confident in him to lead on this.

—A

REPLY

Okie dokie, jeez, don't mean to shit on your friend/CEO choice, you 2 need some time alone?

Srsly tho lets talk tech on this. Esp bc even when you were in the pits of crankin on your thesis, YOU told ME how far QC was from being at a place to make this remotely workable.

REPLY

N—

Of course, I would not be embarking upon this journey if my mind had not been changed on that front.

It was, my first week working at Google.

Not just changed. Blown.

It quickly became apparent to me that quantum processing

(at least, in the rarefied space of highly funded commercial ventures)

was MUCH further along than I'd imagined.

The quantum supremacy announcement from 2019,

that's nothing compared to where they're at today.

Check out the attached doc.

Just need a materials lab and hardware expert, and we'll be up and running.

—A

(The aforementioned "attached doc" has been REDACTED, but refers to Quantum Computing Research Protocols, which Chaudry downloaded from Google servers before his exit.)

REPLY

OOooohhhohoho lookit you, Scooby Doo, absconding w the planz to the Death Star!

For real tho, how many people even know Google is this far w quantum? This is nuts.

OK maybe swing on by Monday and let's beat out what this would cost. I could probably get you a lab and call in some favors with the manu team. Leeet's do the TIME WARP AGAAAIIIIN!!!!

CHAPTER 4

EXPERIMENTAL REPORT — 1/22/2021

Prototype 1
Materials Cost: $3,229
Manu Cost: $4,812
Test Result: N/A
Notes: Power supply insufficient for quantum-processing needs.

EMAIL

From: Ben Boyce
To: Adhvan Chaudry

Hey man what's the deal with this Nikolai guy you're bringing on? He seems like a prick. I'm the CEO, that means I'm his boss, but every time I come around the lab for an update he starts talking tech just to point out how I don't understand it. You know how that condescending shit gets to me.

REPLY

B—
No surprise that you and N are not exactly simpatico.
But trust me.

You know how these CS guys are—
can't measure dicks so they measure brains.
It's just how he rolls.
Plus he's the one with lab access.
To build out what he's providing us with for basically no upfront cost, we'd need a couple hundred K.
Let me deal with him.

—A

EXPERIMENTAL REPORT—1/29/2021

Prototype 2
Materials Cost: $5,103
Manu Cost: $3,994
Test Result: N/A
Notes: Quantum processor failed to run OS.

EMAIL

From: Ben Boyce
To: Adhvan Chaudry

Dude when I stopped by after dinner, Nikolai was sleeping on the floor, I think deadass passed out. Like he didn't wake up until I practically yelled in his face and then he looked like shit and was semi incoherent. I think he was on something.

REPLY

B—
It's probably bc we worked on the build all through last night.

Yes, he uses pharmaceuticals.

So does almost everyone on the dev side.

Cut him some slack.

—A

EXPERIMENTAL REPORT — 2/1/2021

Prototype 3

Test Result: Failure

Materials Cost: $2,895

Manu Cost: $5,059

Notes: Finally, our first real failure. System succeeded in booting up and performing basic Q-processing. Unstable but ran OS. Clearly, no evidence of transtemporal data transmission, but hey, we're just getting started.

EMAIL

From: Ben Boyce

To: Adhvan Chaudry

OK man what's with this? I knew it wasn't gonna be easy but three prototypes in, I'm almost maxed out, and you're celebrating a failure bc it booted up? $25K to what, run Windows? I'm all in on this but my "all" isn't that much.

REPLY

B—

First, fuck Windows, I built this OS myself.

Second, we need runway, and I dunno how long it'll take.

We've already simulated it. It should work.

"Should work" is when the work starts.

How much more? Good question.

Nikolai and I figure, back-of-the-napkin calculation, another $25K to start.

And that's with no one drawing any salary.

We need to be able to ride this out.

What about Lei's family?

—A

EXPERIMENTAL REPORT — 2/6/2021

Prototype 4

Test Result: N/A

Materials Cost: $1,895

Manu Cost: $3,469

Notes: Failed to boot. In trying to minimize cost, we're back to a machine that won't even boot. Shocking, I know.

EMAIL

From: Ben Boyce

To: Thomas Keener

Hi Thom,

Hope you are doing well! Really looking forward to seeing you guys again soon and meeting the newest addition to the fam. Congratulations, Grandpa! You must be so thrilled.

I think that Leila may have already told you a bit about the situation, but I am writing to let you know about an investment opportunity for an exciting tech startup business that I am developing with my good friend Adhvan Chaudry (he was my best man at the wedding).

Now, I still remember the advice you gave me on my

first two startups, though I wasn't ready to hear it then: Find your unfair advantage. And in this case, I know what that unfair advantage is. Adhvan. He is truly a once-in-a-lifetime genius at computer engineering. I went to school with a lot of smart people, and I feel confident in saying—I have never met anyone who matches Adhi for raw creative problem-solving ability. Combined with my business acumen, we've got the team to hit this out of the park.

Our Seed Round will involve raising several million to build the business, but before we even get started on that, we need to get a prototype up and running, and that means capitalizing the business at around $50K for basic physical material costs. So I am seeking that amount as a small-business loan, with expectation to repay in 12 months at 18% return (I know that's high, but I am quite confident in our revenue by that time).

No pressure, of course! I just know how much you've wanted to bring Leila into your own family business, and I am hoping perhaps my startup could become a bit of a family business as well.

Let me know!
Ben

EXPERIMENTAL REPORT — 2/11/2021

Prototype 5
Materials Cost: $2,413
Manu Cost: $5,223
Test Result: Failure
Notes: Frustrating anomaly. We are booting and showing quantum-entangled data states, but still no data transmission. Not clear why no response when we ping future timeframe.

EMAIL REPLY

From: Thomas Keener
To: Ben Boyce

Ben,

It's nice to hear from you! Hope to do so more often, and ideally when money is not involved. But I do know you are very focused on career right now. Just remember to balance it with family. It will be very nice to see you guys again soon, and for you to meet sweet little Jada. Honestly she looks just like her aunt Leila did as a baby.

When it comes to technology, I'm certainly not the savviest, as you may have noticed whenever I've tried to send you photos on the phone. Phonos, as I like to call them, though the term hasn't really caught on yet.

That said, I do have considerable experience working with startup tech businesses; it comes with the territory, as a partner at one of the largest legal firms here in SF. We have had some success exchanging legal services for stock options/ownership stake. Some of those have amounted to nothing, of course, but a few paid out.

So I would propose, rather than a simple loan, why don't we discuss me coming aboard as a partner? Seems like that's the way to really make it a family business.

Best,
Thom

EXPERIMENTAL REPORT — 2/15/2021

Prototype 6
Materials Cost: $3,475
Manu Cost: $6,069
Test Result: Failure
Notes: We might be getting close. All indications were positive until transtemporal connection initiated, at which point data over-

load shut down system. Need to find a way to contain/restrain/
limit data flow.

TEXT MESSAGE EXCHANGE

LEILA KEENER-BOYCE
February 16, 2021 2:31 PM

My dad just called me into his office for a chat.
Are you taking on investment from him?

BEN BOYCE

I asked him about a loan.
He's the one who suggested investment.
Partnership stake, actually.

Come on, hon. You should know, money in
my family comes with strings.

Yet you're the one working for him.

Yes, and I'm also planning to get out of here ASAP.

He seems genuinely interested.

The strings are emotional, not financial.
I guarantee, he will involve himself in every
aspect of the decision making.

I didn't realize this was a Godfather-type
situation.
Should I be worried about an offer I can't refuse?

Please, for the good of your company and our
marriage, I'm asking you to find money elsewhere.

EMAIL

From: Ben Boyce
To: Thomas Keener

Hi Thom,

Thanks for your generous offer! I totally understand where you're coming from here. However, after talking it over with my co-founder, we're just not comfortable taking on an additional partner at this stage of the business. I fully appreciate what you are doing, and am eternally grateful. See you soon!

Love,
Ben

REPLY

Ben,

It is disappointing to hear that you would want my money but not my considerable expertise and experience. However, that is certainly your prerogative. Best of luck. Will see you soon, hopefully.

Thom

EMAIL

From: Nikolai Guriev
To: Adhvan Chaudry

Sooooooo this whole thing feels like it's circling the drain. I was kinda into the prospect of trying to invent some next-next-level shit here, but what we got so far is not even a remote indication that this is gonna work. And meanwhile your power-tripping bff is breathing down our necks while having no clue what quantum spin even is. Plus I'm gonna get audited soon by the department on how I'm using the lab, soooo . . . time to call it, I think. Let's finish up the current trial and then put it to rest shall we?

EXPERIMENTAL REPORT — 2/20/2021

Prototype 6.2

Test Result: Failure

Materials Cost: $585 (Reused Prototype 6 hardware with minor modifications)

Manu Cost: $1,219 (Same)

Notes: Insufficient funds to build new prototype; reusing with minor additions. Result is similar shutdown. Transtemporal data transfer appears to be working, but inundates the system quickly and leads to crash. Need a way to restrain/specify destination/target.

TEXT MESSAGE EXCHANGE

ADHVAN CHAUDRY

February 21, 2021 5:07 PM

Nikolai is pulling the plug.

BEN BOYCE

Are you kidding me?
He CANNOT just do that.

Oh right, I should've reminded him.

Fuckin junkie.
I swear he's high off his ass half the time.

He said we can stay in the lab till the end of
next week.
Then we gotta find new facilities.

Where's this coming from?

I don't think last week's "pep talk" really
inspired confidence.

Well, his attitude doesn't inspire confidence either.
And neither does his pill-popping.
This is bullshit.
He agreed to a fixed period of time.
Do we have a contract for him?
I'm gonna talk to Leila about suing for breach.

5:25 PM

Dude you still there?
Relax I'm not really gonna sue him.

5:45 PM

A?

Sorry.
Fixed period of time!
FIXED PERIOD OF TIME!

Uh, what?

It was so obvious.
I'm going to the lab I'll hit you back later.

OK. Keep me posted.

7:15 PM

Hey man what's the word?
Dude I'm gonna keep calling till you pick up . . .

EXPERIMENTAL REPORT — 2/28/2021

Prototype 6.3

Materials Cost: N/A (Reused Prototype 6.2 hardware, only performed software modifications)

Manu Cost: N/A (See above)

Test Result: Success

Notes: Prototype is operational, albeit with slightly limited functionality, compared with the initial outlook. Able to achieve stable data transfer by stipulating a fixed time gap of one year, thereby achieving relay with specific date. Layman's terms: holy fuck, it actually works.

CHAPTER 5

PROTOTYPE SEARCH HISTORY — 2/28/2021 (THE FIRST DAY OF FUNCTIONALITY)

top stocks of the year
The Future company
The Future stock price
The Future company IPO
The Future release date
Powerball March 2021
Best Picture 2021
best albums of 2021
World Series 2021
Justin Bieber married?
celebrity deaths this year
COVID stats 2021
COVID new outbreak?
top news stories of the year
Ben Boyce instagram
LinkedIn still a thing?
New Star Wars trailer
Bitcoin price
Half-Life 3 announcement
Red Dead Redemption 3
VR technology
TikTok still a thing?
Apple WWDC announcements

Popular men's hairstyles
Air Jordan releases
Adhvan Chaudry
Ben Boyce
Adhvan Chaudry girlfriend
Ben Boyce net worth
The Future company headquarters
The Future company news
The Future company founder profile

TEXT MESSAGE EXCHANGE

BENJAMIN BOYCE
February 28, 2021 10:48 PM

Hey Princess.
I'm still at the lab with Adhi.
Gonna be a little late.

LEILA KEENER-BOYCE

OK. I'll prob be in bed.

Don't be pissed.
Especially cause you have so much to look
forward to:)

?????

Yep.
IT WORKS.

Congrats! OK now I guess I need you to
explain to me what that actually means.

How bout check your email right now
I sent you a little something.
From next July.

WIRED ARTICLE—PUBLISHED JULY 14, 2021
(Downloaded on February 28, 2021)

THE WIZARDS OF TOMORROW
by Fiona Glazer

I believe that it may be utterly unique in the history of journalism to meet a subject who has already read the piece you are planning to write about him. But that was the case when I sat down with Ben Boyce in the offices of the buzzy startup he has created with his co-founder Adhvan Chaudry.

Boyce speaks with a relaxed confidence that is easy to mistake for hubris. Within 30 seconds of shaking his hand, he said to me, "I've read the article you're going to write. Great work, in advance." Initially, I found the claim and the compliment to be laughable—the Valley version of a snake-oil sales pitch. I was quite wrong.

First, let me dispel for my audience the main question that readers will be hoping I get to: yes, yes, yes, their technology is undeniably and unequivocally real. They have created a machine that can see the future.

How do I know? For three days in a row, they allowed me exclusive (albeit supervised) access to the Prototype of the consumer-technology product they intend to sell as early as next year. They challenged me to look up information about the near future, and then let me watch as the news stories I read came true in real time, exactly as predicted.

I arrived with my doubts, certainly. Having reported on Theranos for three years—having witnessed one big bust after another—I imagined that there must be some smoke and mirrors at play. But a peek behind the curtain has eradicated any shred of doubt.

When you first enter the headquarters of The Future, it is not easy to imagine it is home to a typical Valley startup aiming at disruption. Perhaps the Uber of diapers, or a dating app for modern Millennials. Their offices are in a high-ceilinged loft space in the heart of downtown Palo Alto, featuring a mixture of standing desks, bean bags, and vintage arcade games.

The main difference comes if you (as few ever have) get access to the technology—or as they prefer to call it, the Prototype. After passing through a series of security protocols, which can only be navigated with one of the two co-founders accompanying, you are finally brought into a small, all-white office.

The Prototype itself rests on a standing desk and is initially underwhelming. It looks, more than anything, like an iMac from 10 years ago, but the body is as deep as an old CRT television, allowing space for the array of quantum-computing boards positioned inside. It runs a simple Linux-based operating system, which feels throwback, but was selected so the device would never fall out of sync with future versions of itself.

Boyce was quick to point out that, by the time the product comes to market, the interface will be more slick, and the physical design will be more slimmed down. Chaudry was quick to add, "But not by much." Such is the nature of their dynamic: Boyce playing the role of the relentlessly optimistic visionary while Chaudry wades through the weeds of real engineering challenges.

Boyce has already become a minor celebrity in the tech world, though he hardly looks the part. He eschews the hoodie-and-Allbirds casual-Friday feel of most startup CEOs, preferring to don a sharp Tom Ford suit whenever he's in the office. "I take my role in the company seriously," he explains. "Especially as a Black entrepreneur, I need to communicate that I'm here to stay."

Indeed, Boyce has, in a short time, become one of the highest-ranking Black executives in the predominantly white world of Silicon Valley. But when you meet him, you quickly understand why. He is strikingly handsome, in the mode of a high school star athlete, and his boyish enthusiasm is infectious. While Boyce's hero (like any entrepreneur of his generation) was Steve Jobs, his vibe is much more generous, upbeat, and friendly than the feared-but-revered guru of Apple.

While Boyce deservedly takes the spotlight, his co-founder has mostly remained hidden behind the scenes. But Chaudry is a fascinating character in his own right. Born to Indian-immigrant parents, his features are soft, and his curly brown hair falls to his shoulders. He looks out at the world from behind surprisingly long eyelashes, with a curiosity that permeates every interaction—almost as if he were an alien, come in peace, discovering humans for the first time.

Chaudry's modest office belies his eclectic interests. Sci-fi memorabilia (including a life-size Yoda) sits alongside spiritual icons (including a gold-embossed statue of the goddess Shiva). But Chaudry sees little tension between the two. "You look at the history of science fiction, it basically came along when religion fell out of favor with the intelligentsia," he explains. "But it's concerned with the same things. Sci-fi is not primarily about science—it's about our purpose in the cosmos. The big questions. All the stuff that used to be the purview of religion, that's what I care about."

Together, these two have created a company, and a technology, with the potential to permanently alter our fundamental understanding of the world. But detractors have attacked the strategy of shrouding their technology in secrecy before coming to market.

Boyce acknowledges the frustrations his approach has caused, but is confident they will be assuaged as soon as consumers get their hands on the device he's building. He seems well prepared to weather insults and naysayers, which he attributes to growing up in East Oakland. "The neighborhood I come from—if you're good in school, if you try to do anything great—there's haters coming out of the woodwork to cut you down. But my mom taught me to believe in myself. I'm doing this for her."

Boyce's father left the family when he was eight years old, so he was mostly raised by a single mother, who died of cancer while he was in high school. Chaudry's father took his own life when his son was only 10. The two boys were both only children, shaped by trauma; perhaps as a result, the bond they formed when they met in college has been a more intense friendship than either had known before.

On the surface, they are an unlikely odd couple. But on a deeper level, their pairing—Chaudry's remarkable intelligence alongside Boyce's outsized charisma—is the perfect balance of traits to lead a company in the modern Silicon Valley. And it is hard to think of any innovation more well suited for two men shaped by tumultuous childhoods than a device that can see the future.

Today, the public is asking if the company will be ready for their proposed launch date. But having viewed the technology at work, it became clear what question people *should* be asking:

Is the world ready for The Future?

TEXT MESSAGE EXCHANGE

BENJAMIN BOYCE
February 28, 2021 11:16 PM

LEILA KEENER-BOYCE

OK, I don't totally get what I'm reading here.
This is an article about the company you guys
are going to build?

This is going to be published 5 months from now.
It is LITERALLY from the future.

Babe, if this is real, this is utterly insane.

IT IS REAL!
And yes insane.
Wanna see a pic of the vacation home we're
gonna have in Hawaii?

Um, yes please!
Please tell me this is not some big practical joke,
I will be super not amused.

It's not!

Come on down to the lab!
Pick up bubbly on the way:)

Oh my god, totally shook. On my way!!

EXCERPT FROM CONGRESSIONAL HEARING — DECEMBER 1, 2021

SEN. BARBARA CAHILL (R-DE): Once you had a working prototype, how would you characterize the mood of the company?

BOYCE: The mood . . . like that first night? I mean . . . Imagine the first time you won an election. Then times that by a thousand. We were through the roof! It was incredible. We'd just invented something that people have been dreaming about for centuries. Being able to see the future, that's mythic. Literally! Prophets, oracles, seers—we had built a machine that did all that.

SEN. BARBARA CAHILL (R-DE): The celebrations . . . it was you and Mr. Chaudry, and . . . Mr. Guriev?

BOYCE: Well, we didn't tell Nikolai right away. But Leila, my wife, she came to the office. We popped champagne, you know, and got a little rowdy. Leila put on some music. Adhi had these fake Vulcan ears, like Spock from *Star Trek,* and he put them on and got up on a desk, like in *Dead Poets Society,* and he started reciting that poem, "Oh Captain! My Captain!" Doing it to me, kind of. It was awesome.

SEN. BARBARA CAHILL (R-DE): It sounds like at this moment of discovery, there was no concern whatsoever for the potential consequences.

BOYCE: Come on, when Einstein finally nailed the theory of relativity, do you think he didn't have a couple beers to celebrate? We weren't using the technology frivolously. We were just blowing off some steam that night in the lab. And the next morning, it was back to work.

SEN. BARBARA CAHILL (R-DE): What "work" was that?

BOYCE: The work of turning a single, fragile prototype into a functional, global business. I was eager to get out there and start raising capital, but Adhi insisted we had to take a beat and prove out the concept. QA testing, he said, so we'd have solid data to take to our investors.

SEN. BARBARA CAHILL (R-DE): And that's where you began to encounter problems with the technology not working.

BOYCE: No, that's not accurate. It wasn't that it didn't work, it was more *how* it worked. The issue we ran into was . . . unintended consequences.

CHAPTER 6

QA REPORT — 3/4/2021

PREDICTIVE-ACCURACY VERIFICATION

Experiment 001

HYPOTHESIS: Data from the Prototype will hold true—in the sense that events predicted by it will come to pass, at the exact time and way predicted, and said data will be uploaded online in accordance with predicted/reported time-stamping.

PROCEDURE: Research team sought to verify accuracy using news stories published online. On 3/1/2021, we used the Prototype to search for and view ten different news stories from two days in the future (that is, 3/3/2021). The short time window was selected for quick and responsive verification. They were chosen from different regions, different publication outlets, even different languages, to allow for consistent results across variables of publication, and to ensure research team was definitively separated from any involvement with reporting of said stories.

The following ten news stories served as data points (full text in appendix):

- Mudslides in Malibu Cause Major Delays on PCH
- Florida Man Arrested for Assault in KFC
- *Wall Street Journal* Announces New Round of Layoffs

- Philippines President Duterte Threatens Extrajudicial Killings
- Long Beach Port Authority Discovers $600 Million Meth Stash
- Volvo Announces Plans for New Electric Vehicle
- Manchester Teens Arrested for Brutal Assault of Elderly Woman
- Cape Town: New Road Construction Frozen Amid Union Battle
- Dutch Study Disputes Purported Health Benefits of CBD
- Huawei Looking into American Telecom Merger Possibilities

RESULTS: On 3/3/2021, we used a regular Internet-connected device to search for these same stories. All ten were discovered to have been published exactly as predicted, with zero discernible change to the text or particulars of the content. We also verified each story by obtaining a secondary reporting source, which confirmed all relevant information. Additionally, where possible, we found corroborating media, such as YouTube videos of the mudslides in progress.

EMAIL—MARCH 12, 2021

From: Adhvan Chaudry
To: Nikolai Guriev

N—
I know you gave us an ultimatum about getting out of the lab.
BUT: we have now made some serious progress.
I can assure you, it will be in your financial interest to give us more time.

—A

REPLY

Assure me, eh? If entrepreneur promises were redeemable currency I'd be a gazillionaire. And I got Dean Bullock going full Darth Vader on me about freeing up lab space. But as you are a legit coder I will give you one shot to share some data that validates the financial viability of what you got going on, otherwise these boots are made for shutting your lameass lab down.

REPLY

N—

Attaching the results from our most recent experiment.
Keep this to yourself.
Pls don't let Ben know that I showed this to you.
I trust you but he is very cautious.
I'm confident this will buy us some time.

—A

Attachment:

PREDICTIVE-ACCURACY VERIFICATION

Experiment 002

HYPOTHESIS: We can use financial information obtained through the Prototype to profit by risk-proof speculation.

PROCEDURE: Using the Prototype, we identified three stocks that were going to experience sizable jumps in the coming week, from the period of 3/5/2021–3/12/2021; specifically, two stocks that would have strong increases—NXP Semiconductors, which was announcing a new chipset, and Tesla, whose Q4 Earnings Report would be better than projected— along with one company (GM) which would experience a sizable loss, off the announcement of labor disputes with workers in foreign plants.

Based on these projections, we made the following purchases from a new trading account:

Purchase: NXP Semiconductors 10 shares @ 155.70
Purchase: Tesla 10 shares @ 305.11
Purchase: Short on GM, 10 shares @ 34.30

RESULTS: As of market closing on 3/12/2021, the prices for all three stocks exactly matched Prototype-predicted prices, and all positions were sold off.

Sale: NXP Semiconductors 10 shares @ 189.40
Sale: Tesla 10 shares @ 322.90
Sale: Short position on GM, 10 shares @ 29.20

 For 1-week gains of—

$337.00 on NXP Semiconductors
$117.90 on Tesla
$51.00 on GM

REPLY

From: Nikolai Guriev
To: Adhvan Chaudry

You certainly have my attention. If these results are the real deal, they are Very. Fuckin. INTERESTING. Carry on with use of the lab, I'll buy time with the administration. I'd like to reevaluate the scope of my involvement. I'm sure I can be helpful to you guys.

REPLY

N—

I appreciate your support.
However, now is not the time to bring you in more intensively.

Let Ben and me finish up our run of validating experiments.

Then we'll talk, once we're building the team out.

—A

EMAIL

From: Ben Boyce
To: Adhvan Chaudry

My dude . . . these results are fucking beautiful. It's not a lot of money (yet) but it is rock-solid evidence that we've got the formula for success and we are gonna be RICH. And seriously it's not just the money that I care about. It's the fuck-them of it all.

When I was a kid I used to make-believe fight the bad guys and I would look at the newspaper to get a good fake name to give the arch villain, so sometimes it was like Hussein or Milosevic, but mainly I remember it was Dow Jones. That's a damn fine villain name, almost as good as Dr. Dark. And my dad got a big kick out of it and said you got that right. I didn't get why at the time but later on, after he lost his job and took off, I thought about that sometimes, and it felt like yeah, you know what, Dow Jones was the motherfuckin villain. He got my dad, but he wasn't gonna get me.

When I was in college I thought I'd get one over on old Dow Jones. Spent my entire stipend playing the market, cause I thought I was just smarter than the rest and I'd beat the system. Course you know how that turned out. Broke as fuck, eating a lot of ramen, and taking on some extra shady-ass loans just to get through school.

But now we finally got a way to beat Dow Jones. Power to the people.

REPLY

B—

That is a lovely story about your dad.

However, let me balance it out with one of my own.

My father was infatuated with the American Dream.

With a belief that he could make his own luck.

But when he did not find that opportunity in the labor market, he looked for it in a Hindu concept: the wheel of fortune.

Only, not in his roots in India, but rather, at an Indian casino.

If you have not seen it at work, it is hard to convey the extent of just how unbearably *sad* gambling addiction is.

Because the gambler is not addicted to winning, as you would think.

He is addicted to losing.

No matter how much he gets up in one exciting run, he will invariably bury himself.

My father did.

When he took his life, it was a mercy.

For him, for my mother, and for me.

I do not intend to follow in his footsteps.

I do not intend to pin my fate and success to chance, or investment.

To the roll of the dice, or the rise and fall of the market.

I intend to bet on myself.

—A

REPLY

Dude I hear you 1000% but you're seeing it all wrong! Bc we have found the most perfect way to bet on a sure thing.

These are not degenerate sucker-bets any longer. There will be no hoping and praying for things to go well. This is ingenuity and innovation providing a competitive edge!

REPLY

B—

I wish that were true, but I know in my heart that it's not. More specifically, I know those are rocky waters for us.

I've been digging deep on our financial future, and I have some good news:

a year from today, we're going to be stupid-rich.

But I also have some bad news:

we are going to be under SEC investigation.

In other words, we already know we're going to get in trouble for using this.

Every dollar we make in this way becomes a problem for us. This cannot be our primary revenue stream.

—A

REPLY

Hey Adhi, I hear you on that, that said I am wondering, how inevitable is this SEC investigation? I mean, it's not gonna come from the literally like $500 we made on this test, right? So you think we could figure out where, in the current projection, we're crossing the threshold that puts us on the SEC radar, and just don't go there? Like maybe if we make 50 mil but don't get too greedy and don't go over 100 in a year, then we'll be cool? Or we pepper in some losses with our guaranteed gains? I get that it looks suspicious if we only win every time.

Point being, knowing what we know about the future, let's do it different, and avoid those consequences.

REPLY

B—

You are bringing up a much more fundamental question:
When we see the future through the Prototype . . .
Can we change it?

—A

REPLY

There ya go dude, you just nailed what's gotta be our next experiment, right? We pick out some event from the news that we see through the Prototype and then we change it. Like maybe something bad where we can prevent it. We can be heroes too:)

REPLY

B—
Yes.
But.
We should not try to be heroes.
To start, for the purposes of experimentation, we need to select something as innocuous and trivial as possible.
I have found a good candidate (see the attached).

—A

TUMBLR BLOG POST — "FARRAH THE FRESNO FOODIE"
Published 3/15/2021

I STAN This Frozen-Custard Stand

So picture this, fellow Fresno foodies. It's last night. Hubs and the kid-dos have finished off my low-carb chicken parm. And they are DYING for dessert, telling me they DESERVE it after that healthy dinner . . . and let's be honest, I am dying for it too, been hungry all day due to IF plus Keto.

I remember I've seen Tony n Tina's Frozen Custard Stand since it opened up on Lark Street at the beginning of the year. I was initially put off by the lines and rather garish decor, and feared it might just be a throwbacky gimmick. I've had a few people asking for my take, and was eager to deliver.

So we hopped in the Windstar and headed over. First off, the lines have died down, and it was a manageable 20 min wait. I went for the Death by Chocolate, a glorious confection of delectable excess, with chocolate custard, layered with dark-chocolate crisps, topped with milk-chocolate chips and sprinkles, along with a rich Godiva chocolate hot sauce. It was devilishly delicious, and I am a changed woman.

I also quality-tested the dishes of the rest of the fam. Hubs went for a brownie sundae, and the vanilla custard was rich enough to keep pace with the nutty brownie. Sam got a strawberry milkshake, which was so thick it took him a while of working the straw before he tasted a single sip. Yum! Kaylee went Cookies n Cream, and I tell you, they are REAL chunks of Oreo.

My verdict: Worth every penny, and more important, worth every calorie (and trust me there were plenty of those!)

REPLY

Yo are you kidding me? This is . . . I don't even under-stand. Some suburban mom who's reviewing fro-yo places in her area? I wanna get out there and raise $100M, I don't see how this gets us any closer to that goal. We need big BLOCKBUSTER results!

REPLY

B—
Yes. It is the food blog of some rando in Fresno.
The point is: she published this/will publish this the morning of 3/15/2021.
That means she will go to that establishment and have that dessert the night of 3/14/2021.
Can we prevent this from happening?
If so, we have our answer.

—A

REPLY

Bro who even cares what she has for dessert and writes about.

REPLY

B—
"who even cares" is exactly the point.
We want the most inconsequential event possible.
This is all to know that we have the power—meaning, the FREEDOM—to alter the course of her life.
We start small and work our way up to bigger changes (IF it works).
So, I have sent her the following email, from a made-up throwaway address:

Quoted Text:

((Hi Farrah! We here at the Wilde Food Group are big fans
of your blog! Want you to know that we would sincerely
be HONORED to have you come by and write a review of
Mulberry's House of Pies, which is located in your area.
Stop by tomorrow evening at 8, and we'd be more than
happy to give you and your family all the free pie you like!

David Hastings,
Regional Manager—Wilde Food Group))

And here was her reply:

Quoted Text:

((Well hi David—that sounds lovely! Thanks so much for
the kind offer. I know my kids will be beyond excited.
Very excited to write a review of your establishment:-)

Yay!
Farrah))

So now, instead of custard, she'll be having pie.
    Make sense?

—A

REPLY

From: Ben Boyce
To: Adhvan Chaudry

Dude that's cool and all but what happens when she gets
there and there's no one giving her free pie?

REPLY

B—
I called in and gave them a credit card and a fake name.
We're paying for her and her ridiculous family to have a
free meal.
Small price for proving the existence of free will, I'd say.
She eats pie rather than custard, and then . . . Future:
changed.

—A

QA REPORT—3/16/2021

PREDICTIVE-ACCURACY VERIFICATION

Experiment 003

HYPOTHESIS: Data predicted using the Prototype can be altered. Events that are recorded in the future can be prevented or redirected through intervention, based on information gathered from the Prototype.

PROCEDURE: We selected an online posting at random, taking care to choose one that we had no connection to, and that had no special significance in the world (wanting to ensure that our intervention did not create any adverse consequences).

RESULTS: Mixed. Credit card transaction confirmed that on the appointed date and time, the subject of the experiment was at Mulberry's House of Pies, not Tony n Tina's Frozen Custard Stand. However, Internet search the following morning shows that the exact same blog post was uploaded at the exact same time.

EMAIL

From: David Hastings
To: Farrah Wanekke

Hey Farrah,
I noticed that you came in to Mulberry's, but then the next day you posted about Tony n Tina's and said you'd been there the night before. Mind if I ask what that's all about?

Best,
David Hastings—Regional Manager, Wilde Food Group

REPLY

Hi there David,
Don't worry I haven't forgotten about you! We LOVED Mulberry's, thanks so much! My reviews are usually delayed a week or two so I have time to write them (being a mom is full-time!). I often say "last night" or some such just cause it's better for the story of it.

Hope that my "fudging" the truth doesn't make it fake news. I'll post about Mulberry's next week, I promise!

Yay!
Farrah

EMAIL

From: Adhvan Chaudry
To: Ben Boyce

B—
Looks like we have our answer.
To the small question about her food blog, and to the bigger question:

If we can see the future, can we change it?

(No.)

Or rather: no, we cannot alter the data that will be posted online.

—A

REPLY

Hey A, I get you, but honestly, fuck that. This one seems like a goofy coincidence. We gotta keep trying.

EXCERPT FROM CONGRESSIONAL HEARING — DECEMBER 1, 2021

SEN. DAVIS McHALE (R-WY): Now, the data you have furnished, it seems to indicate that the events predicted by your technology are iron-clad and unpreventable?

BOYCE: As far as we know, yes, that is correct.

SEN. DAVIS McHALE (R-WY): So if you were to see evidence of a particularly terrible event coming in the future, you would not be able to prevent it?

BOYCE: Well . . . Adhi and I have discussed this in the past. What it all means. And I think the best way to look at it is that no, you can't prevent a thing from happening, any more than you can prevent the sun from coming up. But our technology can help you decide how you react to it.

SEN. DAVIS McHALE (R-WY): Uh-huh. So, let's say I get this machine, I could look ahead at whether I'm gonna win reelection. And the answer would be set in stone.

BOYCE: Well . . . yes, that's correct. As a matter of fact, I happen to have seen the future regarding your next electoral cycle. Are you interested in knowing your future?

(AUDIBLE MURMURING IN THE CHAMBER)

SEN. DAVIS McHALE (R-WY): I mean, certainly. I pay pollsters a lot of good money for less information than that.

BOYCE: You can save yourself some money, you're not going to be re-elected.

SEN. DAVIS McHALE (R-WY): Well . . . I disagree.

BOYCE: That's fine, you can disagree with the sun coming up too. You have free will to decide . . . how you're going to lose.

SEN. DAVIS McHALE (R-WY): I'm not interested in losing. Surely I could get the information to figure out how to win.

BOYCE: I mean, you could try. You could devote all your time to fund-raising, try to dig up dirt on your rival, hit the campaign trail tomorrow. But your efforts would not only fail, they would likely end up *causing* the very loss you were seeking to prevent. Do all that, and I bet you'll lose to some drain-the-swamp populist candidate who labels you a do-nothing professional campaigner. You're better off resigning yourself now to defeat, and instead using your remaining time in office to pass meaningful legislation, since you no longer need to pander to your base.

SEN. DAVIS McHALE (R-WY): What you're saying seems to imply that we have no control over our own lives. And maybe you don't, but I do, and I will not be enslaved by your technology.

BOYCE: Sir, I don't think you should lecture me on self-control, when your personal conduct hardly puts you in a position to criticize.

SEN. DAVIS McHALE (R-WY): Excuse me?

BOYCE: Let's just say that your indiscretions are going to come out within the next year. If you wanna push me, I could name names right here and now.

SEN. DAVIS McHALE (R-WY): Mr. Boyce, I don't know where you get the nerve, but I would remind you that your conduct here subjects you to charges of Contempt of Congress.

BOYCE: I mean no disrespect, sir. I am merely trying to convey the gravity of our results.

SEN. DAVIS McHALE (R-WY): Your results hardly seem definitive to me. Three experimental verification tests, that's all you needed?

BOYCE: Sir, I can assure you, there were many other tests after that. In fact, we continue to do QA testing to this day. But some of our results have been redacted from the record, due to certain . . . sensitivities.

EMAIL—MARCH 17, 2021

> From: Nikolai Guriev
> To: Ben Boyce, Adhvan Chaudry
>
>
> GENTS! Trying you both since I have not heard back in a couple days. What is the deal? I'm excited to hop in the kiddie pool and help out. At the very least let's mix things up in the market.

REPLY

> From: Adhvan Chaudry
> To: Ben Boyce
>
>
> B—
> Just ignore Nikolai's email.
> I told him about Experiment 2 a little bit.
> But I'll deal w him.
>
> —A

REPLY

Bro why'd you tell him about ANYTHING?! I'm worried we should move the Prototype and untangle from him as much as possible.

REPLY

B—
I can handle Nik.
Right now, we don't have anywhere else to go.
Running a quantum computer is a massive power drain and requires a fully controlled clean-room environment.
We can't just move and set up in a garage.
Let's focus on finishing our run of QA experiments.
This is the data we need so we can secure investment.
As soon as we can afford it, we'll move out.

—A

REPLY

Fine. Keep an eye on him or I will.

So listen, I've been on the Prototype looking through next week's news trying to find a better example of something to change, something that's not just bullshit blog posts. I get that you don't want me to set off World War 3 or some shit, but we gotta do something that actually MATTERS and makes this shitty world at least a little BETTER.

I found this article (attached) and it's in my head now.

This is small and local like you wanted but it's something where I know we can actually make a difference.

Attachment:

MOTHER MURDERED IN FRONT OF CHILDREN, AGES 3 AND 5
East Bay Times—March 19, 2021

OAKLAND—26-year-old Keisha Porter was killed in her home on the 11000 block of International Blvd., in a brutal attack witnessed by her two children, aged three and five years old.

The victim's ex-husband was taken into custody as a person of interest. Police sources reported that he was apprehended in his home, and that a set of bloody clothes in the trunk of his car may connect him to the crime.

The couple divorced two years ago, and have been engaged in an ongoing dispute over custody of their two children. Neighbors said that police have been called to the home on multiple occasions, and that the ex-husband has a history of showing up intoxicated.

Nothing was taken from the home, suggesting the motives for the slaying were personal or domestic.

At present, the victim's children are in the custody of their grandparents, pending the resolution of the criminal investigation. The family has set up a fund to help pay for Ms. Porter's funeral, and appreciates any donations.

REPLY

B—
There are too many variables here.
I get what you're saying, but this is a slippery slope.
How many tragedies are there every year?
Murders? Mass shootings? Terror attacks?

Are we going to intervene in every one?
We need to start smaller.

—A

REPLY

Slippery slope my ass, they told us in frosh philosophy that that's a logical fallacy and you know it. This is happening tomorrow and it's one where we can intervene in a simple way. I am DOING IT for sure, I hope we are doing it together. Benny-Boy to the rescue, callin on Dr. Dark for the team-up! Don't sell yourself short man you can be a hero, we're the next Batman and Robin, let's do this!

REPLY

B—
Very disappointed in you . . . bc Robin sucks.
If we're going to be the next anything, we're Professor X and Wolverine.
Brains and brawn. United. Unstoppable.
Meet me in the lab in the morning, we'll make a plan.

—Dr. D

QA REPORT—3/20/2021

PREDICTIVE-ACCURACY VERIFICATION

Experiment 004

HYPOTHESIS: Data predicted using the Prototype can be altered. Events which are recorded in the future can be prevented or redirected through intervention, based on information gathered from the Proto-type.

PROCEDURE: We selected a news story about a woman who was murdered in her home the evening of March 18, 2021.

That afternoon, we went to the woman's house, and waited for her to return home from work. We knocked on the door to her home and told her that she was in danger, and that while we could not disclose how we knew, we were aware of a credible threat to her safety on that particular day. Immediately, she asked if this was connected to her estranged ex-husband; it was apparent that threats of violence were not new. We told her that it was, and that she needed to leave her home and go stay somewhere she would be safe for the night. She agreed.

We remained nearby, and waited to leave until we saw her depart her home with her two children in tow. At that point, we concluded the experiment was a success, and assumed our hypothesis would be confirmed in the newspaper the following day, when the predicted story did not publish.

RESULTS: Failure. The subject of the experiment was murdered in her home, as narrated/predicted by the article we selected for experimental basis.

The following day, research team spoke with police and neighbors in an effort to understand the circumstances. We learned that, after our intervention, the subject first took her children to a local restaurant for an early dinner. Then she went to her sister's home nearby, expecting that was a place she and her kids could safely stay for the night. Upon arriving, she apparently discovered her ex-husband there, and it became apparent that the sister and ex-husband were having a romantic relationship. A fight erupted, and the subject left in a hurry, after vowing, according to neighbors, that her ex-husband would never see his children again. He pursued her in a rage back to her home, where he broke down her door and shot her twice, killing her in exactly the manner described by the article.

NOTE: Further investigation is warranted, to attempt to determine whether or not use of the technology was causally connected to the subject's death. And by extension, whether or not it could be asserted that experimental team is responsible for the death in question.

(The final NOTE from previous report was later REDACTED from the version of the report saved to company servers.)

CHAPTER 7

EMAIL

From: Adhvan Chaudry
To: Ben Boyce

B—
Saw you called, but I need some time.
Not ready to talk yet.
Trying to wrap my mind around this.

—A

TUMBLR BLOG POST — MARCH 20, 2021

THE BLACK HOLE: ANONYMOUS MUSINGS OF A
SCI-FI SUPERFAN

"In Defense of Frankenstein"

People should read *Frankenstein*.
  It is not only the very first work of science fiction,
  it is still one of the very best.

Victor Frankenstein is not the wild-eyed mad scientist of the film.
  In fact, he is not even a doctor.
  He is a humble student, a seeker of truth,
  sensitive and thoughtful.

Driven not by a god complex to create life, but by the shocking death
of a parent (his mother).

He seeks to remake the world in defiance of that tragedy,
so others will be spared the suffering he has known.
When his creation gets out of control and starts to kill,
he is wracked with guilt, tormented to his core—
and he devotes the rest of his life to making things right.

Moreover, the creature he creates is not a soulless monster.
It only kills because it is misunderstood and persecuted.
The true villain is not the reanimated life-form;
it is the cruel, small-minded world he occupies.
In the book, the creature is thoughtful and articulate,
not the groaning hulk immortalized by Boris Karloff.
It is desperate for connection. For friendship. For love.

Superficial moralizing may see *Frankenstein* as a cautionary tale,
and indeed, its subtitle is *The Modern Prometheus*.
But ought we really see Prometheus as merely a warning?
The fire-stealer suffered, certainly, from an eternity of liver-eating,
but that is the price he paid on our behalf,
so that we all could keep warm and cook our food.

Similarly, was Frankenstein really a villain, simply because of the unintended consequences of his creation?

Is "playing God" so wrong, in a world that seems devoid of meaningful divine interventions?

Someone needs to do it.

Where would we all be, in a world without those who dare to try what was previously thought impossible?

It is not the scientist's responsibility to anticipate every eventuality his discovery may produce.

It is his duty to fumble in the dark for the light of knowledge, and to do his best to shine it nobly in the world.

EMAIL

From: Ben Boyce
To: Adhvan Chaudry

Hey A, I totally understand where you're at, I'm right there too. Yesterday Lei asked me what was wrong. I said nothing just thinking. She pointed out I'd been sitting out in the cold for like 45 minutes. Then we watched some CSI-type shit and I busted out crying in the middle of the autopsy scene.

I'm sending the money we got off the second experiment to the family to help kick in a little bit for the funeral. I dunno what else to do. Pay for those kids to go to college if/when we get this shit up and working like predicted?

REPLY

B—

Please be sure to make the donation anonymously.

I've been thinking about this a lot too . . .

and I've come to a place of peace with what we've created.
But it is clear to me, to be free of guilt:
we need some guidelines for how to proceed with using
the Prototype.
I'm going to take a crack at a working version of what
those might be, will share with you later tonight.

—A

EMAIL

From: Nikolai Guriev
To: Adhvan Chaudry

What is going on, friendo? You been away from the lab for
a few days and WHY?! Is the data you sent me a hoax?
Am I being fucked with to try to buy you a little extra
time? Or are we legit holding the keys to the kingdom?

REPLY

N—
The technology works.
The data was not a hoax.
However, we are evaluating key functionalities, as they
pertain to interacting with the data.
And we are developing a set of guidelines for responsible
usage.
Stand by, more soon.

—A

EMAIL

From: Nikolai Guriev
To: Adhvan Chaudry, Ben Boyce

+ Your boy Ben, since it seems like he should be in on this convo too—

I hate to burst yall's bubble on this but uh . . . I am a co-owner of this company and this tech, that's what an equity deal means. If you're writing up guidelines on how to use it, I need to be consulted. I mean look I get that you're pre-rev, but the data you're showing me means we could be making rev, like, tomorrow. And instead of a business plan you're writing up a set of self-imposed handcuffs?

REPLY

From: Ben Boyce
To: Nikolai Guriev, Adhvan Chaudry

Hey Nikolai, interesting points, but also, go fuck yourself. These guidelines are not coming from us hating money. They're not coming from trying to cut you out. They're coming from you have no fucking idea what, so maybe bite your tongue for a minute here. We guarantee revenue, and we will buy you out generously as soon as humanly possible.

GOOGLE DOC

CREATED AND SHARED BY ADHVAN CHAUDRY

Commented on by Ben Boyce

GUIDELINES FOR USAGE OF THE FUTURE PROTOTYPE

1. Speculation: Information obtained through usage of the Prototype is not to be used for the purposes of speculative financial investment or gambling.

> BEN: *Hear you on this but what are the limits of "speculative"? The whole endeavor of the company is one big gamble.*

2. Usage: While company is in R&D phase (i.e., before commercial product-launch), the Prototype is ONLY to be used by the co-founders, Ben Boyce and Adhvan Chaudry.

> BEN: *Agree for now but we should leave it open down the line, and for others w/ supervision.*

3. Intervention: Information obtained through Prototype usage should be construed as an accurate prediction of the future. Any effort to alter future outcomes predicted by the device must be approved by both co-founders.

> BEN: *Word.*

4. Sharing: Information obtained through the Prototype should all be re-garded as Intellectual Property owned by the company. It shall not be sold or otherwise disseminated to the general public, or any persons outside the company, without express joint approval of the co-founders.

> BEN: *These seem good but before you start to send through to Nikolai I would make it crystal clear to him he's not a "co-founder." Or maybe we just need to define that term in here as me and you?*

EXCERPT FROM CONGRESSIONAL HEARING — DECEMBER 1, 2021

SEN. BARBARA CAHILL (R-DE): Now, these guidelines . . . you came to these purely on your own? Unprompted?

BOYCE: Well . . . yeah, basically. I mean, shortly after we got it working. They were in response to certain events that happened . . . certain data that we obtained, and what came next.

SEN. BARBARA CAHILL (R-DE): It would be helpful to our understanding if you would simply share that data. Those "events."

BOYCE: I am confident that it is best for the public good if we don't.

SEN. BARBARA CAHILL (R-DE): Let the record show, the witness again declines to share data. As you're aware, we are working on a subpoena of all those records. And it strikes me that the "public good" seems to have a lot in common with the self-interest of your company.

BOYCE: Look, I'll be honest, I wasn't initially pumped about the guidelines. But Adhi was talking about the world-altering potential of this thing. How it could create . . . an imbalance. Power in the hands of a select few, which would be unjust and unsustainable. Morally, we felt a responsibility to restrict its usage. And even on a practical level, we knew that without limits, we would draw unwanted attention.

SEN. BARBARA CAHILL (R-DE): Which, it appears, you have ended up doing anyway.

BOYCE: You could look at it like that. But I would argue that the present hearing is an opportunity for all of us to have a conversation about responsible usage of the technology.

SEN. BARBARA CAHILL (R-DE): I'm sure. And is it your plan to enforce these rules for everyone, subsequent to the release?

BOYCE: No way. We know people are gonna use it how they use it. But once everyone has it, or at least has a shot at it, there's no more unfair advantage to how it gets used.

SEN. BARBARA CAHILL (R-DE): Assuming your device makes it to market, that is. I would remind you that we are weighing legislation which might affect the legality of selling this device at all.

BOYCE: Of course, yes, I respect that. But we are confident—supremely confident—that after this hearing you will see the public value of this technology. We know, because we have seen the outcome here. So why would I bother betting on basketball or winning the lottery when that's just going to draw a ton of attention, and put us at risk of going to jail?

SEN. BARBARA CAHILL (R-DE): And the creation of your guidelines . . . did that have anything to do with the incident involving Mr. Guriev?

BOYCE: No. I mean, not exactly. We created the guidelines, before . . . what happened. I think Nikolai didn't appreciate them, really.

SEN. BARBARA CAHILL (R-DE): It sounds like you are avoiding the question.

BOYCE: You're asking for straightforward linear causality. And I'm telling you, when it comes to this technology, things don't always work that way.

TEXT MESSAGE EXCHANGE

ADHVAN CHAUDRY

March 23, 2021 10:12 AM

Hey B.
You around?

BEN BOYCE

Yeah bro what up?

Nikolai is dead.

Wait, what?

He overdosed.
His girlfriend couldn't get hold of him.
Came into his place, found him in bed.
Painkillers and alcohol.

Whoa.
Are the police looking into it?

Probably? I dunno.

Shit man I'm sorry.
I know you guys were buds.
Keep me posted.

EMAIL

From: Adhvan Chaudry
To: Ben Boyce

B—

I went through the search history on the Prototype.
It looks like Nikolai was using it last night, searching for
info about himself.
He found the attached, which will be published two days
from now.
He read it.
Went home.
Overdosed.
And died.

—A

Attachment:

OBITUARY FROM THE *MERCURY NEWS*, PUBLISHED THURSDAY, MARCH 25, 2021
Downloaded through Prototype on March 22, 2021

Nikolai L. Guriev, age 33, passed away in his home in the early hours of Tuesday, March 23, 2021. He was born on January 12, 1986, in Kiev, Ukraine, and came to the United States as an undergraduate student at Massachusetts Institute of Technology. Nikolai distinguished himself as a computer engineering PhD student at Stanford University, and stayed on as a post-doc research fellow. Memorial services will be held at the Aldrich Funeral Home, at 2 p.m. this Sunday, March 28. His cause of death is reported as an accidental overdose from pain medication.

REPLY

Whoa what the fuck. Lemme get this straight. He breaks into the lab to look shit up and see what's gonna happen to him. He sees this article that says he's gonna die from an overdose "tonight." He gets high and overdoses and dies. That makes no fucking sense whatsoever.

REPLY

B—
It's not that different from Experiment 004
Think about it this way.
He tries to see his future.
It tells him he's going to die (tonight).
He freaks out. Gets high to deal with the anxiety.
Goes too far this time, chasing relief . . .
and in the process, he overdoses.

—A

REPLY

I'm sorry man. I know you were tight with him, take some time if you need it to deal with all this.

REPLY

B—
I don't need time, I just need to know:
Were you there with him that night?
I looked at the security log and you swiped in a little while
before he did.

—A

REPLY

Yeah man I was in there with him for a bit earlier in the
evening. I don't want to talk shit on a dude that just died,
but he was on his whole trip about what we owe him,
started threatening to sue for a stake. I told him to fuck off
and my wife's a lawyer. He said he'd let it go if I just let
him use the Prototype. So fine I let him use it, told him to
lock up when he's done.

Guess he didn't like what he saw.

REPLY

B—
Why didn't you tell me this sooner?
This certainly does not look good.
The police will find out about our connection to him.
And our tech.

—A

REPLY

Hey man, we can't let that happen. There's no reason the police gotta find out we were working with him really. We should probably look into moving the Prototype soon. I'm sure the university's gonna shut down his lab.

Why'd you hook us up with this sketchball anyway? This was supposed to be you and me, we can't be too careful who we trust.

REPLY

B—
You are my friend, but Nikolai was too.
He had his troubles but he was a good scientist and a good person.
I know you and Nikolai didn't see eye to eye . . .
but your secret-keeping and half-truths are troubling.

—A

REPLY

No man are you fuckin KIDDING me? I should be asking you the same thing. You sure don't seem very TROUBLED by any of this, you're the one who never wants to talk face-to-face, you're the one who seems to be hiding something. And I hate to say it but you're the one who doesn't even seem to FEEL anything about any of this, who is acting like a total ROBOT when now there are two people who have DIED in ways that we are mixed up in.

TUMBLR BLOG POST—PUBLISHED MARCH 27, 2021

THE BLACK HOLE: MUSINGS OF A SCI-FI SUPERFAN

"The Voigt-Kampff Problem"

In *Blade Runner,* Replicants are robots
  that are nearly indistinguishable from humans.
  The opening scene of the film shows a Voight-Kampff test,
  where someone is interrogated by a machine,
  answering questions to determine if he's a Replicant.
  A computer studies him closely, not for his verbal answers
  so much as a close reading of subtle, irrational, emotional reactions.
  "Proper" emotional reactions are proof of humanity,
  while reacting improperly is evidence of being a Replicant.
  A monster. Cold, unfeeling, evil.
  Judged, apparently, by a momentary flicker in his eye.
  The movie speculates:
  What if there were a Replicant who could pass as human?
  But the more dangerous question to ask is . . .
  What if there were a human who couldn't pass the test?
  What if some people simply have the wrong wiring?
  What if the programming of childhood never gave us the proper
tools?
  Should we be destroyed for failing to show emotion on *their* terms?
  What if it's the test that is broken?

The film is considered one of the finest works of sci-fi ever made,
    but at the time, the studio didn't understand it.
    They found it to be overly intellectual—
    Cold, emotionally distant, convoluted, and opaque.
    It was over budget, a monster out of control,
    so they took control of it away from the director,
    and added a lame voiceover so people would know how to feel.

In the original theatrical ending,
    Deckard solves his case and defeats the Replicants.
    Humanity triumphs over the cold, unfeeling robots.
    But ten years after the original, a new Director's Cut was released,
    which stripped the hoary voiceover and added a few key moments . . .
    and the new ending suggested a new wrinkle:
    that Deckard himself was a Replicant.
    So good at passing, perhaps, that even *he* didn't know it.
    These ideas were advanced even further in the Final Cut from 2007.
    Fans have exhaustively debated which version is definitive,
    and the proper meaning of the ending.

What matters is this: *Blade Runner* is a film about robots
    that get out of control and turn on their creator.
    Yet it was the film, ironically, that got out of its creator's control
    and left us with a jumbled mess.
    More than a robot, but not quite human either.
    A movie that doesn't pass the Voight-Kampff test.
    The conflicted offspring of conflicted parents, wrestling for control,
    plagued by an overabundance of ideas
    and cursed with a struggle to show emotion "the right way."

EXCERPT FROM CONGRESSIONAL HEARING — DECEMBER 1, 2021

SEN. BARBARA CAHILL (R-DE): It strikes me that you and your colleague do not seem particularly grief-stricken over the death of your colleague Nikolai Guriev.

BOYCE: Nikolai was Adhi's friend, not mine. And Adhi . . . I mean, he just doesn't deal with things the same way as most people.

SEN. BARBARA CAHILL (R-DE): The manner of Guriev's death is puzzling. It was an accidental overdose, yes? Which happened to coincide with him learning of his own death . . . by accidental overdose? Wouldn't he read that obituary and then, I don't know . . . not use drugs that night?

BOYCE: That is what you would intuitively assume. But he was a junkie, and as we've seen with this opioid epidemic, it's pretty common for junkies to do things, hurtful things, that don't make any sense.

SEN. BARBARA CAHILL (R-DE): Is it possible, in your mind, that his death may even have been triggered by the information that he learned?

BOYCE: Absolutely not. Certainly not that the technology *caused* his death. It merely made him aware of what was going to happen.

SEN. BARBARA CAHILL (R-DE): And when the police investigated . . . there were no indications of homicide?

BOYCE: Of course not. Homicide? It was an overdose.

SEN. BARBARA CAHILL (R-DE): We are just trying to be clear on all the circumstances. The two of you . . . you were in a business relationship with Mr. Guriev, and . . . there had been conflict. Did the police ever question you about that? Or did you make a statement?

BOYCE: No, and . . . I mean, we're not gonna call up the police and volunteer to be suspects when we didn't do anything.

SEN. BARBARA CAHILL (R-DE): Does this case imply that the individual using the machine has no agency to change the outcomes seen through the technology?

BOYCE: Look, this thing didn't come with a manual for how to work it and what it means in society. Not any more than social media. It's tech, it's out there in the world; the only way to learn how we relate to it is to use it.

SEN. BARBARA CAHILL (R-DE): The question we are endeavoring to answer is whether or not it *should* be out there in the world.

BOYCE: Well, it's going to be, no matter what. And I'm just trying to be clear and up-front here, so we get it out there in the most responsible way.

SEN. BARBARA CAHILL (R-DE): And the most lucrative for you, I'm sure. Because as far as I can tell, you hardly paused before moving forward with the project.

BOYCE: Sharing information isn't hurting anything, and that's all that it does. And when this happened, we were already underwater. We were just doing what we could to keep our heads up and not go broke. We had a working time machine and we still couldn't get arrested in the Valley. We had to set aside all the philosophical questions and step up our fundraising just to stay afloat.

SEN. BARBARA CAHILL (R-DE): I see. So the ethical issues and life-or-death danger took a backseat, while you focused on . . . getting more money.

BOYCE: No, that's not what—

SEN. BARBARA CAHILL (R-DE): Thank you for your testimony, Mr. Boyce. I'm satisfied to yield the balance of my time.

CHAPTER 8

EMAIL—MARCH 29, 2021

To: Ben Boyce, Adhvan Chaudry
From: Y Combinator Admissions

Mr. Boyce and Mr. Chaudry,

Thank you for your application to participate in Y Combinator's 2021 class. It was a very competitive year, and ultimately you were not selected to participate in the Incubator Program.

On a personal level, we are interested in you as entrepreneurs. Y Combinator values diversity and seeks to promote voices outside the Valley mainstream.

In terms of the project, however, our selection committee was uncertain how to regard your proposal. One common reaction was "Are they trolling us?" Others were more convinced of your sincerity, but regarded the project outside the scope of reasonable scientific feasibility.

We wish you the best of luck, and would encourage you two to reapply in the future with a different idea.

Sincerely,
Arnold Teaford
Director of Selection Committee
Y Combinator

TEXT MESSAGE EXCHANGE

BENJAMIN BOYCE
March 29, 2021 9:33 AM

You see the email from YC?

ADHVAN CHAUDRY

Yeah.
Not really a surprise.

Value diversity my ass.
We gotta go straight to the source.
VC cash.

You really think that's the way to go?
In this economic climate?

Still plenty of rich people lookin to get uber-rich.
And in a world that's super uncertain and
scared of what comes next, our tech is EXACTLY
what those people are looking for.

Maybe so.
But do you have access to them?

I'll get it.
That's what I do:)

EMAIL—MARCH 29, 2021

From: Ben Boyce
To: Gerald Bellflower

Mr. Bellflower,
Hey, this is Ben Boyce! I met you briefly at the Disrupter
Ball last year, and got your contact info from Alan Silver,
who suggested I reach out. I've been a big fan of your

work ever since seeing what you did with Fiverr, and I've been hoping we could work together. I think the time has come.

My partner Adhvan Chaudry (PhD in CS, longtime Google vet) and I have been cooking up a next-level game-changing idea involving quantum computing for a completely novel application. We're just starting our Series A pitches and would love to get in front of you. My asst is CC'ed to help coordinate.

Talk soon,
Ben Boyce
CEO of The Future

REPLY

I'm traveling extensively and not hearing pitches now. Good luck.

EMAIL

From: Ben Boyce
To: Emma Karas

Ms. Karas,
Hey, this is Ben Boyce! I met you briefly at the Planned Parenthood fundraiser last year, and got your contact info from Paolo Ventrini, who suggested I reach out. I've been a big fan of your work ever since seeing what you did with Kaleidoscope, and I've been hoping we could work together. I think the time has come.

My partner Adhvan Chaudry (PhD in CS, longtime Google vet) and I have been cooking up a next-level game-changing idea involving quantum computing for a completely novel application. We're just starting our Series A pitches and would love to get in front of you. My asst is CC'ed to help coordinate.

Talk soon,
Ben Boyce
CEO of The Future

REPLY

Hi Ben,
Sorry but I'm not hearing Series A pitches at this time.

Best of luck,
Emma Karas

EMAIL

From: Ben Boyce
To: Sanjay Parnathy

Mr. Parnathy,
Hey, this is Ben Boyce! I met you briefly at the DNC fundraiser at the Hilton last year, and got your contact info from Cynthia Benn, who suggested I reach out. I've been a big fan of your work ever since seeing what you did with the Instagram sale, and I've been hoping we could work together. I think the time has come.

My partner Adhvan Chaudry (PhD in CS, longtime Google vet) and I have been cooking up a next-level game-changing idea involving quantum computing for a completely novel application. We're just starting our Series A

pitches and would love to get in front of you. My asst is
CC'ed to help coordinate.

Talk soon,
Ben Boyce
CEO of The Future

REPLY

Just talked to Cynthia Benn. She doesn't remember making this connection. Good luck with this.

EMAIL

From: Ben Boyce
To: Heidi Collette

Mr. Bellflower,
Hey, this is Ben Boyce! I met you briefly at the Cavalcade
launch party last year, and got your contact info from
Greg Simeon, who suggested I reach out. I've been a big
fan of your work ever since seeing what you did with
BoHo Shopper, and I've been hoping we could work together. I think the time has come.

My partner Adhvan Chaudry (PhD in CS, longtime
Google vet) and I have been cooking up a next-level game-
changing idea involving quantum computing for a completely novel application. We're just starting our Series A
pitches and would love to get in front of you. My asst is
CC'ed to help coordinate.

Talk soon,
Ben Boyce
CEO of The Future

REPLY

Hi Ben. You seem to have left "Mr. Bellflower" in the salutation, while sending your thinly disguised form emails. I'm not sure how you got my personal email address, but please lose it.

EMAIL

From: Ben Boyce
To: Paolo Ventrini

Mr. Ventrini,
Hey, this is Ben Boyce! I met you briefly in the SalesForce box at the Warriors game last year, and got your contact info from Emma Karas, who suggested I reach out. I've been a big fan of your work ever since seeing what you did with the BluePill deal, and I've been hoping we could work together. I think the time has come.

My partner Adhvan Chaudry (PhD in CS, longtime Google vet) and I have been cooking up a next-level game-changing idea involving quantum computing for a completely novel application. We're just starting our Series A pitches and would love to get in front of you. My asst is CC'ed to help coordinate.

Talk soon,
Ben Boyce
CEO of The Future

REPLY

Well hello there "Ben Boyce."

I'm in a meeting with Emma right now, and we were both surprised to learn that we had recommended you to one another. You certainly did not invent this ploy, but yours is a superlatively ballsy version of it. For future reference, space out the timing of the emails, and be mindful of the connections in your network. And do a little SEO on yourself, the results are embarrassing.

—Paolo

REPLY

Oh and in case that wasn't clear, "superlatively ballsy" is a strength in my book. Send me your term sheet and prospectus today, and I'll meet you at Chromatic Coffee tomorrow, I have a window from 2:30-3.

—Paolo

ARTICLE—*TECHCRUNCH*—APRIL 1, 2021

GREYWALL SINKS $10M INTO "THE FUTURE"

Paolo Ventrini, managing partner at Greywall Capital, has made a seed-stage investment in "The Future LLC," according to insider sources on Sand Hill Road. The fledgling Valley startup is new on the scene and fronted by co-founders Benjamin Boyce and Adhvan Chaudry.

This is the first public news of the company, which is positioning itself in the emerging quantum-computing space, combining unique hardware and software solutions. The field has long been recognized as a hypercompetitive one to break into, since Amazon, Facebook, and Google are clearly positioned to lead the way, with the infrastructure for large-scale research.

At this time, no information has been offered about the nature of the technology The Future will deliver, but it is described as a consumer-level application of quantum computing.

According to Ventrini, "These guys have come up with a truly game-changing technology. We're keeping it under wraps for the time being, but I'm excited to debut to the public when the time is right."

The founders are Stanford alums and college friends. Boyce is a serial entrepreneur, whose first two startups folded in 2018 and 2020. Chaudry is a CS PhD who worked briefly at Google before leaving to undertake his first standalone venture.

According to Boyce, "This is a true passion project, and we are confident that we will change the world within the next 12 months." As of press time, the world remains relatively unchanged, but we will post updates as they emerge.

COMMENTS

TheCarltonDancer: I heard it's 10M at a 100M valuation? Ventrini has lost it. Grasping at straws trying to stay relevant.

WallStBetsy: Is this an April Fool's joke?

PiraTech: This is another blatant quantum cash grab. Smoke and mirrors. Greywall needs an engineer on the team to help evaluate or they're gonna keep getting taken.

DefCon5000: Paolo is a solid dude. Often ahead of the curve. Worth watching.

TamaguchiKid: "Confident that we will change the world within the next 12 months." Hmmmm. Spoken like a true snake-oil salesman. Start digging the grave now.

MAGAMan: Fuckin snowlfakes.

YourMomSays: Never heard of these guys. Expect that I never will again.

EMAIL—APRIL 5, 2021

From: Paolo Ventrini
To: Ben Boyce, Adhvan Chaudry

OK, boys, we're in this boat together now.

First off: your tech is amazing. That said, question is, how to make money from it. That's where I come in.

I reviewed your business plan (in a nutshell: sell time machines, right?) and I see a number of red flags. Regulation, for one. Infrastructure for another. To undertake extensive R&D, and scale to manufacturing and retail size, would be prohibitively expensive.

My proposal: Toss it. You want to get into the hardware business, really?

Early on, I like to ask: What is a startup? To me, it's not about size or tech or the Valley. A startup is a capitalist science experiment. We are testing the viability of a new business model. So defining that model is crucial, and it is worth considering all the variables here.

Does this have to be consumer-facing at all? Couldn't this essentially work as the basis for a hedge fund? We'll be infallible for next-level returns. It's the ultimate investment algorithm, and at a moment when investors are desperate for certainty, we can actually deliver it. Whatever social good you conceive can be better accomplished simply by making a ton of money and donating to worthy causes.

Think about it.

Paolo

REPLY

From: Adhvan Chaudry
To: Ben Boyce

B—

What the fuck did we just sign up for?

Seriously wondering if we should give the $ back.

Or better yet, just ignore him.

Day 1 and he's trying to change the whole direction.

—A

REPLY

From: Ben Boyce
To: Adhvan Chaudry

Hey man, chill out. We've got a lot more time with this, a lot more sunk cost and heart and soul, we're seeing it in ways he's not yet. I totally hear you. I don't want to compromise our vision.

That said, what if we open ourselves up to diversifying the possibilities for what the business could be? Every business book says that the critical moment is when you pivot. Is this our moment? Worth considering . . .

REPLY

From: Adhvan Chaudry
To: Ben Boyce

B—

No. It's not the time to pivot.

It's the time to hold fast.

Integrity.

Go back and read the letter you sent (will send) yourself.

—A

REPLY

From: Ben Boyce
To: Adhvan Chaudry

Word. Let me reply though. I can speak his language and manage this.

REPLY TO ORIGINAL EMAIL

From: Ben Boyce
To: Paolo Ventrini, Adhvan Chaudry

Hi Paolo,
So excited to be getting started!

We hear what you're saying about the challenge of using this tech for a consumer hardware application. But that is the vision of the company—to sell a device that lets *anyone* see the future. We're introducing a technology with the potential to fundamentally shift our relationship to the world . . . and it's important to us to keep alive the possibility that anyone has access to it.

Moreover, we know it can be done! I know many recent unicorns are either software-based or infrastructure-based, but how to explain Tesla? What if Elon had just licensed his tech to other car manufacturers? We think we're in that camp and we've got something that's iron-clad going to market.

REPLY

From: Paolo Ventrini
To: Ben Boyce, Adhvan Chaudry

Hey, boys, no offense, but you're not Elon Musk. I'm sure you have dreams of being Jobs and Wozniak, but the built-in-my-garage billionaire myth is a generation out of date. You need to get your business working in the real world, and that's where I can help.

REPLY

From: Adhvan Chaudry
To: Paolo Ventrini, Ben Boyce

P—

You're right, we're not Elon.

Elon is a preening, self-important prick masquerading as an engineer.

I've done the heavy lifting on this already.

We've got a working prototype.

We're ready to go into deep R&D and roll out within the year.

To use your cynical analogy of a capitalist science experiment—

let's not change our hypothesis before we at least get some data.

This business model is what we pitched you, and what you signed up for.

Get on board or get out of the way.

—A

REPLY

From: Ben Boyce
To: Adhvan Chaudry

Duuuuude come on. You literally just took a shit on ten MILLION dollars. I can't just jump in and smooth this over. We have to be a united front. Send him an email and apologize, say you're sorry and you overreacted, then I'll follow up and we can get back on the same page, maybe see if we can arrange a face-to-face to discuss the direction in person.

REPLY

From: Adhvan Chaudry
To: Ben Boyce

B—
I will not apologize.
If we lose him, we lose him.
Nikolai didn't die for us to start a hedge fund.

—A

REPLY (DRAFT)

From: Ben Boyce
To: Adhvan Chaudry

This is such bullshit why am I always cleaning up your messes. You fuck up and get caught, I save your ass. You lose your mind in grad school I'm there to get you back on your feet. And Nikolai didn't die for anything other than being hooked on Oxy. I'm not gonna let you drag me down any

The previous draft email was left unfinished. During the time it was being composed, the following was sent:

REPLY

From: Paolo Ventrini
To: Adhvan Chaudry, Ben Boyce

Hey boys,

Well, I must say, I've never been addressed that way by anyone to whom I just wrote a giant check. And frankly, I admire your conviction. You will have to learn to compromise to go all the way, but I like that you are talking about VISION. That is the essence of any venture. And while I do not yet share your vision here, I respect the fact that you have one.

Where I net out is, I will support you in pursuing this direction for our little experiment, but with two caveats:

Number one: if you want to build a retail/hardware/sales-driven business (like Tesla) you will need a LOT more money. We'll get into the details but I would guess that you need the full $100M of your initial valuation to get to the starting line. $100M pre-revenue would have been a lot to ask for even in the good old bubble days, and becomes a vastly more challenging proposition amid the current market conditions. Besides, if we do succeed, it will mean diluting all of our ownership stake.

Number two: you don't close the door on my idea completely. We try your idea, with the understanding that you will try my idea if we're not getting traction (meaning, not getting the investment capital we'll need).

Buono?

REPLY

From: Adhvan Chaudry
To: Ben Boyce

B—

I can get behind this, as long as he's actually supporting us getting the traction he's talking about.

Not just stringing us on.

Seem good to you?

—A

REPLY

From: Ben Boyce
To: Paolo Ventrini, Adhvan Chaudry

Paolo,

Thanks for hearing our passion and totally understanding! We both think that this compromise sounds like a GREAT solution. We will totally continue to explore the possibility you discussed, but yeah, we'd love to have a fair crack at realizing the initial vision that we got excited about. You start getting us in some more VCs' faces, we'll showcase what the Prototype can do; we have no doubt that we'll be drowning in money in no time.

Thanks!
Ben

REPLY

From: Paolo Ventrini
To: Ben Boyce, Adhvan Chaudry

Boys,

Excellent excellent excellent. I will absolutely open all the doors that I can. However, I want you to know, what you're getting into is a different type of beast, and a different type of company. You want to launch in stores (maybe even your own stores?) within a year.

That's doable but requires you to build in a way that is public-facing. That means branding, marketing, communications, corporate infrastructure—and it's not like people will just give you $100M and expect those things to get figured out.

In other words, it's time to take this enterprise out of the garage.

Yours,
Paolo

BRANDING REPORT

GOOGLE DOC CREATED BY CARRIE CHAN—APRIL 12, 2021

Reviewed and commented on by Ben Boyce and Adhvan Chaudry

MISSION

THE FUTURE seeks to bring time-machine technology to the world by developing, marketing, and selling innovative consumer products to a global audience.

Brand Strategy

Our goal is to roll out a singular, unified messaging campaign that electrifies the imagination of the popular consciousness.

Phase 1: Starting with key influencers and launch-potential plat-forms, we will educate the public on The Future and its revolu-tionary technology.

> *ADHVAN: The word "influencer"*
> *gives me douche-chills.*

Phase 2: We will grow a media presence based on a combination of bold public announcements and evocative advertising placements.

Phase 3: Once product becomes available, we will continue to build excitement through FOMO-based consumer-testimonial targeted ads.

> *BEN: FOMO, MOFO!*

Voice and Personality

When it comes to all consumer-facing messaging, we propose an ap-proach as indicated by this in-voice style manifesto:

The Future is <u>confident</u>.
Bold. Unapologetic. Precise.
Statement-oriented.
Text that is direct and simple.
Sentences that hit hard.
Clear vocabulary and diction.
Uniform messaging across platforms.

> *BEN: This kinda sounds like we're selling Dodge trucks.*

> *ADHVAN: WTF does statement-oriented mean?*
> *Doesn't bother with complete sentences?*

Marketplace Comps

Apple: The high-water mark for lasting brand identity, especially in the consumer-electronics space. Makes technology feel clean, beauti-ful, simple, intuitive.

Uber: Brand feel is high-end, high-tech, sleek, powerful. Conveys sta-tus over universality. Markedly in contrast to Lyft, which aims for more personal, lo-fi, user-friendly, accessible.

Tesla/SpaceX: Similarly, an aspirational consumer product, with a bold mission statement, cultural cachet, and charismatic founder personality.

> ADHVAN: *Charismatic founder personality—just one? Gee I really wonder which one of us she's referring to.*

> BEN: *How much did we pay someone to tell us we should be the next Apple, Uber, or Tesla?*

Brand Colors

Chrome—to evoke the physical device

> BEN: *Shiny!*

Green—as found on a digital clock

> ADHVAN: *Digital clock, so futuristic.*

White—suggestive of the light of knowledge

> BEN: *Little bit of casual racism here, yeah?*

Company Name

As a name, "The Future" is potentially a bit unwieldy. SEO is problematic; Google results are all over the place, and will be difficult to displace. Moreover, virtually no Fortune 500 companies have names that include an article. The following name alternatives are good possibilities to consider:

Prescient

Lesser-known word (therefore SEO-friendly) which means "having foreknowledge." Sound is scientific and technical, with a hint of magic.

> BEN: *Prescient? No, too hard, this one is a mouthful.*

> ADHVAN (reply): *That's what your mom said.*

Peek

A more personal and accessible option. Conjures the notion of "peeking" at the future. Homonym means pinnacle, which connotes success. Emotional connection to the voyeuristic feeling which users might reasonably seek, in line with social media usage.

> *BEN: Sounds like a camgirl porn site.*

> *ADHVAN: Should we maybe start that site? I'd pay for Peek.*

> *BEN (reply): Who pays for porn you weirdo?*

Crystal

Subtly conjures a crystal ball, looking into the future. Also evokes the high-end feel of tableware. Exclusivity suited to a higher price point.

> *ADHVAN: Oh yeah, really subtle.*

> *BEN: Why do we keep getting ideas that suggest magic?*
> *We have to hit home that this is science.*

Quant

Another high-tech option, which leans into the quantum technology at the core of the product. Unique and SEO-ownable.

> *BEN: Isn't this a term for a financial analyst?*

> *ADHVAN (reply): It's the math world's word for a sell-out.*

<u>Logo</u>

Feel should be clear, clean, high-tech. Evoking "see the future" functionality.

Images to consider:

An eye
A clock
An hourglass
A calendar
A telescope

> *BEN: Can't we get something a little more inviting?*

> *ADHVAN: Meaning . . . vaginal? Like airbnb?*
> *Just turn the eye sideways.*

EMAIL — APRIL 12, 2021

From: Paolo Ventrini
To: Ben Boyce, Adhvan Chaudry

Boys . . .

This branding report was undertaken by a top-flight agency. Carrie is one of the best. She came into my office and ripped me a new one over the juvenile comments on her work. If you don't like it, fine. But you also declined to provide her with a jumping-off conversation, which means she was feeling her way in the dark.

We need to get this figured out soon if we're going to hit any of our targets. I have a dinner but I'll try to get out early and meet you in the office by 7:30 so we can hash this out.

Paolo

TEXT MESSAGE EXCHANGE

BEN BOYCE
April 12, 2021 5:23 PM

Hey babe gonna be a little late tonight
Adhi and I just went through this branding report
It's terrible.
And now we gotta go sit down with Paolo.

LEILA KEENER-BOYCE

Oh, OK. How late are we talking here?

I dunno prob 9-10ish?
Don't wait up, I know you gotta be up early
I'll be quiet as a mouse.
Or a ninja.
Sound OK?

TEXT MESSAGE EXCHANGE

LEILA KEENER-BOYCE
April 12, 2021 5:24 PM

Hey A! Hope you're well. Big plans tonight?

ADHVAN CHAUDRY

Hey Lei.
I'm supposed to do a meeting with Paolo,
he wants to go over our branding strategy.
But if you need anything, I can bail on that,
it's not a big deal.

No that's OK, I was just saying hi. You and Ben
are doing that together, right?

Oh. Yes. I see.
Next time you can just say you want to
check on Ben.

Sorry.

TEXT MESSAGE EXCHANGE

BEN BOYCE

I'll be quiet as a mouse.
Or a ninja.
Sound OK?
April 12, 2021 5:29 PM

LEILA KEENER-BOYCE

OK NinjaMouse, have a good time. Certainly seems like
you guys are having fun.

Not really it's a lot of work.
And I miss you.

I'm not upset you're having fun, I'm glad.
Seems like things between you and Adhi are
more like how they used to be.

Yeah I guess so.
Startup life is a little like college.

That's great. Just don't go FULL college-Ben.

I won't. Sleep tight.

TEXT MESSAGE EXCHANGE

BEN BOYCE
April 12, 2021 7:58 PM

Hey Carrie.
Good start with the branding report.

CARRIE CHAN

Good start, huh?
Based on the comments, I'd hate to see what
a bad start looks like

Yeah, sorry about that.
Adhi and I like to joke around
We don't always think about all the work that
goes into things.
Just had a sit-down with Paolo and realized I
was being a jerk.
I'm new to all this!
Being a founder is like 10 jobs in 1.
And I have experience with none of them.

It shows.
But yes, I know it's not easy.

I think we should start over.
I want to take a more personal approach.

How bout we grab drinks and
I talk you through the vision?

> Sure.
> How bout right now?

Oh. Yeah, I could meet in like an hour?

> Great. Haberdasher on Ellsworth.
> See you there.

EXCERPT FROM CONGRESSIONAL HEARING — DECEMBER 1, 2021

REP. ALEXANDRA DELGADO (D-CA): So—Ms. Chan, her ideas about the look, the branding, all of it . . . you knew it was wrong . . . because you had seen what it was going to be already. Right?

BOYCE: That's correct. And I mean, her ideas were not totally off-base. Our website *is* sleek and minimal. It's more Apple than the Apple site, in some ways. And our logo is actually in line with a couple of her ideas. It's an *F* for Future, formed by the hands of a clock. So you can imagine, the feedback she was giving, it could've conceivably led to the results we ended up with. But we had seen the end result already, so . . . we knew more than she did.

REP. ALEXANDRA DELGADO (D-CA): When you consulted on the look and branding of the company . . . did you ever just show her what you'd seen? If you knew that's where it was going to end up anyway?

BOYCE: By this point, we had started making an effort not to do that. Adhi had this theory about what happened to Nikolai, that it was this thing he called a causal loop. Information from the future, looping back in the timeline, causing itself. And he thought the more that happened, the more room there was for . . . you know, trouble.

Think about it; if Carrie looked at the website from the future, and copied that design to make the website, which then *is* the website in the future . . . where'd those ideas *come from*? Reality is serving the information, not the other way around.

REP. ALEXANDRA DELGADO (D-CA): Thank you, Mr. Boyce. You have articulated, very succinctly, one of the primary problems with allowing this technology to go public. I don't think any of us want a world in which our reality is subservient to our gadgets.

BOYCE: But it's not, as long as people make informed choices about how they use it! It's up to the user to decide when to look. And once they do, that choice becomes part of the system of choices they were always going to make. I get that it's tough to wrap your head around, but we are actually *increasing* personal freedom.

REP. ALEXANDRA DELGADO (D-CA): Oh, I understand perfectly. Setting aside the confusing circularity of it all, I am simply pointing to the fact that empowering people with a dangerous tool and trusting them to make perfect choices is a recipe for disaster. Look at your own brief history with this technology. Whenever you hit a roadblock to success and profitability, you wasted little time in turning to the technology, regardless of any supposed philosophical concern with a so-called causal loop.

EMAIL — APRIL 15, 2021

From: Paolo Ventrini
To: Ben Boyce, Adhvan Chaudry

Boys, I've been out on Sand Hill Road beating the war drum, but we can't even get into the right rooms unless we have something to catch the attention of our audience. I know you guys are reticent to release any content into the public sphere, but I need something we can selectively share.

Paolo

REPLY

From: Ben Boyce
To: Paolo Ventrini, Adhvan Chaudry

Hey Paolo,
We talked it over and hear where you're coming from. How's this?

Ben

(The following news article, dated January 2, 2022, was attached.)

THE FUTURE LAUNCHES STRONG IN U.S.

After months of hype and rampant speculation, The Future stores around the country opened on New Year's Day to lines around the block and strong sales. Insiders were expecting solid numbers, since over 50,000 people had pre-ordered the Future 1 units online, which were available Sunday for pickup and shipping. Since the company reported estimates that another 55,000 units had sold in its 22 locations, it's clear that expectations have been met or exceeded.

"It's a strong rollout," said Ben Boyce, the company's boisterous young CEO. "But we're just getting started here."

Given the necessary geographical clustering of the stores, some believers drove over 500 miles and camped out overnight to get their hands on the F1's.

"It's a revolution on par with the Internet," said Wendy Romero, a customer who bought two. "It's going to totally change the way the world works. I mean, I'm going to see my future tonight. Are you?"

The company expects sales to stabilize and remain strong for months to come and is projecting revenues north of $80 million in its first quarter of operation. But some business analysts are skeptical about the company's long-term prospects.

"Their business model is simply unsustainable," commented Eduardo Ortiz, a financial-sector forecaster. "This company is starting out so deep in the R&D hole, they'll need to normalize sales figures on par with Apple if they're going to be in this for the long haul."

Others have voiced doubt about the long-term stability of the technology, with initial reports trickling in of widespread technical issues. But Boyce dismisses these as overblown Internet chatter by jealous discontents. "We've had a few technical glitches, yes. But this is our first day getting the product in the hands of the public. A lot of times, it's an issue of user error. Our solution will be a combination of great customer support, continued public education, and a commitment to keep improving our product."

It remains to be seen if The Future has the long-term staying power to compete with the giants of Silicon Valley. But it's undeniable that the company has completed a spectacular launch, and public demand for the product is sky-high.

REPLY

From: Paolo Ventrini
To: Ben Boyce, Adhvan Chaudry

This is real? This is a news article, from the actual future? These are the numbers we're going to do rolling out at the start of next year? Fuck me we have some work to do, boys, but raising money is certainly not going to be the hard part.

CHAPTER 9

EMAIL—APRIL 16, 2021

From: Paolo Ventrini
To: Ben Boyce, Adhvan Chaudry

Well, boys, I spoke too soon. Turns out sharing the news piece ended up having the opposite of the desired effect. Most of the VCs I sent it to thought it was a hoax.

We're in a bind now because we're not getting public traction without funding, and we can't get funding without a perception of public interest or at least acceptance. Let's brainstorm on how we can get back in the game.

REPLY

From: Ben Boyce
To: Paolo Ventrini, Adhvan Chaudry, Carrie Chan

Hey Paolo,
Sounds good, let's schedule a group sesh. Adhi, you want in on this? If you want to focus on the tech, we can take care of these PR-type situations, I know it's not your thing. Also, I'm adding Carrie to the mix.

REPLY

From: Paolo Ventrini

To: Ben Boyce, Adhvan Chaudry

My goodness, Benjamin, are you, dare I say . . . managing? Using your team in skill-area-appropriate ways? Should I possibly think that you might have read one or two of those management books that I sent your way? Bravo, bravo, bravissimo.

REPLY

From: Adhvan Chaudry

To: Ben Boyce

B—

Yeah, I want in on this.

And Carrie too? Really?

Seems like a situation where we can get a plan going on our own, then bring her in later to execute.

This is our company.

—A

REPLY (TO BOYCE'S EARLIER REPLY)

From: Carrie Chan

To: Ben Boyce, Adhvan Chaudry, Paolo Ventrini

Hey Guys,

Thanks for looping me in. If you want to get this out there, you need to start a conversation about your product, especially among the tech-influencer community. I've got some ideas about how to make that happen fast.

Carrie

REDDIT AMA — APRIL 19, 2021

Hey Reddit, we are Ben Boyce and Adhvan Chaudry, and we invented a time machine! Read all about how it works **HERE.** It'll be on sale in less than a year!

Our CCO Carrie will help us out here and post proof momentarily. Ask us anything!

FortniteFuckery: Why do you call your tech a time machine? Based on the link, it's not exactly gonna take me to any different time, it's just gonna let me see how boring and shitty the world will be next year . . .

> Adh_Ball: We call it a Time Machine because Quantum Computing Device for Trans-Temporal Data Transmission didn't have quite the same ring to it. QCDTTDT is a hell of an acronym.

> BenBoyceAMA: Bro it's a machine that lets you see through time! Maybe try it out before you get all ungrateful-whiner about it. This isn't the latest Marvel trailer, it's a device that's legit gonna change the world.

Hiphophippocampus: Catapult or Trebuchet?

> Adh_Ball: Trebuchet is the superior siege weapon, of course.

> BenBoyceAMA: Uhhhh what kind of question is that?

BernieFlandersLeft: What's a day in the life for you guys? How much do you use the machine?

> BenBoyceAMA: We use it all the time! You get up and check the news from today, I check the news one year from now. You read your email, me too, but I also read the email I'm sending and receiving 365 days in the future. It's crazy and exciting and gives you an edge on everybody.

> Adh_Ball: That said, we also have strict protocols about how we are using the technology. It's important to be thoughtful, ethical, and self-policing in our scope.

> Adh_Ball: But also . . . it is pretty f-ing cool.

Power4Words: Is the future you "see" with your computer the guaranteed only real one?

BenBoyceAMA: Yes indeed. The device is 100% accurate, as it is talking DIRECTLY to itself in the future. No margin of error!

Power4Words: Just to be clear, this means that free will doesn't exist. Bc whatever you see, it means you can't change it.

BenBoyceAMA: No no no, bro, it means you get to see HOW you will end up USING your free will. It's a tricky business but it's exciting!

Power4Words: Is it just me or is that not what free will means at all?

Adh_Ball: Ben and I see this one differently. I think free will is a fairy tale. It's a pretty well-settled scientific question actually. Read Yuval Noah Harari or Benjamin Libet. Some people still argue about it bc it feels like they have free will, but within a year of releasing our product, we'll clear it up pretty solidly.

RunLowlifeRun: Holy shit are they really saying their product will destroy free will?

DicktionaryDude: Are you guys gonna stay friends in the future?

BenBoyceAMA: Yeah bro, we're day 1's, go back 10 years, ride or die.

Adh_Ball: As long as Ben doesn't fire me.

PurrpullDrank: Will PrequelMemes still be a thing in a year?

Adh_Ball: As long as they still have the high ground.

BenBoyceAMA: This some deep-cut nerdery?

Dedditordie: Can you show us a picture from the future?

BenBoyceAMA: We could but we'd have to kill you;-)

Adh_Ball: Serious answer—we have an intense protocol for keeping our data under lock. We're still developing this technology and figuring out the implications. We guarantee that it works and won't launch a product until it's ready, but we're wary of the effects of feeding information from the future into the public sphere until we've diligently evaluated the consequences.

PearlPopper: Im gonna go ahead and recommend you answer this one. Based on how this AMA is going you're gonna come off looking pretty weak-sauce if you don't share something decent.

RatMeetCage: either too pussy or too full of shit

BenBoyceAMA: (Removed)

TheCarltonDancer: Did anyone see the pic before he deleted it?

DeuceTakerTwo: It was up for like 2 mins but I screenshotted it. Anybody PM me and I'll get it to you. EDIT: I'm now getting legal threats from the Communications girl if I continue to share the pic. Obviously not stopping!

PerfectPersimmons: Pic is Boyce at some PR event for launch of the new company offices. Standing on a big stage smiling like a dummy. The Communications girl is there too. And Elon Musk, lookin all chummy with them.

RobbinRobinHood: Total Photoshop job.

Topathemorningtoya: I dunno- can anyone find where they sourced the pic of Elon? Reverse-image-search didn't turn up shit. Looks pretty legit to me.

Blazeitupnow: Hey all compare/contrast their AMA announcement photo with the one they leaked. Boyce got a wedding ring first one, no ring in the "future" one.

MKUltraDude: This is exactly the type of Easter Egg hunt they're tryna get us on.

inigomontoyahere: What a disaster for these idiots

TEXT MESSAGE EXCHANGE

LEILA KEENER-BOYCE

April 19, 2021 4:11 PM

Wow, it looks like you got a bright future with
your buds Elon and Carrie from Communications.
Not me though, huh?
Helllooooo?

BEN BOYCE

Hey babe, sorry, been crazy here
Look those people are colleagues in the future
I mean Carrie is a colleague already
And hey—you always said you wanted to
meet Elon . . .

Do you think I'm gonna skip over you not
wearing a ring?

I dunno, maybe I'm just not wearing it
Maybe I go to the gym that day and forget to
put it back on
Wouldn't be the first time.
I'm forgetful! I suck! Absent minded.

I gotta get back to work.
We'll talk about this later.

TEXT MESSAGE EXCHANGE

BEN BOYCE

April 19, 2021 4:19 PM

Dude this is so fucked
I'm like the first guy in history getting in trouble
for cheating that hasn't even happened.

ADHVAN CHAUDRY

A: that's not true, this isn't even the first time
it's happened to YOU.
I know how Lei gets.

Haha fair enough.

And B: hasn't even happened?
You sure?

Dude, no.

I'm just saying . . .
I know you and Carrie have been out together
a bunch.

Yeah, working our asses off.
Genital contact level: 0

No emotional cheating? No flirting?

Lay off Dr. Phil.
It's not my fault if she's into me.
Now I'm paying for some shit I haven't even
done yet.

Yet?
Resigned to your adultery already?

No. You know what I mean.

Look, I don't want to rub it in, but . . .
None of this would have happened if you
hadn't put the picture up
We have protocols on this for a reason

Fuuuuuuuuck Yoooooouuuuu

TEXT MESSAGE EXCHANGE

LEILA KEENER-BOYCE
April 19, 2021 4:22 PM

Hey A.
What do you think about all that?

ADHVAN CHAUDRY

I think your husband has remarkably thin skin
And jeopardized our whole business bc of
some troll

You know what I mean. The ring thing, and
the possibility of what might happen. Am I
overreacting here?

Honestly, I'm not sure.
It sort of depends on a fundamental question
about free will and how the universe works.

Right. So either, Option 1: My marriage might
be fine, and we have agency over our choices.
Or Option 2: My marriage is fucked, and free
will is an illusion, and nothing we decide matters.
Call me naïve, but if I got a choice here, I'm
gonna go with #1.

Fair enough.
But if that's the case, our technology doesn't
really do anything.

Maybe it helps people avert disaster.
Helps people make better choices.

Maybe.
Or maybe quite the opposite.

TEXT MESSAGE EXCHANGE (CONT'D)

BEN BOYCE

Fuuuuuuuuck Yoooooouuuuu
April 19, 2021 4:28 PM

ADHVAN CHAUDRY

Hey man.
One more thing about the photo.
Aside from all the crap about your ring.
Notice anything else missing?

Uhhh like another inch of my hair?
Is that what you meant?
Guessing not.
What'd you have in mind?

Nothing.

You don't mean you, do you?

You tell me.

Bro it's a public event.
You've been crystal goddamn clear
You don't want anything to do with any of
that noise.

Seems surprising.

Look, we saw your bio on the future website
CTO and Co-Founder.
You're not goin anywhere till you want to.
You're the top secret behind-the-scenes code
ninja!
Besides, you think my mom knows who Steve
Wozniak is?
No way.
And guarantee that Woz likes it that way.

Yeah.

Totally.

I dunno what I'm worried about.

Don't let your brain get the best of you.

Word.

Listen Carrie's got a good idea I think for our
next step.
But it's even more public, not less.
If we're gonna make it work, I need you behind
me all the way.
Ride or die.
You up for it?

Of course.

I'm the genie, you make the wishes.

The GENIUS GENIE!
This is gonna be good . . .

TRANSCRIPT OF TED TALK — DELIVERED APRIL 24, 2021

BEN BOYCE—"THE FUTURE IS YOURS"

0:00

When I was a kid, I used to love thinking about the future. About going to the moon, robots cleaning my room, living forever. But when I was twelve years old, my mom got cancer. And all of a sudden, I wasn't dreaming about the future anymore, I was dreading it. What would the coming year bring? Healing and remission? Or more pain, more metastasis? Every birthday, I wondered if it was the last one I had with my mom. I couldn't live in the present, much less plan for the future.

00:30

Mom fought hard for five years, in and out of chemo and remission, before she passed away. The year before I started college.

Ever since she got sick, I have been scared to death of the future. Of what the coming year might bring. And like many of us, I've immersed myself in work, in an attempt to create some lasting legacy, some deep wealth, some impervious relationship. Some safety and insurance against the slings and arrows of outrageous fortune.

00:55

We all live with the uncertainty of not knowing what's coming. We can never be fully *present* because we're so fixated and fearful about what's next.

But it doesn't have to be that way. Because I've been working together with leading scientific minds to build a technology that lets us see into the future.

01:25

In a nutshell, it's a computer, the size and shape of a typical desktop machine. Just like the one you already have, in every way except one. This machine can connect to itself, one year in the future. Through the joined principles of quantum computing and quantum entanglement, it's possible to receive email from your future self and browse websites that don't exist yet.

01:50

Of course, the proof is in the pudding. And I wouldn't be standing on the TED stage if I didn't have something to show for myself. You're probably wondering, what's it gonna be? What's he gonna show us from the future? Stock reports? News stories? Highlights from the Super Bowl, for a season that hasn't even started yet?

02:20

Well, you came here to see TED Talks—to be the first ones to see what's new in the world of ideas—so how about a little preview of next year's TED stage?

VIDEO PLAYS: *In which Ben Boyce is visible on the TED stage, in different clothes, with different facial hair.*

That is me. Giving a TED Talk. *Next year*. Ten months from now. Want to hear what I have to say?

02:55

ONSCREEN: Now, when I gave my talk last year, The Future was still in its infancy, and many were struggling to wrap their minds around the possibilities of what it could do. Today, the consensus has come around to acceptance, and many are using our product on a daily basis as they make decisions about every aspect of their lives: where to work, who to marry, how to spend their time, and so much more.

But we have a long way to go if we want to ensure a world where time-travel technology remains stable and beneficial. Which is why educating our users is so important. And that's why I'm launching a new initiative—

VIDEO ENDS

I know, it's a tease! But the whole talk is available on our website, along with a selection of other downloads from the future, and links to some of the science validating our methodology. That's just a peek at the vast wealth of what will be available through your very own personal time machine.

04:25

We live in an age where a small group of companies have nearly complete control over our lives. Technology is intertwining with every facet of human existence, and the means to build it are consolidating into the hands of a few. They all know what's coming, they're making it happen, and we're just checking the news to find out what our lives will look like tomorrow. Google, Facebook, Amazon . . . they have a monopoly on the future.

05:10

But that ends today. By creating an affordable machine that gives everyone access to their own future, we are leveling the playing field. Now I no longer have to be afraid of the unknown. Of what's coming next. And as a result, I'm dreaming big again. I hope you'll join me. Thank you.

APPLAUSE

TWEETS

@HEYBENBOYCE

So excited I can finally share what I've been up to! Check out my TED Talk (Link) and learn about the revolution that's coming! #TheFuture #SeeTheFuture

@TEDCHRIS

Thank you @HeyBenBoyce for one of the most revolutionary talks in TED history! Long live #TheFuture

@RAYKURZWEIL

An unexpected wrinkle in our transition to the singularity. #TheFuture

@ELONMUSK

Revolutionary potential here. The underlying scientific principles are sound, but share your code and design specs if you really want us to get onboard! #TheFuture

@MICHAELPOLLAN

A game-changing new technology that could vastly expand the bounds of human potential. #TheFuture

@NASA

Well worth a watch for anyone who cares about the future of tech! #TheFuture

@KANYEWEST

Did I not tell yall this was comin? #TheFuture

@KARASWISHER

Bold claims here. Anyone else think that two years from now we'll be deconstructing how he got us all to believe the hype? #TheFuture

@ALGORE

Thank you @HeyBenBoyce for an inspiring vision of change. Finally, a technology that climate-change deniers will be unable to ignore. Imagine what we can do to care for our planet when we have the power to see what's coming. #TheFuture

@IAMWILL

This vid is fire. My boy @HeyBenBoyce out here showing us all what is UP! Much love, much support, long live The Future! #TheFuture

@ARIANAGRANDE

can't even believe wut i'm seeing lol this dude is a straight-up genius #TheFuture

EMAIL

From: Adhvan Chaudry
To: Ben Boyce

B—
Congrats.
You're officially viral.

—A

TUMBLR BLOG POST—APRIL 25, 2021

THE BLACK HOLE: MUSINGS OF AN ANONYMOUS
SCI-FI SUPERFAN

"The Loneliness of the Wookiee"

At the end of *A New Hope,* our team of plucky adventurers succeeds in saving the galaxy and blowing up the Death Star.

Luke, Han, and Chewie stand upon a dais . . .

celebrated before a massive crowd . . .

And Leia presents medals to Han, and Luke, and . . .

That's it. Seriously.

No medal for Chewbacca.

The end of *Rise of Skywalker* acknowledged the oversight,

    (only 42 years late)

    which really begs the question: why did it happen in the first place?

    I suspect it's a matter of how we understand heroes.

    Luke is an archetype we respect—a dashing young dreamer, saved by faith.

    So is Han—the roguish scoundrel, redeemed by love.

    But Chewie? The steadfast loyal friend who kept the *Falcon* running?

    There's no arc, because none is needed.

    So there is no celebration.

    And he is expected to be grateful.

The sidekick is always a second-class citizen,

    even though he plays as much a role as anyone else.

    When Han comes back heroically in the end,

    are we supposed to believe that's entirely his idea?

    We have Chewie to thank.

    He is the moral center and soul of the team . . .

    but is treated as a subhuman animal.

In the final shot of the film, he snarls in his guttural language . . .

    And I think we've all assumed it means something like "Go team!"

But perhaps what he means is, "Where the fuck is my medal?"
Only, there is no sympathy for him.
He is isolated and unable to communicate.
Even as he stands beside his friends, before an adoring crowd,
he is fundamentally alone.

TEXT MESSAGE EXCHANGE

LEILA KEENER-BOYCE
April 25, 2021 7:24 PM

Hey A.

ADHVAN CHAUDRY

Hey Lei. How you been?

Good thanks.
I just wanted to say, I saw the TED Talk, and I
thought the way Ben handled it was pretty shitty.
Talking about the company and the tech like
it's all his. He left you out of the story and I'm
sure it doesn't feel great.

It's OK.
We strategized on it with Paolo and Carrie.
Everyone agreed: personal story, single
founder, stronger message.
And I always wanted to stay behind the scenes.

I know what you're doing to protect yourself,
but I also know that it hurts.
Whenever you want someone to talk about
the feelings with, I'm here. I won't even say
anything to Ben.

Thanks Lei.
It means a lot.

I'm worried if I start talking like that it'll open
a dam and all flood out.

What will all flood out?
April 25, 2021 7:45 PM

You there Adhi? I've seen a lot of bubbles appear
and then vanish.

Sorry I'm just tired.
Thanks for checking in.
I'm good though.
Have a good night.

You too.

EMAIL — APRIL 26, 2021

From: Paolo Ventrini
To: Ben Boyce, Adhvan Chaudry

Hello Gents,
Congrats on the TED Talk blowing up the Internet. Looks
like it's already having an impact. I'm getting hit up by
VCs all over town, including some of the assholes that
wouldn't even take my call last week. My asst is into setting meetings; take a look at the calendar, we want to go
back to back on this momentum.

Paolo

TEXT MESSAGE EXCHANGE

LEILA KEENER-BOYCE
April 28, 2021 8:13 AM

Knock em dead today A.
I know you guys got a full one lined up.
These guys should be so lucky to get a piece of you.

ADHVAN CHAUDRY

Thanks Lei.
Just trying to focus, not get in my head.

Oh sorry.
Your head can be a scary place, don't get lost!
Good luck.

TEXT MESSAGE EXCHANGE

LEILA KEENER-BOYCE
April 28, 2021 8:15 AM

Knock em dead today babe! Saw the pic you
posted on Insta, the new jacket looks awesome.

BEN BOYCE

Thanks Princess.
I'll update you when I hear more.

April 28, 2021 5:02 PM

Hey Princess.
Do you see me as more of a Bentley guy,
or a Maserati guy?

!!!!
How much?

7M.

Wow that's a great start!

From Welder Bachman Kane.
They were on the low end.
6 meetings, 6 investors.
All on board.
Today . . . total . . .
(Drumroll please . . .)

Babe, don't do me like that.

102.
MILLION. DOLLARS.

Fuck me.

Soon as I get home:)

I'm so happy for you!
Is A happy too?

Yeah, I think so.
I mean he's not exactly SMILING but still.

Well, that's not his style.

He says it's all Monopoly money at this stage.
But it's a LOT of Monopoly money.

Give him a big hug.
Or manly back-slap or whatever.

Come give him one yourself!
We're having a little impromptu celebration tonight
I think I can arrange to bring a +1 ;-)

Oooh so flattered you picked me.

And hey, maybe this could be a good
opportunity to start our little Operation Cupid?

You want me to bring one of my friends
to meet Adhi, on like 3 hrs notice?

It's worth a shot.
Come on, for the good of the company.
He'll be easier to work with if he's getting
laid on occasion.

Gross. I don't even want to think about that.
But yeah I guess I can ask at least. Amy?

Eh. I don't think she's really his type.

Babe we have no idea what his type is.
We've literally never seen him date ANYONE.

How bout Cali?

Kayleigh. Yes she's single and smart but maybe
a little out of his league?

My boy is a millionaire now!
Don't give me that league shit,
he just got drafted into the pros!

Haha alright I'll give it a shot with Kayleigh.

Great. Reserved the lounge at OPAL. 9:00.

Hon, you hate Opal. You said it's a bougie hellhole
full of douchey VC money

I don't hate the place, I hate being looked down on
But those days are OVER

Now that you got douchey VC money of your own?

Exactly. See ya tonight

TEXT MESSAGE EXCHANGE

ADHVAN CHAUDRY
April 29, 2021 11:22 AM

Hi Kayleigh.
It's Adhi.

KAYLEIGH MILLS

Hey. Wow didn't really expect to hear from you.

Sorry.
Hope it's OK I'm reaching out.

Of course.
I'm just saying, it wasn't an obligation.

Just wanted to clear the air.
I'm sorry last night was a little weird.

No need. We both had a lot to drink.
The party was fun.
Congrats on your success, I'm happy for you guys.

Thank you.
It's not really something I typically do.

You don't raise 100 million dollars EVERY week?
Come on you gotta step up your game!

No. I mean going home with someone.

Yeah, that much was clear.
Look, I came out last night bc Leila said you were a great
guy.
And I can tell, she's right.
But you're also completely unavailable.

Well you seem like a lovely person.
I'm just not the romantic feelings type.

Actually you seem to be quite in touch with your feelings.
It's just that they're not for me.
Pro-tip, don't let a friend set you up if you're
already in love with her.

Sorry about that.
I'd appreciate if you don't tell Leila about how things went.

Lips are sealed.

Just out of curiosity . . .
You think I should tell her how I feel?

NO. Jesus. Definitely not.

That's what I thought, just checking.

Look, I don't know you well or anything,
but can I give you a little unsolicited advice?
MOVE. ON.

Oh brilliant idea, I hadn't thought of that.

I'm sure you have but it doesn't show.
You just started a business with her husband!
It seems like you're either playing some long con to
try to get with her, or you're trying to punish yourself.
Maybe both.

Right. Thanks for the armchair expertise.

Take care of yourself Adhi.

CHAPTER 10

EMAIL — MAY 1, 2021

From: Adhvan Chaudry
To: Prisha Chaudry

Mom—
I am sending you some money.
The company Ben and I started is doing well.
We're building a new type of computer.
People invested a lot.
I'm going to send you more like this every month.
You should quit the dry cleaners, I know it has been terrible for your back.
Thank you for raising me well.

—A

REPLY

Hello Adhvan thank uou for the kind of message. You are good at computers can uou please help sit up my phone when you are here next. Photos are on it but sending them does no. I will make biryani. I can not quit of the cleners they are only the money but thank you.

Now that your have some money you think to find nice girl to marry?

REPLY

Mom—
I'll be over for biryani tomorrow night.
I would be happy to help you with your phone.
Someday I will try to get married, I promise.
I am sorry that my heart has not made it easier.
I love you.

—A

EMAIL

From: Ben Boyce
To: Adhvan Chaudry

Dude check this out. Got a DM on my Twitter this morning. From my dad. No joke. Checked him out, looks legit far as I can tell . . .

Quoted Text:

Benjamin! Long time no talk! I'm sorry that it's been a while. I'm sure it's strange to hear from me now. I saw your online video recently of giving a public talk about a new technology, and I've read everything I can about it. Amazing! Seems like you are really taking over the world. I'm so proud of you and always knew you were meant for great things. Sorry I fell out of your life, at the time that felt like the only option, and when I was ready to be part of it again, your mom convinced me it was better to leave you alone. But I regret the years that I missed. My email is cboyce17@hotmail.com, I'd love to hear from you son.

REPLY

B—
Whoa.
Amazing.
You excited about this?
Have you shown it to Lei?

—A

REPLY

I dunno how to feel about it. And no I haven't told her . . . I mean, I'm just worried she's gonna say I gotta go to therapy with him or some shit. Like right now I could just pretend I never saw this and ignore it, but soon as I tell her it's gonna be a whole thing.

What do you think? Is it worth engaging?

REPLY

B—
Up to you obviously.
The timing is certainly a cause for some concern.
I don't want to disparage him.
But reaching out now is a little starfucky, if not outright golddiggy.
I took the liberty of gathering what I could from the Prototype.

From what I can see (social media, what's available online . . .)

It doesn't look like your dad will be in your life next year.

So, you can let that inform your decision as you see fit.

—A

REPLY

Dude wtf?! I didn't ask you to do that. I was looking for
your input as a FRIEND, your opinion as a fucking
HUMAN. I don't want all my choices all tied up with our
data.

REPLY

B—

My apologies.

I assumed you wanted that information.

I had hoped it could spare you the difficulty of a tough
decision.

For what it's worth, the data is not definitive in this situation.

Maybe he's present in your life, but not in the content
you're posting.

I can certainly give you my "human opinion" instead.

Bc more than I know the future, I know *you*.

And I know what it's like to grow up without a father.

I know you'd love nothing more than for him to be proud
of you.

But I would hate for you to chase that, and get hurt or
used in the process.

So I advise you, as your friend, to proceed with caution.

—A

REPLY

Yeah how bout I live my own life, and you do the same.

EMAIL

From: Ben Boyce
To: Carl Boyce

Hey Carl . . . or should I call you Pops or something? I'm gonna go ahead and keep it at Carl for now. It's definitely a little overwhelming to hear from you. And I'll be honest it opens up some tough old memories. But I'm not totally shut off from starting to talk at least. Maybe we could hop on the phone sometime?

REPLY

Benjamin,

Great to hear from you! Absolutely, we can take it all in stride. I know there's a lot of history to move past. But I'd love to see you and catch up in person, that's just how I roll, I'm a lot better in person than the phone. I'm living out in Philadelphia now, and truth is, it's been a rough couple years. If you could wire me a small sum (a loan I will repay soon of course), I could catch up on a couple things around here, then perhaps get a ticket to fly out and see you and your lovely wife. It would be really good to catch up, son!

REPLY

Hey, it's a busy time for sure on my end, we're hiring a lot right now trying to scale up fast, but I could definitely make time for a short visit, either in Philly or out here. Meaning I could be the one to travel if that's a burden. That said, I'm not really in a position to make a loan at this point.

REPLY

Benjamin,

I know you're in a crazy busy exciting time with all that's happening at work, I just saw a new article about you online, and the guys at the garage are talking about your technology all the time! I don't want to infringe on your life too much. Captain of industry! Mover and shaker! I love it!

So I'm not sure what you mean about not in a position. The articles I saw certainly indicated otherwise! I wouldn't be even mentioning it at all if it wasn't a tough time for me, I've had multiple health situations the last couple years, and that stuff adds up. I know it's been quite a while, but we're family, and family is sacred. Also I hope you do realize, I sent money to you and your mother for several years. Maybe she and her parents didn't tell you about that but I did. They never liked me. I know it's easy to paint me as a bad guy when I had to leave like that, but I honestly tried to do right by you, and I hoped you would try to do the right thing with me.

REPLY

I certainly was never aware that you sent any money. If that was kept from me, I'm sorry about that. We certainly could've used some money at the end when Mom was sick.

As for what I can and can't do, I understand how it looks from the outside but let me just try to shed some light on the truth of how startup money actually works. You see a headline about 100M and your eyes go wide. But that is money that the COMPANY has. And most of it isn't in the bank, it's just committed. As partial owner, I have a PORTION of that (which isn't as big as you might think). But that money is not cash. It's like stock in something that I can't sell. Bc for one thing, we're not publicly traded, and number 2, if a founder starts selling off his stake privately it looks REALLY bad, the value will quickly plummet, AND I would probably get pushed out of my job real quick bc the optics of it suggest I'm not serious about the co.

What I do have is a SALARY. And my salary has to be approved by the Board, based on what I've made/could make other places. And it's generally agreed in Silicon Valley that if you believe in your company then you try to take the lowest salary you can.

So I'll be fully transparent here, I'm paying myself a healthy paycheck, equivalent to low six figures for the year. Which, given the cost of living here, does not leave a ton of money lying around. I'm also still paying off a hefty chunk of student loan debt, as well as credit cards from the months I committed to this before there was ANY income. Plus my wife Leila and I would love to START saving for a house! If you want me to buy you a plane ticket, I could do that, but I'm not going to send you cash.

REPLY

Benjamin,

Look son, I never knew about what was happening with your mom until years after she passed, I'm so sorry about that and wish her parents would've reached out to me. I want to be in your life now I'm just not in a position to go hop on a plane. I'm an old man and I got a bad situation here. You're sitting on millions, married to millions, I know you can afford to share a little. If you want to wait until I can afford to leave work and fly across the country just to visit, then I guess we're back where we started. It's sad for me see that my own flesh and blood puts no stock in family.

REPLY

You are un fuckin believable. There's a million things I wanna say to you now, but I'm gonna cut to the chase and say the one that matters.

THANK YOU. Thank you for leaving all those years ago and freeing me from your toxic bullshit. Thank you for showing me that I had to take care of myself bc that's what made me who I am today. Thank you for showing me that family's not just what you're given, it's what you CHOOSE. And today I got a wife who's with me no matter what and a friend and partner who's like a brother. That's MY family. And the last thing I need is an old man crawling out of the fuckin woodwork to take what I've earned.

So yeah, thank you, now fuck off.

FORWARD OF PREVIOUS EMAIL THREAD

> From: Ben Boyce
> To: Adhvan Chaudry
>
> Hey man, check out the "convo" w my dad. Turns out you were right. Guess you know me too well. Bums me out that that's what I come from, freaks me out that it's what I might turn into someday. So yeah I'm just telling you so you'll like fuckin SHOOT ME if that starts to happen.

REPLY

> B—
> This is one time I take no pleasure in being right.
> I'm sorry if I stuck my nose in prematurely.
> I only wanted to help.
> I know a thing or two about deadbeat dads, and you are better off without him.
> More importantly, you are NOT him.
> As a husband already, and someday, I'm sure, as a father.
> I don't need the Prototype to see, you are better.
> Your future will be different.
> And yes, I promise to shoot you if necessary:)
>
> —A

EXCERPT FROM CONGRESSIONAL HEARING, DECEMBER 1, 2021

BOYCE: Look, I'd rather not dredge up all these situations from my personal life. It's an old, familiar story, OK? I got some money, and it made some problems. I don't think we need to get into the soap opera of it all.

REP. MICHELLE BAXTER (D-GA): Mr. Boyce, our interest in these matters is not prurient. We are taking a look at how this technology will affect millions of users. It absolutely *does* matter how it tangles with human relationships.

BOYCE: You can't ban a technology because of how it could, *potentially,* affect people's relationships. Cell phones, dating apps, none of these things are subject to congressional oversight. We're not talking about life and death here.

REP. MICHELLE BAXTER (D-GA): You are not in a position to define the scope of congressional oversight. And your own testimony has pointed to ways in which the technology actually *does* create life-and-death situations.

BOYCE: OK, yes, but we anticipate that overall the device will improve human life and safety.

REP. MICHELLE BAXTER (D-GA): Overall? . . . Mr. Boyce, since you can see the future, let me ask you: Are there people who will die as a result of your technology?

BOYCE: Well . . . It depends what you mean by "as a result."

REP. MICHELLE BAXTER (D-GA): That answer hardly inspires confidence.

BOYCE: Look, this is a Waymo situation.

REP. MICHELLE BAXTER (D-GA): Excuse me?

BOYCE: Self-driving cars. Everybody knows they're coming, the only question is when and how. People argue about what's the threshold for putting them on the road. How safe is safe enough, right?

Thing is, they're ready to go already, they're actually safer than human drivers. For every hundred million miles of human driving, you have around two fatalities. In a self-driving sample set, the rate drops 30 to 40 percent. That means going fully autonomous would save hundreds of lives a year in the U.S. alone. But we're so scared of people dying *from* technology, we won't make changes that will allow technology, on the whole, to save lives. Which, I think, is comparable to the effect we could expect from widespread adoption of The Future.

REP. MICHELLE BAXTER (D-GA): I will simply repeat my question, Mr. Boyce, and remind you that you are under oath and compelled to be truthful: Based on the data you've gathered, are there people who will die as a result of your technology, who would not die otherwise?

BOYCE: A more sensible way to look at it is like this: Our technology will be adopted. And I anticipate that fewer people, overall, will die as a result of the adoption. But yes, of course, some people, in somewhat related ways, and certain situations . . . yes, people will die.

CHAPTER 11

EMAIL — MAY 3, 2021

From: Ben Boyce
To: Adhvan Chaudry

Hey man I checked the news today, see the article attached. Kinda freaking out about this. We gotta take a look and figure out what we can do.

Attachment:

NEWS ARTICLE DOWNLOADED THROUGH TF1 PROTOTYPE

FLOODING AT "THE FUTURE" STORES BLAMED ON CYBERATTACK
May 3, 2022, San Francisco, CA

Customers were just starting to stream into the company's flagship retail location in the Mission District at the beginning of the day when alarms suddenly sounded and overhead fire-control sprinklers were activated. As a downpour drenched the store, workers moved quickly to escort customers outside and cover as many of the floor-model units as possible. Major damage was done, both to the expensive inventory and to the company's already-embattled reputation.

Nearly identical scenes played out at five other retail locations around the country, in Los Angeles, Las Vegas, Austin, Chicago, and New York, all at the exact same time. Officials report that there was no actual risk of fire at any of the stores. Rather, it is believed that the systems were activated by a coordinated hack, which resisted attempts at override.

As a result, water continued to pour down on the interior of each store for hours, until fire crews arrived and were able to manually override the systems. Based on initial reports, there were no injuries, but it is estimated that more than $5,000,000 worth of inventory was destroyed.

Police and FBI investigators are still attempting to determine who was responsible. "Based on preliminary evidence, we're confident it was a deliberate attack," said Police Chief Raymond Bautista of San Francisco. Investigators are scouring the store locations for physical evidence, which they say could take several days, while the FBI's Cyber Terrorism Task Force has opened an inquiry as well.

The multiplicity of attacks appears likely to have been the result of a coordinated operation, carried out by a group with agents operating in several cities. The Future CEO Ben Boyce appeared to affirm this view: "We are being targeted by a fringe group of Luddites, who do not reflect the widespread enthusiasm for our technology." He added that customers have nothing to worry about. "Moving forward, we will be re-evaluating our security protocols, both in our stores and online."

Since it became available to the public at the beginning of the year, The Future technology has been highly divisive. While many early adopters hail it as a giant leap forward for the information economy, think tanks have warned of the device's potential to sow widespread chaos. Some religious groups have viewed it as an indicator of end times, and certain fringe sects have vowed to oppose it by any means necessary. Government watchdogs continue to debate regulation that would dictate how and if the devices could be sold at all.

At present, there are no plans to cease sales of the product, The Future 1, or to disrupt operations of the company.

ADDENDUM:

As of press time, this paper has declined to participate in publication of future-projected information obtained from The Future 1 sources. Until we are confident in The Future 1 as a stable information source, we will not present such prognostications as news.

REPLY

> B—
> Yes, this is certainly unfortunate.
> But not particularly surprising, given the resistance we've anticipated.
> And knowing the way our technology works . . . what can we do?
>
> —A

REPLY

Dude, this means people are gonna be actively trying to SABOTAGE our company. And look at how they're doing it! It's like the prank in the library back in the day. It's somebody who KNOWS US and is trying to fuck with our heads. We gotta figure out who's gonna do it and stop them.

REPLY

B—

The connection to the library . , . maybe.

But this is a fairly common way to carry out a cyberattack with IRL results.

More importantly, why bother trying to preemptively investigate, when we know there's nothing we can do about it?

Or to put it another way—if there is anything we can do, then the technology we've created is useless.

Then what it sees is not the future, but one possible future. If that is the case, then our whole business plan will collapse.

—A

REPLY

I disagree, I think there's a LOT we can do. Beef up security protocols. Figure out who's gonna do it and stop them! We've got a year, so let's be the heroes that solve the mystery and SAVE THE DAY. I'm gonna loop in Paolo and get his help to figure it out.

REPLY

B—

Do not send this to Paolo. Or anyone.

Do not try to get more info about who is responsible.

Doing so will only entangle your fate with theirs.

Think about the mother we tried to save in Oakland.

You will only re-create that situation.
You need to forget it and delete that article.

—A

REPLY

NO. WAY. Not OK. I'll leave out Paolo yeah, fine, but we gotta figure something out, I'm not about to just sit on this.

REPLY

B—
Look at what happened to Nikolai.
He looked into his own future . . .
and as far as we can tell, doing so merely caused his own death.
Moreover, think about your own role in that situation.
If you hadn't been there and argued with him about the technology . . .
if his state of mind had been different . . .
then his fate (and the future he foresaw) might have been entirely different.

—A

REPLY

Yo man, that is a low blow bringing up Nikolai and honestly so fucked up I don't even know where to begin.

Are you seriously not gonna take any action here? Super disappointing. That's not the Adhi I know. The Adhi I know is a fuckin ENGINEER. And when I asked you what that really meant freshman year, you told me it means a PROBLEM SOLVER.

So, it's time for a next step. We need a machine that goes beyond just "information." One that lets you actually CHANGE things. Otherwise, we're on a collision course with an iceberg of inevitability.

In short . . . yeah, we got a problem here. Both of us, together. Now, are you gonna run out and leave your friend holding the bag on this? Or are you gonna strap in and do your best to find a SOLUTION?

TUMBLR BLOG POST — MAY 6, 2021

THE BLACK HOLE: ANONYMOUS MUSINGS OF A
SCI-FI SUPERFAN

"Krishna Was an Alien"

I would like to advocate for classifying religious texts as science fiction.
  We have learned enough to dispense with any factual claims they make . . .
     but they may still entertain us, even enlighten us,
     if we can view them as made-up stories about extraterrestrial beings.
     Sci-fi, like religion, is concerned with the big questions, the cosmos,
     epic metaphors to explore the human condition.
     The last time a "major" religion was invented (50 years ago)
     it was called Scientology, and was created by a failed sci-fi writer.
     Perhaps we can all agree to view the Bible less as sacred scripture,
     and more as the precursor to *2001* and *Dune*.

Being versed in the Hindu religion of my family,
  I have found myself drawn recently to the *Bhagavad Gita,*
  which becomes far more readable when viewed as a story of alien visitation.

The whole thing begins with Arjuna, sitting on a ridge,

    preparing to lead his men into battle.

    Desperate to win, to prove himself.

    Then the many-headed god Krishna descends to Earth in a flying chariot

    (clearly a spaceship, described in the language available 2000 years ago).

    Krishna is a 4-dimensional being, timeless,

    able to see all events past, present, and future

    (much like the Tralfamadorians in *Slaughterhouse Five*).

Krishna reveals to Arjuna the outcome of the battle,

    and even worse, the meaninglessness of the war he is engaged in.

    The illusion and vanity of all human endeavors.

    After this wisdom is imparted, Arjuna is prepared to leave it all behind—

    to call off the battle, and go home with his men.

But Krishna tells him no.

    If he leaves, he will leave alone.

    He must fulfill his dharma (his duty).

So it is Arjuna's burden to fight, and drown the battlefield in blood,
even when he knows better.

Most scholars see his dilemma in terms of destiny,
    but I would call it the curse of enlightenment—
    seeing the futility and meaninglessness of it all,
    but still gripped with the need to win.
    Still desperate to prove his mettle.
    Still attached, by the bonds of human connection, to his army.
    He has no choice but to lead them into the fray,
    because if he does not do his duty, he does not know who he is.
    The knowledge and wisdom of the gods do not save him—
    they merely alienate him from his men,
    and leave him deeply, fundamentally alone.

EXCERPT FROM CONGRESSIONAL HEARING — DECEMBER 1, 2021

SEN. ELEANOR BALLENTINE (R-NC): Mr. Boyce, have you considered, in the least, the larger implications of this technology, on a moral and spiritual level?

BOYCE: Excuse me?

SEN. ELEANOR BALLENTINE (R-NC): Meaning what this might mean for the *soul* of the person using it.

BOYCE: No, ma'am, I do not see it as really the purview of a science and technology hearing to get into . . . religious questions like that.

SEN. ELEANOR BALLENTINE (R-NC): I can feel you snickering at my question, and I'm aware that a California liberal like yourself might not give much thought to such matters. But as the representative of my constituents, 90 percent of whom self-identify as Christians, and all of whom will be affected by your technology, I think you ought to consider how a machine that effectively destroys free will might impact the eternal souls of all of us.

BOYCE: Is there a question for me to answer here?

SEN. ELEANOR BALLENTINE (R-NC): The Book of Revelation refers to the rise of "a charismatic leader who will deceive the world with his gift of Prophecy."

BOYCE: Oh, so I'm one of the horsemen of the Apocalypse.

SEN. ELEANOR BALLENTINE (R-NC): You're the one who said it. Matthew tells us that there is no virtue without choice, yet your machine takes that away. And our nation is built on the value of freedom, yet you give us a technology that tells us we have none.

BOYCE: Listen . . . I'm not the bad guy here. Our technology is not destroying the fabric of the cosmos, it is just delivering information. And I have been actively engaged in trying to protect the possibility of choice, from the very beginning. I am confident, in time, when we get to another level with our technology, we will actually open up a whole new level of personal freedom.

SEN. ELEANOR BALLENTINE (R-NC): What's that mean, another level?

BOYCE: I'm sorry, but I am neither able nor willing to discuss that at this time.

REPLY (TO BOYCE'S EARLIER EMAIL) — MAY 7, 2021

From: Adhvan Chaudry
To: Ben Boyce

B—
I have been giving the matter of agency and inevitability
some thought.
Here is where I net out . . .

Our invention seems to affirm a Newtonian view of the
"clockwork universe."

One big, interlocked machine.

All the pieces, all the atoms, working together,

in a way that is fundamentally unchangeable.

Nothing can be changed by the technology we've created,

because only *information* is transmitted through time.

In order to "change things," you would need to disrupt
the machine.

Throw a wrench into the gears, so to speak.

You would need a device that lets you *physically* travel
through time.

Which, as I've said before, is theoretically impossible.

Now, before you get all excited . . .

"theoretically impossible" does not just mean "very difficult."

It means mathematically, it does not make sense.

It means we'd need infinite energy density (on the order of
a black hole).

These are DeLorean-level fantasies.

Best to put them out of your mind.

—A

REPLY

Come on, I believe in you. And right now, we got a working product, a surplus of funding, and a guaranteed success of our first launch. We hired that Evelyn chick out of
Microsoft last week, you said yourself she's even better at
CS than you—so put her in charge of day-to-day maintenance . . .

And meanwhile, we'll set up a little side lab for you,
some top-secret shit, and you just go in there a few hours
a week, and do some Einstein magic on the whiteboards
and whatnot . . .

I got you a little present, it's being delivered tomorrow:)

REPLY (THE FOLLOWING DAY)

B—
Thank you for the DeLorean.
It is the most ridiculous thing I've seen in my life,
and I love it.

At the end of the day, my duty is to serve.
You're the boss. The God of the Future.
If you say this is the way, I believe.
I'll get started, on an exploratory basis,
to see if we can break the clockwork universe.

—A

CHAPTER 12

SEC FORMAL COMPLAINT — SUBMITTED JUNE 4, 2021

Dear Sirs:

We are writing to inform you that the Securities and Exchange Commission has opened an Active Investigation into the business or enterprise incorporated under the name The Future LLC.

The Future has been brought to our attention by anonymous individuals who have reported that its technology may have been used in breach of the Insider Trading and Securities Act of 1988 (Title 17 CFR 240.10b5-1).

You are advised that subpoenas of relevant information will be forthcoming, and encouraged to employ legal counsel. You are also advised that as of this notice it is a criminal breach to destroy, remove, or suppress any documentation which may be relevant to this inquiry.

Martin Sloe
Senior Investigator
Federal Securities and Exchange Commission

EMAIL — JUNE 7, 2021

From: Ben Boyce

To: Leila Keener-Boyce

Hey Princess, thanks for taking a look at this. I know I was freaking out when I called you earlier but I'm calm now, and I just want to say I really appreciate any help you can give, and sorry if it seemed like I yelled at you. I just don't know how big this is gonna be.

REPLY

Babe, I understand that you're feeling really triggered here. A startup is like your baby, and your autonomic nervous system is kicking in because it feels like your child is being threatened. Just keep in mind, it's not me that poses the threat. I'm on your side.

For some perspective, I would just let you know that this is perfectly normal. About 1 in 3 new businesses go through a significant legal hurdle in their first year or two. In the Valley, it's more like 1 in 2. The reason they're coming after you is because they know you've got something big and they're afraid of it.

REPLY

Totally. I just think, maybe your dad's firm could be helpful? You could be the one to bring the case in, maybe he could just sign off on it. I'm gonna need all the firepower I can get to fight this shit.

REPLY

That's a perfectly understandable response, but if you want to engage my dad's firm, then I will likely step away from this personally. I just can't be involved with him any more directly than I already am. All the small, subtle familial dynamics that already permeate my work life would only be cranked up to 11 if you were involved.

Also, purely on a practical basis, I would advise you that his firm has a history of getting unpleasantly entangled with some of their clients. Meaning, he ends up owning a large chunk of the startups he represents. And candidly, I know he is still hurt that you turned down his investment offer (which for the record was 100% the right choice).

But it's totally up to you, I know this is a large attractive firm.

REPLY

No no no you're right. I took a walk and got my head on straight. I can't afford to have some big legal team monkeying around in all our shit. We have a MASSIVE security liability, if anything leaks during this process we are straight-up FUCKED. Not worth it. For the company or for us.

I trust YOU. That's the bottom line. And there's barely anybody I can trust right now. So I went and talked to Adhi and Paolo and they're cool with this, so I wanna propose—how bout come work for us?

Dead serious. Quit your job, quit working for your dad period. We'll bring you in with CLO title and appropriate comp (I think like 250K is appropriate and doable at our funding level) plus stock options. Start tomorrow. We're gonna need someone full-time for sure, you know what's involved.

I don't wanna pretend it's gonna be anything other than a fuckton of work. You already know Goliath is coming after us . . . and there's a limit to how many people we can bring in under you. Both funding-wise, and security-wise.

BUT on the bright side, we WILL get to spend a lot more time together. I know this isn't what the Love Language book meant by "quality time" but at least SOME of it will be.

REPLY

Hey babe, this is super sudden and drastic. I mean first off, thank you very much for the offer. It really means a lot that you believe in me enough to propose that. And I do think it could be fun working together, as long as it's me working with you and not for you.

But you know that for me to work my way up, I need time in-office at a reputable firm, which means riding this desk for at least another 9 months. I'm not saying no, I just need some time to think about it, and to prepare a transition plan if I'm going to pursue a change.

REPLY

Of course, sure. I guess I hoped you believed in me and this company enough to pull the trigger. If you're not in a position to do so, I get it, it's cool, but prob we will move on and offer to someone else, cause with this SEC shit I mean we need someone like yesterday.

Here's the thing. I've gotten a legit glimpse into the future of this company—the future of this WORLD, and this company's role in it—and I know it's gonna be bright. I want what's best for you and wouldn't be offering this if I didn't think it was a golden opportunity.

I know we're a balance for each other, I'm the gas and you're the brakes, I'm the dreamer and you're the realist, each one has its ups and downs, that's why we're so good. Just consider it.

Five years ago I told you I didn't wanna get married till I had my future figured out . . . and you convinced me, love means sometimes making a leap. Maybe this is one of those moments. Love me . . . love The Future:)

REPLY

I don't think you've ever written me a card or a letter as heartfelt as that email. But I knew what I was signing up for when I married you, and I don't want to miss out on this opportunity, or the chance to build something great together. So yeah . . . I'm in:)

OK I'm gonna go draft a letter of resignation. Fuck, my dad is gonna be so mad . . .

EXCERPT FROM CONGRESSIONAL HEARING — DECEMBER 1, 2021

SEN. ELIZABETH BYRNE (D-FL): Mr. Boyce, would you talk us through the decision to hire your wife as your chief legal officer?

BOYCE: I mean, it was a no-brainer. She's the best lawyer I've ever met. And one of the smartest people, period. She wins, but also . . . she does it with heart, and character, and dignity. What more do you want?

SEN. ELIZABETH BYRNE (D-FL): Were there any other individuals considered for her position?

BOYCE: We needed to fill the position fast. And—look, if you're saying this was a case of nepotism—no way. Leila was young, sure, but so were we. And she was incredibly qualified. Top of her law school class, cum laude as an undergrad. And she came to us after distinguishing herself while working at a top-tier law firm.

SEN. ELIZABETH BYRNE (D-FL): Where she was, to be clear . . . hired by her father.

BOYCE: Yes. And . . . so what? Look, Leila's great at her job, she's whip-smart and super savvy, and . . . she was in a unique position to be able to help.

TEXT MESSAGE EXCHANGE

LEILA KEENER-BOYCE
June 7, 2021 3:14 PM

Hey A, it looks like we're gonna be working together again. Just like back in college, right?

ADHVAN CHAUDRY

Yeah.
Guess nothing really changes.

Ha. Except my hair, thank God. And come on, you've changed plenty.

Doesn't feel like it.

If nothing else, you're a millionaire now.

Doesn't feel like it.

You OK Eeyore?

Yeah sorry just tired.
Ben asked me to brief you on the tech.
I'll send over specs in a few.
And the original research paper is a good start.

OK, but it's all gonna be Greek to me. Do you
think we could meet up later? It would be a lot
easier if you could walk me through it all in person.

Just like freshman year.

Ha. Yeah. Well, nothing really changes, right?

I'm in back to backs with my engineers.
Swing by the office at 6, we'll get started?

Great, I'll bring Thai. You still do pad see ew
with beef?

Chicken now.
I guess one thing changes—my metabolism.

Lol see ya then.
June 8, 2021 7:18 AM

Hey . . .
Sorry about last night.
You there?

June 8, 2021 7:35 AM

I shouldn't have said all that.
I'm not sleeping enough.
Not thinking straight.
I'm gonna get back to seeing my therapist.
And exercising regularly.

June 8, 2021 8:13 AM

Hey A. Sorry, I just got up.
Look, it's OK. I'm not going to say anything
about it to Ben. I had no idea how much you'd
been keeping to yourself, I'm sure that's been
really hard. But just to give my two cents and
some perspective, what you've been building
up inside your head is not the reality.

Basically what I'm trying to say is, I'm not all
that you think I am.

Yes you are.
But it was wrong of me to say all that.
I don't want to make you uncomfortable.
It's prob better for me to do everything email
from now on.

So you can hide behind the screen?

Something like that.

Whatever you need. I'm working on the letter now,
I'll share it for you to review later.

No need I'm sure it's great.
Fire away.

TUMBLR BLOG POST—JUNE 8, 2021

THE BLACK HOLE: ANONYMOUS MUSINGS OF A
SCI-FI SUPERFAN

"The Curse"

Vampires have generally been consigned to the realm of fantasy,
    but if my small readership will indulge me today,
    I would argue for their inclusion in the sci-fi canon.
    First, because (if you set aside the magical bat-transformations)
    the rules are scientific: A bite. An infection. Changed biochemistry.
    Extended longevity in exchange for new appetites.
    Even though these stories originated as Gothic Romance,
    the personal truth in them is illuminating and profound,
    which is why we keep coming back to them, year after year,
    from Victorian England to modern teenage television.

I think it is fundamentally because we all relate
    to their endless, selfish, ravaging *hunger*.

The way vampires love—that is how we all fear that we love.

With an endless desire that will only drain the object of our affection.

The way Dracula loved Mina,

that is the curse of the vampire—

the knowledge that desire, if indulged, will only bring misery.

Love, for the vampire, needs to be an impossible hunger.

Which is why, as much as I may offend diehard fans,

and lose nerd cred for saying it . . .

the best it's ever been expressed is in *Buffy*.

The impossible will-they-won't-they of a vampire and a Slayer

was simple, elegant, sexy, and fun.

Buffy and Angel were equally matched enemies who became unlikely allies—

and for all the torture of frustrated desire,

the tension between them was exquisite.

It built until they finally indulged and consummated their love.

But in the moment (S2E14: "Innocence") when Angel tasted true bliss—

he was not saved.

He was ruined.

And he reverted into a monster.

It was for mumbo-jumbo story reasons related to an ancient gypsy curse,

but even those of us who have never met a gypsy know . . .

if I am a vampire, love and happiness are not for me. Never will be.

This is why the *Twilight* books are such an abomination.

It is not the mediocre prose so much as the arc of the story

which presupposes that, by becoming a vampire herself,

Bella gets a happily-ever-after with Edward.

The fantasy is juvenile for its suggestion

that love can heal and redeem the darkest among us.

Anyone over the age of 15 cringes—

not at the story's faux-darkness, but at its optimism.

THE EVOLUTION OF VAMPIRIC ROMANCE

If vampire stories teach us anything, it is the truth about love:
    that it is not a destination of contentment,
    so much as an endless yearning.
    And if there is happiness and purpose to be found in this life,
    it will be in a frustrated friendship—
    suppressing the urges I know will be destructive
    in order to protect, from myself, the object of my affection.

FORMAL REPLY SUBMITTED TO THE SEC

June 9, 2021

Dear Sirs,

I am writing in regard to your notification of an Active Investigation into The Future LLC (hereafter designated as "The Company") operated by Benjamin Boyce and Adhvan Chaudry (hereafter designated as "The Partners").

As Chief Counsel, I am writing to request an immediate dismissal and disavowal of this Investigation, on the grounds that

1) Invocation of the Insider Trading and Securities Act of 1988 (Title 17 CFR 240.10b5-1) is inappropriate in this situation, since the Company is not (at the time of this Investigation) a publicly traded entity, and therefore is not subject to provisions of the ITSA.

2) The Company and its Partners have not engaged in any speculative investment, except for investment in their own company. The ITSA has been used to prosecute inappropriate share-dumping, but never has it been used (nor should it be used) to prosecute entrepreneurs investing in their own ventures.

3) The additional Investors who have speculatively provided seed-funding and ownership-stake investment have done so in good faith, only with knowledge about the Company provided by the Company, which therefore cannot be considered "Insider" status.

On these grounds, we decline the request to turn over proprietary data and information, which is of substantial private value and constitutes Trade Secrets, until such a time as a Federal Circuit Court Judge has issued and upheld any subpoena.

Respectfully,

Leila Keener-Boyce
Chief Legal Officer
The Future, LLC

EXCERPT FROM CONGRESSIONAL HEARING—DECEMBER 1, 2021

SEN. KAREN WILSON (D-NV): Mr. Boyce, the ongoing investigation by the SEC has bogged down in a legal quagmire, which cannot be—

BOYCE: Hold up, I just want to say one thing about that. That whole case is a hatchet job. They've been coming after us on everything they can think of, even though it makes no sense, just because we're disruptors, and they're in the pocket of all the entrenched power structures. Meaning Wall Street. What we're doing is not insider trading, it's—

SEN. KAREN WILSON (D-NV): Listen, I've read the briefs from your lawyer, all the relevant arguments. What I'm asking is . . . what will be the *outcome* of that particular legal situation?

BOYCE: I don't know, obviously.

SEN. KAREN WILSON (D-NV): But you're able to see the future. You've raised money off utopian visions of your own success. Surely you can foresee the outcome of important struggles like this one.

BOYCE: Well . . . the window of our product is one year. So beyond that—

SEN. KAREN WILSON (D-NV): I'm aware of the "window." I've reviewed this concept with a number of scientists. They've all assured me, there is no reason, if your technology is real, why you wouldn't be able to create a Prototype that views a two-year gap. Or that communicates with itself even further in the future.

BOYCE: Yeah. Theoretically, yes, that is true. But in practice, that is not the case.

SEN. KAREN WILSON (D-NV): And . . . why not?

BOYCE: That is a question Adhi would be better equipped to answer. But the short and long of it is . . . we are not entirely sure.

EMAIL

From: Ben Boyce
To: Adhvan Chaudry

This SEC shit is keepin me up at night. Where are we on gettin a look at a further-off horizon? We gotta keep a competitive edge.

REPLY

B—
Based on your question, it appears that you never opened any of the progress reports I sent your way.
And you redirected my efforts from the longer-horizon Prototype
to the fantastical project of investigating physical travel through time.

—A

REPLY

Hey man, come on. I'm sure you could handle both, I didn't mean to totally abandon that. And no offense but why would I read progress reports when you told me yourself that we were making no progress?

REPLY

B—
Sometimes it is worthwhile to explore the nature of failure. Consider: we made a Prototype that can talk to itself 1 year in the future.

But we have never been able to make a Prototype that talks
to itself 2 years in the future (or 3, or 4, or more).
So we ought to consider possible reasons
why the prototype receives no data signal
when we attempt to connect across a greater time-gap.

1. Some theoretical limit, akin to light speed.
   -However, we have no other data to support this possibility,
   and I can think of no mathematical basis for one.
2. The Prototype does not exist 2 years in the future.
   -Which means it has been destroyed, and we must ask—why?
   And by whom?
3. The Internet itself does not exist 2 years in the future.
   -Which similarly means there has been some catastrophic destruction,
   and we need to consider who perpetrated it? And why?

Given that it is clear our technology will provoke significant blowback,
the second and third possibilities are both deeply troubling.
I would say the most likely explanation is:
the world is on course toward some cataclysmic event
that will effectively destroy our entire informational infrastructure
on a time horizon somewhere between 1 and 2 years in the
future.

—A

REPLY

Dude you are giving me such a headache here. Maybe it's
just a glitch? And you're thinking too small. If there's a
limit to how we connect to the Internet of the future,

maybe it's just because there's a different type of connection?

We all get information, and we make a choice about HOW WE SEE IT. I want The Future to be a corporate culture that is positive, optimistic, hopeful. So turn off your gloom and doom, and let's get cracking on how to create positive change. Maybe our invention will be the thing that SAVES THE MOTHERFUCKIN WORLD!

REPLY

B—
Or, perhaps, quite the opposite.

—A

CHAPTER 13

NEWS ARTICLE—THEINFORMATION.COM—JUNE 28, 2021

ALPHABET MAKING $3B BUYOUT OFFER TO STARTUP "THE FUTURE"

Multiple anonymous sources from the tech giant (the parent company of Google, YouTube, and more) have confirmed that the offer is coming soon, and is expected to be in the $2–$4B range. Offer is for complete ownership of the company and all underlying rights to its technologies.

The Future has been in the news extensively ever since its founder Ben Boyce gave his famous "The Future Is Now" TED Talk. VCs have flocked to the company and it is estimated that they have raised $250M in the past few months, though little is known about a timeline for bringing their product to market.

Alphabet has tried to keep the offer quiet, probably in order to avoid a bidding war with other potential buyers, who have not, as of press time, weighed in.

More as this one develops.

SELECTION OF RESPONSES ON TWITTER

@HARVARDBIZ
If #TheFuture tech is for-real then this price would be a bargain. Gotta be a vetting process.

@KARASWISHER

This is insane. Theranos-level scam happening here. Boyce is doing a bait-and-switch. Guaranteed this is exactly what he wants. #thefuture #siliconvalley #bs

@LIN_MANUEL

Anyone else feel like this is some elaborate performance-art hoax satirical social commentary, and @HeyBenBoyce is gonna laugh in all our faces when it's over?

@EMILYNUSSBAUM

A company called The Future sounds more like a Bond villain than a legitimate enterprise. Silicon Valley has officially jumped the shark.

@ELONMUSK

Hey @HeyBenBoyce I don't know about 3B but I will pay 1B cash right now for your company and we will have way more fun than you ever would with google. #TheFuture

@PATTONOSWALT

Wish I'd bought futures in #TheFuture.

@KANYEWEST

Pay attention, this the moment Big Tech LITERALLY gets control of the future. We all fuckd. #thefuture #techpocalypse #finalact

EMAIL

From: Paolo Ventrini
To: Ben Boyce, Adhvan Chaudry

Boys, I'm sure you read the article this morning. I've been back-channeling to verify and am confident that it's legit and we will see an offer later this afternoon. They are upset that this leaked, which could be both good and bad for us. Bad bc they will try to tie a firm clock to it. Good bc the need for them to resolve quickly might lead them to overpay. Let's discuss.

REPLY

From: Ben Boyce
To: Paolo Ventrini, Adhvan Chaudry

Hey man, wow BIG NEWS. Holy shit. Let's think about conditions here, and price of course. This leak will be good. Let's see if we can get some other offers on the table. This could be perfect timing for an acquisition. I would try to get up to more like $10B if we can. I know that's crazy for a startup but nobody's ever seen anything like this. And we want to be involved too not just some handoff.

REPLY

From: Adhvan Chaudry
To: Ben Boyce, Paolo Ventrini

B&P—
We are not selling.
No way.
We have literally seen the future,
and we know that we're not selling
so let's just nip this in the bud.

—A

REPLY

From: Paolo Ventrini
To: Ben Boyce, Adhvan Chaudry

Boys, I appreciate your passion, however this is now a bigger situation than just you. We've taken on over $250M in VC at this point and we have a fiduciary obligation to do what's best for those investors. At the end of the day, the Board will vote in the interest of the stakeholders. I know you're among that group but you have 2 of the 5 votes, and I'm confident in how Samantha and David are going to vote. I don't want this to be adversarial, I want to support you through the transition, just get on the right side of this.

Yours,
Paolo

REPLY (DRAFT)

From: Ben Boyce
To: Adhvan Chaudry, Paolo Ventrini

OK y'all let's just take a deep breath here, I'm sure there is a solution that we can all get behind if we just

The previous draft was not completed or sent, apparently because while it was being composed, the following was sent.

REPLY

From: Adhvan Chaudry
To: Ben Boyce, Paolo Ventrini

P—
Are you honestly trying to strong-arm us into selling our own company?

I always imagined corporate villainy would be, I dunno . . . a bit more subtle?

—A

REPLY

From: Paolo Ventrini
To: Ben Boyce

Ben . . . your co-founder is treading on dangerous ground here. I'm reaching out directly in the hope that you can bring him into line.

REPLY

From: Ben Boyce
To: Adhvan Chaudry

Dude, you're pissing off Paolo something fierce. And why aren't you even open to this?! You've been looking for ways to change the future, alter the timeline or whatever, get out of this . . . we just got one HANDED to us.

REPLY

B—
After our last discussion, YOU convinced ME
Not to abdicate responsibility here.
Not to settle for a lesser role in this history-making endeavor.
I didn't quit Google to end up working for them again six months later.
And you didn't build this company to be an out-to-pasture middle manager.

—A

REPLY

Come on man, this could be HUGE. And I mean, I don't think I need to point out, your ownership stake is still at 30%, meaning this goes through, you will be a BILLION-AIRE. Before 30. Don't write this off so quick. And don't let your pride get in the way. Getting paid a literal BIL-LION dollars is not the same as being a cubicle bitch. Be-sides, Alphabet has the infrastructure to help us scale up and get to market.

REPLY

B—

Do you want to be a billionaire, or do you want to be someone who matters?

If this goes through, you really think they're gonna keep you on as CEO?

No way.

You wanna be Andrew Mason/David Karp?

Most ppl don't know who the fuck they are anymore.

Or do you want to be Zuck/Elon?

The Future won't be the same if it's just one more Google sibling.

Look at Insta after the FB acquisition.

You've got money, you don't need to sell your soul.

I came over here because I believed in you.

I still do.

—A

REPLY

From: Ben Boyce
To: Paolo Ventrini

Listen Paolo, Adhi's not gonna bite on this. Maybe if we can go back to them and change up the nature of the offer? But it might just be a done deal. Do you think this could also fuel another round of growth investment?

REPLY

No. It is extremely naïve to imagine Alphabet will pursue/accept anything other than outright acquisition. And right now, we don't NEED more investment. We have plenty of runway. We either need REVENUE (which is still far off) or a leveraged BUYOUT (and this is a pretty great one).

I expect you will understand these points, but I want you to consider something seriously here. Does this company work with Adhi in a position of managerial authority?

We're living in a strange moment in the history of business, when it is common for engineers and technologists to find themselves running billion-dollar firms. But the skill set that enables someone to envision and realize new technology does not prepare them for the tasks of hiring, deal management, cost control, PR, etc. For every Zuckerberg success story, there are a dozen flaming wrecks on the shoulder of the information superhighway.

You need to ask yourself: does Adhi have the temperament to manage?

Of course not. YOU DO. That is your talent and your unique skill. If you want this company to achieve its true potential, you need to realign the power structure, or he

will always be a limiting factor on the growth potential of
The Future.

REPLY

Hey Paolo, I hear what you're saying and I know what you
mean. Obviously it's delicate. Just so I understand, what
exactly are you proposing?

REPLY

I recommend taking Adhi off the Board. Let him keep his
CTO role for now but tell him that he will henceforth take
a backseat on issues of corporate governance. Trust me,
he will get richer in the process, and honestly, he will enjoy
his life more.

   I'm coming to you candidly here, because I already
know my co-investors are aligned with this position,
which means we have the Board votes to unseat Adhi already. But doing so against the wishes of the CEO is a bad
look for all of us. So let's line up on this, and make the
transition as smooth as possible.

REPLY

It's a dicey proposition, but it does make sense to me. I
know we need at least 5 on the Board, so we'll obviously
have to replace him. Now that Leila is part of the company, I think we could move her into position in his place.

   Now, I know what you want to say about the optics of
putting my wife in that slot, but I need someone in there
who I trust. And yeah, we'll probably be together on most

things, but if you think Leila sides w me on every issue, you don't know my wife. Besides, you and your little finance crew will still outnumber us 3-2. Plus I think as long as we're a board of 5 grown-ups who want to make money, we'll be able to work together. I'll support ousting Adhi if you'll support bringing in Leila.

REPLY

Are you making this an explicit quid pro quo? Fine. As long as your wife is aligned with the sale, we will support her.

CORPORATE MEETING MINUTES

Call to Order:

June 30, 2021, 1:05 PM

ROLL CALL

Present: Benjamin Boyce, CEO; Adhvan Chaudry, CTO; Paolo Ventrini, Director; Samantha Vargas, Advisor; David Lee, Advisor and Secretary

NEW BUSINESS

Motion

To Adopt New Board Member: Leila Keener-Boyce
Proposed by: CEO Ben Boyce
Seconded by: Director Paolo Ventrini
Votes in Favor: Ben Boyce, Adhvan Chaudry, Paolo Ventrini, Samantha Vargas, David Lee
Votes Against: None

RESOLVED—The Adoption of New Board Member Leila Keener-Boyce

CHANGE IN ATTENDANCE: New Board Member Leila Keener-Boyce joined the meeting 1:14

Motion

To Remove Board Member: Adhvan Chaudry
Proposed by: Director Paolo Ventrini
Seconded by: Director Samantha Vargas
Votes in Favor: Paolo Ventrini, Samantha Vargas, David Lee
Votes Against: Ben Boyce, Adhvan Chaudry, Leila Keener-Boyce
Per Corporate Constitution, Tie Vote Fails to Pass
Motion DENIED

Motion

To Accept Proposed Acquisition Offer from Alphabet
(Deal Memo Attached, Addendum A)
Proposed by: Director Paolo Ventrini
Seconded by: Director Samantha Vargas
Votes in Favor: Paolo Ventrini, Samantha Vargas, David Lee
Votes Against: Ben Boyce, Adhvan Chaudry, Leila Keener-Boyce
Per Corporate Constitution, Tie Vote Fails to Pass
Motion DENIED

CHANGE IN ATTENDANCE: Paolo Ventrini departed from meeting 1:23 following failed Motion to Accept Proposed Acquisition Offer from Alphabet.

ADJOURNMENT

Board agrees to Adjournment until next meeting: July 15, 2021

Minutes Recorded By:
David Lee, Secretary

Approved By:
Ben Boyce, CEO

EMAIL

From: Paolo Ventrini
To: Ben Boyce, Adhvan Chaudry

Well boys, I hope you're happy. With your little *Succession* antics, you just flushed a billion dollars down the toilet and alienated your entire executive team. And if you think Alphabet will simply lie down and let this go, you haven't been around like I have.

I and the other Board Members (and honestly all of your stock-option employees) have cause to sue you. Ben, you may have insulated yourself from direct action, but we are asking you to voluntarily step down from the CEO position at the next Board Meeting, or we will consider legal action against you.

REPLY

From: Ben Boyce
To: Paolo Ventrini, Adhvan Chaudry

Hey Paolo, I appreciate your warnings and such, but honestly we grew up on a different HBO show, and it's Omar that said it best: "You come at the king, you best not miss."

You missed your shot bro! Now, you're still in position to get filthy fucking rich, so just lay back and wait to reap the benefits while we do the work.

REPLY

> From: Adhvan Chaudry
> To: Ben Boyce
>
> B—
> Quoting *The Wire* was a little cheesy.
> But also . . . awesome.
> I know this whole thing could've gone a different way.
> I know it's hard to walk away from the quick money.
> Thank you for trusting me and getting my back on this.
>
> —A

REPLY

> You got it man. Benny-Boy teamin up with Dr. Dark! An
> immortal alliance! See ya on Monday, we still got a lot
> to do.

EXCERPT FROM CONGRESSIONAL HEARING — DECEMBER 1, 2021

SEN. KAREN WILSON (D-NV): Mr. Boyce, who is "Dr. Dark"?

BOYCE: That was . . . that's not a real person. I mean, it's Adhi, but . . . OK, when we were first getting to know each other, Adhi told me how kids used to make fun of him in high school, and they called him Dr. *Dork*. Glasses, comic books, computers, it wasn't that clever. But I told him, we're the generation where dorks run the world, and he shouldn't shy away from it. So we tweaked it a little and it became more like a positive, and he used it for his handle when we were gaming.

SEN. KAREN WILSON (D-NV): And you were "Benny-Boy"?

BOYCE: Yeah, I used that for mine, and it became this inside joke, where we talked about turning ourselves into superheroes and writing a comic book. We even took a crack at actually making it a couple times in college, just for fun, but we never got real serious about it.

So then after the whole situation with Paolo trying to kick Adhi off the board, Adhi gave me a little gift, to say thanks for having his back. He paid an artist to make a comic-book cover, for issue number one of *The Adventures of Benny-Boy and Dr. Dark*. I was really touched. It came out looking great and we put it up on the wall of the office.

SEN. KAREN WILSON (D-NV): I may not be a comic-book expert, but don't you think the name Dr. Dark sounds a bit more like . . . a villain?

BOYCE: I mean, sure. But like I said, it was just meant as a joke.

SEN. KAREN WILSON (D-NV): I'm sure it was hilarious. But now we are here evaluating whether or not the technology he created poses a serious threat to the future of our civilization. Don't you think a more apt title might have been *Benny-Boy* Versus *Dr. Dark*?

BOYCE: You're reading into this way too much. I never saw Adhi as a villain, and he didn't see me . . . Well, you'll have to ask him how he sees me sometime. But yeah, sure, the pressures of a startup . . . I guess the way things ended up, maybe it was more of a "versus" situation.

CHAPTER 14

CEO BEN BOYCE'S SPEECH AT THE FUTURE 2021 FOURTH OF JULY PARTY—JULY 4, 2021

Hey hey Futurinos! Futuramas! What should we call ourselves?

> (Riff, see if anyone has suggestions)

Everybody having a good time tonight?

> (Leave space for applause)

I just wanted to take a minute to say a few words to you all. Our employees. The future of The Future.

We've grown from just me and Adhi to eighty-five employees, in the past six months alone. How 'bout that? I don't know all of your names yet, but I'm working on it. I am thankful for your commitment.

I know that we lost some good folks recently. The startup game isn't for everybody. But I'm confident that those who stuck around are in it for the long haul, and I promise, your loyalty will be rewarded.

Now, I'm sure you're all aware, we keep a pretty tight lid on security around here. We can't be sharing data from the Prototype too freely, until we're in a position for everyone to have free and equal access. But I wanted to take this opportunity to share with you all a couple snippets from next year. 'Cause 2022 is when we're coming to market, and it's gonna be big.

First off, I'll just take this opportunity to invite you all to NEXT YEAR'S Fourth of July party. And if you think this year's off the hook, check out this invite, which I just pulled from the Prototype earlier today—

(Wait for slide projection)

Looks pretty fuckin sweet, right? And I'm taking requests on what carnival rides we get. Gravitron for sure. So you know we're still gonna be here next year, doing well enough to book Sia, partying harder than ever.

Now, real talk, I know some of you have questioned the decision to rebuff the offer from Alphabet. You're looking at your shares, and saying *Come on, Ben, I could've paid off my student loans!*

I totally hear that. But this company isn't called The Future by accident. We're in it for the long haul. And there is money to be made here that is WAY beyond getting out of debt. That's more in the realm of "name a library wing at your university."

So to thank you all for sticking with the team, I am giving everyone in the company an additional 100 shares of equity. When those shares vest, and when we go public at a price of $144— which we *know* will happen—the value of those 100 shares will be almost fifteen grand, and only going up more over time.

And what we're doing here, it's not limited to getting rich. We are going to be active participants in the Copenhagen Climate Change Summit—an international conference convened specifically to look at how data from The Future 1 machines can be used to positively impact climate studies and public policy.

On top of that, we're going to form a partnership with the CDC, to identify, prevent, and manage disease outbreaks. Thousands of lives can be saved by this technology. By getting it into the right hands. By getting it into *everybody's* hands.

But none of that will be possible if we cave to the pressure of the obstacles we're facing, and sell out to the Big Tech powers that be. So before we launch the fireworks, I would just leave you all with the words of President Thomas J. Whitmore, aka Bill Pullman, at the climax of my favorite movie of all time:

"We cannot be consumed by our petty differences anymore. We will be united in our common interests. We will not go quietly into the night. We will not vanish without a fight! We're going to live on! We're going to survive! Today . . . we celebrate OUR Independence Day!"

WEB ARTICLE FROM THEINFORMATION.COM

STARTUP FOURTH OF JULY PARTY ENDS IN PUNCH-OUT
July 5, 2021

Red-hot startup The Future threw the Valley's most ridiculous party of the summer, and the fireworks weren't limited to the planned ones in the sky over the Bay, as the co-founders traded blows in a drunken rage.

The outdoor venue was extravagantly decorated in homage to the '90s movie *Independence Day,* with replicas of aliens and flying saucers from the film, and a large White House cake that CEO Ben Boyce cut.

The party was a transparent attempt to rally employees and investors after founder Ben Boyce publicly (and preemptively) rejected the possibility of a sizable buyout from Alphabet, which would have been a windfall for everyone involved.

By all accounts, it was a boozy night for all, and many reported that the co-founders seemed like the old friends they are known to be. But late in the evening, approximately 1 A.M., an argument erupted between them, which culminated in a full-on fistfight. Employees had to separate the two, who both declined to file charges.

Reports differ on the reason for the tiff, but my most reliable source says it was more personal in nature than professional. Will keep you all posted as I learn more about this embarrassing Silicon Scandal.

TEXT MESSAGE EXCHANGE

LEILA KEENER-BOYCE

July 5, 2021 1:13 PM

Hey A. You there? What the hell happened at the party???
When I left it looked like you and Ben were totally buddy-buddy,
then I find out two hours later you're attacking him. Alcohol or not, that's not you.

ADHVAN CHAUDRY

Hey Lei.
Ask Ben.
It's really for him to tell.

I wouldn't be reaching out if not for the fact that he's being vague and won't talk about it. I'm spinning out and need to know what's going on here.

Sorry but it's not my place to say.
I genuinely hope he'll do the right thing here.
But it has to come from him not me.

Come on Adhi please. We're friends.

Yes exactly. I am honestly trying to be your friend.
And his too.
You two don't exactly make it easy.

EMAIL

From: Carrie Chan
To: Ben Boyce, Adhvan Chaudry

Hey Guys,

Congratulations on throwing the most expensive party in Silicon Valley history! I'm not talking about the millions you put down to make it happen. I'm talking about the loss in value in the wake of that debacle.

Do you realize when Elon smoked weed on Joe Rogan's podcast, Tesla lost $5B in market cap? They eventually made up much of that, bc they are a real working company with sales. As of right now, you are not. You are a privately traded pipe dream. Until we are in the black, the main product you are selling is your STORY. And after whatever happened at that party, we need to do something to drastically change the narrative here.

I've got a close contact from when I was doing PR who owes me a favor, and she's at *Wired* now. I've arranged for her to do a profile on you guys. It's going to be less focused on the tech, more so on the personal story of you and your friendship (yes, your friendship, believe me it is crucial that we tell THAT story, even if it is hard right now).

Thing is, we need to give her something exclusive. Namely, hands-on use of the Prototype. Supervised, of course, but real, eyes-on proof that it works. I'll have Legal put together an ironclad NDA. Trust me, this will go a long way toward restoring credibility. My assistant will coordinate details once we're all agreed.

Carrie

REPLY

From: Ben Boyce
To: Carrie Chan

Adhi and I had a bit of a blow-up and we're not really talking right now, but I'm down for the article. It's a good idea, and it's gonna be a good piece (I've already read it, in fact, and so has Leila). Don't worry, I know how to play nice with a journalist.

REPLY

From: Adhvan Chaudry
To: Carrie Chan

C—
I get the impression this will happen whether I want it or not.
Ben would never say no to a chance at the limelight.
I'd rather participate than not, so there might be some shred of scientific credibility in play.
In return for my cooperation, I ask only one favor.
Steer clear of Ben.
I saw what happened at the party, and I don't need to ask to know there's more going on there.
Don't make Leila a fool.

—A

REPLY

Thanks for your reply Adhvan. I'll set it up. I think you'll like Fiona.

As for your request? Ben is a grown-up. So am I. Stop worrying about the personal lives of your coworkers, and try having one of your own.

—Carrie

EMAIL — JULY 12, 2021

From: Carrie Chan
To: Fiona Glazer

Hey Fiona,

Read your draft of the story. People are definitely going to be excited about this exclusive. All in all, I think it does a great job of painting a real and human portrait of the guys.

I have one concern, which is the two-paragraph section where you talk about the rumors that have been out there about their personal lives, the party, all that. I happen to know that much of it is untrue, and all of it is unverified. On top of that, it's salacious gossip, and frankly that kind of soap opera is beneath your standards. How about we just cut that little section before we publish. Thanks so much!

REPLY

Carrie,

I appreciate the exclusive. But this is, in the end, a piece of journalism. And while I'm not trying to gossip-monger here, I think that the personal/human story is important, since it potentially impacts the technology, and the structure of the company bringing it into the world.

To be clear, I have chosen to leave your name out of the article, even though it certainly did come up with some of the employees I spoke to, who were definitely speculating about the nature of your relationship with one of the co-founders. I'll keep that to myself, but with respect to the part about these two college-bro buds, let's not pretend they're saints here.

REPLY

Hi Fiona,

Bit of a low blow there, but I should not be surprised. With respect to the personal-life material you're referring to, I would refer you back to your NDA. And based on what you have seen of the capabilities of our technology, do you really want to get into a legal battle with us, when the outcome is uncertain (for you)?

REPLY

This is spilling into overt intimidation. I'm going to report this to my editor, Mark, and will discontinue contact if it persists.

EMAIL

From: Carrie Chan
To: Ben Boyce

Hey . . . We have a situation regarding the article. Fiona is getting all high-and-mighty about journalism, and using this exclusive as a chance for a scandalous scoop. Also it appears there are plenty of employees in your office who are more than eager to mouth off about you and me, and I have good reason to believe Adhi is one of them.

We need leverage to be able to motivate Fiona toward a more favorable portrayal. Otherwise we are both going to come off looking pretty awful, and the company is fucked PR-wise. So maybe get off your high horse about how you use your technology.

REPLY

Damn. OK. Yeah, I can probably find something using the Prototype. Meet me at the office tonight. Need to do this after Adhi leaves or he'll flip out. 9 PM should be safe.

EMAIL — JULY 13, 2021

From: Carrie Chan
To: Mark Santoro

Hi Mark. I'm sure Fiona has talked to you about the story she's doing on The Future. As you can probably imagine, use of the technology has a tendency to bring up personal information that could be sensitive if it were released into the public sphere.

Just as an example: it's easy using the Prototype to find out about your son's arrest for DUI next summer, right before the start of his freshman year at Brown (see the attached). But if that came out now, it could wreck his chances of even getting in. Hardly seems fair, right?

Surely we can all agree that the story ought to respect boundaries of the personal lives of those involved. For all of our sakes, please have a word with Fiona about this.

Thanks,
Carrie

EMAIL

From: Fiona Glazer
To: Carrie Chan

Carrie,

Talked to my editor. Not sure what you said to him, but I'm not interested in losing my job over this, so fine, he's going to press with the story, minus those two paragraphs. I hope they are paying you well over there bc this is some Enron-level bullshit. Lose my number.

Fiona

CHAPTER 15

DISTRICT COURT OF SANTA CLARA COUNTY

July 22, 2021
Case no: 482694-203

Alphabet, Inc.,

Plaintiff

COMPLAINT

Vs.

The Future, LLC,
Adhvan Chaudry
Benjamin Boyce

Defendants

Plaintiff Alphabet, Inc., by and through their undersigned attorneys, bring this complaint against Defendants, alleging that—

1. Defendant Adhvan Chaudry was an employee of Google, Inc., a subsidiary of Alphabet, working under willfully agreed-upon Employment Contract (Exhibit A), for the period of October 2020–January 2021.

2. Defendant Adhvan Chaudry, under the terms of his Employment Contract, agreed that any Intellectual Property generated by him in the field of relevant Computer Sciences was the property of Plaintiff Alphabet Inc. through its subsidiary Google, Inc.

3. Defendant Adhvan Chaudry, during the period of his employment with Google, Inc., did willfully download documents pertaining to the design of Quantum Computing architecture (henceforth herein referred to as "Relevant Google IP"), and disseminated Relevant Google IP in defiance of his Employment Contract.

4. Defendant Adhvan Chaudry entered into partnership with Defendant Benjamin Boyce, and created new technology (henceforth herein referred to as "The Device") using both (A) Relevant Google IP, and (B) original plans and designs developed during the period covered by his Employment Contract.

5. Therefore all value generated by development of The Device falls under the protections of Employment Contract, and is rightfully the property of Plaintiff Alphabet, Inc., through its subsidiary Google, Inc.

6. Additionally, the theft and public dissemination of said technology has caused financial injury against Plaintiff, due to future market concerns no longer available to Plaintiff.

DAMAGES

Wherefore, Plaintiff seeks compensatory damages in the amount of $250,000,000 together with underlying rights to Intellectual Property of the Device (designated in Addendum A) along with attorney fees and court costs.

Dated this 22nd day of July, 2021,
Thomas Keener, Esq.

TEXT MESSAGE EXCHANGE

BENJAMIN BOYCE
July 23, 2021 9:19 AM

Holy fuck what is even happening
Is this a joke?
Why are you not picking up?

Google is suing us for EVERYTHING
And YOUR DAD is representing them.

                                    LEILA KEENER-BOYCE

                                              I KNOW.
                            I'm on phone with him right now.
                    Don't panic I'll call you soon as I get off.

Don't panic yeah right
CALL ME

TEXT MESSAGE EXCHANGE

LEILA KEENER-BOYCE
July 23, 2021 11:04 AM

Hey A, I know we haven't been talking much,
and probably for good reason. But we're
going to need to now.

                                    ADHVAN CHAUDRY

                                  Yeah I gathered that.
                    It's all true. What the lawsuit says.
                          About downloading their IP.

OK let's meet up and talk about it. Meaning
please don't say anything else in text or email,
all this could potentially all end up in subpoena.

                                I don't care. It's true.

Before you freak out, just know that you might
have a stronger case than you think. California
employment and IP law is pretty strongly in
your favor.
Plus I know all the tricks their lawyer is gonna
try to use, so . . .

So you're the ace up our sleeve?

I'm the QUEEN up your sleeve.

Ben is the king.
And I'm the Ace.
Lowest of all.

Cut the vague self-pity. It's not a good look,
and as usual, it's not helping.

Just let me know when and where.
I'll tell you everything.
Open book.
I'm ready to give up.

I'm not going to let you give up. We're going
to figure this out, just like you helped me figure
out physics in college. I'm bringing Thai. Pad
see ew with chicken now as I recall.

Fuck it, if I could lose everything, might as
well go beef.

See you soon :)

EMAIL

From: Paolo Ventrini
To: Ben Boyce, Adhvan Chaudry

Boys, I'm sure you're feeling a little freaked out, and honestly, you should be. But this is a pretty familiar carrot-and-stick approach. What they want is not so much the $250M of VC that we've raised (which of course is down to about half of that right now). What they want is our company. The fact that they offered a buyout first tips the hand. At this point they're not gonna pay more than $1B, but I bet we can still get close to that if we sell now, save them the hassle and headache and expense of the lawsuit (which will drag on a couple years). We can all save face, save stress, and leave this whole thing filthy fucking rich.

REPLY

From: Ben Boyce
To: Paolo Ventrini, Adhvan Chaudry, Leila Keener-Boyce

Hey man, I hear you, but listen, we're gonna fight. We got the best fuckin lawyer in the Valley on our team! (Adding Lei on CC, whatever you wanna say to us, you can say to her.) We got Adhi's big brain too, he came up with this tech himself, I mean it was his dissertation for fuck's sake. We are un fucking stoppable. Drag this shit out for two years, the fight's just gonna keep us sharp. They got the money to outspend us now but give it some time, we are NOT gonna get beat on this. Look man we can already see 1 year out and this shit is just gonna be getting started at that point.

REPLY

From: Leila Keener-Boyce
To: Paolo Ventrini, Adhvan Chaudry, Ben Boyce

Paolo, I'm just chiming in here to be the voice of reason. Ben is right. We are not going to lose. And before you start calling the other Board members, if you haven't already, let's just be clear: Ben and Adhi and I are united on this, and you know where we stand.

EMAIL — JULY 26, 2021

From: Leila Keener-Boyce
To: Thomas Keener

Dad,

Usually it's tough to get you to even read an email, much less respond, but something tells me this one might be different. And yes, I would prefer to conduct our dialogue in this way rather than on the phone or in person. Yes, I'm aware that means there is a paper trail. That is the point.

First off, the fact that you took this client without talking to me is absurd, but let's not even deal with that. I'm sorry for leaving to go work with Ben, but it's petty of you to respond in this way. In a way that genuinely could jeopardize my career, and any potential relationship between us in the future.

Second, we both know the relevant IP and employment laws here, and the fact that both the statutes and the precedents in California are overwhelmingly in favor of individuals, new enterprises, and, above all, innovation—in other words, what The Future is all about.

Acquisition is simply never going to happen. Your best strategy is to outspend and wear down my clients with endless litigation, but they don't have a big firm (like yours) as an expensive albatross around their neck. We are agile and I am willing to go to the mat on this for years to come.

Now, normally here I would propose discussing a modest settlement, but I know that (A) Alphabet doesn't give a shit about that type of pocket change, (B) you wouldn't be willing to lose face like that, and (C) Ben is too stubborn to agree to that type of a loss anyway.

So instead let's discuss an alternative arrangement that's best for both parties, and gets your client what they

really want: access to the technology. The Future is primarily in the business of consumer electronics. *However,*
we may be willing to entertain the possibility of a man-
aged exclusive licensing agreement, wherein a mutually
beneficial partnership could be reached.

    I hope you will do what's right—for the world, for your
client, and for our family—as you make your way to the
bargaining table.

Love,
Leila

REPLY

Leila,
Nice to hear from you. This is certainly not personal. I
serve my clients. It is sad and unfortunate that you chose
your husband's flash-in-the-pan moonshot over a third-
generation family business, but I should not be too surprised.

    Regarding the relevant employment and IP laws, let me
share with you a bit of history, which you may or may not
know. In the 1870s, California was still a fairly new state,
but the influx of Gold Rush money and the expansion of
the railroads put it on the map, economically speaking. The
state and its government were rapidly growing, and they
needed to develop a comprehensive legal code for financial
matters, and quickly. The governor at the time wrote to
New York, asking for a copy of *their* employment codes,
and asked to see them for reference as California developed
their own. The California state legislature received their
codes and, in a hurry, enacted them immediately—without
even reading through them. If it was good enough for NY,
it was good enough for us.

The only problem was, the document they'd received was not actually the NY codes . . . it was a proposed bill for what they might be, offered and supported by a fringe wing of libertarians paranoid about the Gilded Age over-reach of big business.

You would think that a bill so enacted would not last long. But in fact, it proved to be good for innovation. And it is always politically harder to ramp up restrictions on individual liberty. So California is a state in which no non-compete agreement stands a legal snowball's chance in hell. 140 years of legal precedent now supports a set of laws that were passed, essentially, by mistake.

No lawyer has sought to challenge those restrictions in any meaningful way. But the time has come to do so. Look at what has already happened with Facebook, and every other company that has overreached in this field. Popular will is shifting against unchecked technological progress. The tide is about to turn.

I have been personally interested in pursuing a case in this crusade for quite some time. At last, the time has come, as has the right defendant—because what Ben's company is attempting is, on its face, profoundly irre-sponsible.

I appreciate the entrenchment of your position. But please know that this, for me, is just as important, albeit for ideological reasons, rather than personal ones.

My client has no interest in a limited licensing arrange-ment. Chaudry was in their employ when he made the breakthrough that evolved this idea from a grad-school fantasy to a viable technology. He stole hundreds of mil-lions of dollars in research IP to make it all possible. It is flagrantly irresponsible and dishonest.

So, my beautiful girl, I will, as they say, see you in court.

Yours,
Dad

TEXT MESSAGE EXCHANGE

ADHVAN CHAUDRY
July 27, 2021 11:04 AM

Hey Lei.
Proud of you for standing up to your dad.

LEILA KEENER-BOYCE

Thanks. Really hope I'm doing the right thing
here! Any chance you could give me a hint
about how it's all gonna play out? Might help
me sleep better at night.

You know I can't.
Honestly, I'm trying to use the Prototype as
little as possible.
I tend to get down when I do.

Do things really look that dark ahead?

It's not that. It's just . . .
If you hoped for one thing in all the world,
and you knew it wasn't gonna happen . . .
What would you do?

I'd start hoping for something else.

EMAIL—JULY 28, 2021

From: Carrie Chan
To: Ben Boyce, Adhvan Chaudry

Hi Ben and Adhvan,

Our marketing team just completed our latest research
with a focus group, the full report is attached. Two key
takeaways that I would highlight here—

1. In response to the question "How would you characterize your view of the company The Future?" the options

are Favorable/Unfavorable/No opinion, and we've jumped from 22/46/32 (right after the party debacle) up to 38/32/30. That's a massive improvement in a short time, which I primarily attribute to the *Wired* article and subsequent social chatter.

2. That said, another key metric was on the question "Would you be interested in purchasing a product that lets you look one year in the future?" Our Yes/No/Not sure answer split on the latest round came in at 22/48/30. Which is pretty low, especially given that our initial market price (I know we're still hashing it out) is gonna be in the ballpark of double what most people pay for their priciest personal electronics.

I think we should recalibrate our sales goals, and take a more targeted approach with the rollout (if you look at the demo data, it's clear there's a much higher WBR for the coastal early-adopter crowd). Also let's look to significantly step up our marketing budget, so we can tell the world what we've got here. In short: the culture of secrecy is damaging our prospects in the marketplace.

Carrie Chan
Chief Communications Officer
The Future LLC

REPLY

From: Ben Boyce
To: Carrie Chan, Adhvan Chaudry

Hey Carrie,
You know Henry Ford's take on this issue? "If I'd asked people what they WANTED, they would've said 'faster horses.'"

Real innovation isn't something you can run through your little market-testing playbook. We are going to mar-

ket on schedule and at full production. We are going ALL
IN. If we HALF-ASS, we will be dealing with CLONES,
and we risk getting beaten out before we can dominate the
market. Adhi, back me up on this.

Ben

REPLY

From: Adhvan Chaudry
To: Ben Boyce, Carrie Chan

B—
Henry Ford never actually said that.
It's a business-book myth.
He also certainly never used caps-lock.
What people actually wanted back then was less horseshit.
In fact, they still do.
But I digress.
I agree with you that Focus Groups are horseshit . . .
but I agree with Carrie that we can learn from this.

Here's a better way to look at the issue.
A thought experiment.
Put a peephole in a locker room,
and ask guys if they want to look through it.
Most will say no, that's sick.
But put dark paint around that hole,
and see how many guys walk out with dark circles around
their eyes.
Then you have your answer about real interest.
You want to know if/how people will use the tech . . .
you need to start giving it to them.
In other words, we need to go to Beta.
People will use it.
They will be hooked.

Word will spread.

Demand will build.

And we can get a more accurate market gauge before we go into production.

—A

REPLY

From: Carrie Chan
To: Adhvan Chaudry, Ben Boyce

Well guys, it sounds like your minds are made up here, look forward to seeing how the strategy plays out.

REPLY

From: Carrie Chan
To: Ben Boyce

What the actual fuck? When I talked to you about this in person, you seemed receptive. Then as soon as anyone else is around or on CC, you get all high and mighty, playing the part of the maligned entrepreneur boxed in by the small-minded marketing girl. I am genuinely trying to help.

You're running a playbook that you won't let me see. Both in the office, and in your personal life.

Carrie

REPLY

From: Ben Boyce
To: Adhvan Chaudry

Hey man, appreciate you chiming in on the beta test, but you sure we can handle that with real out-in-the-wild users? I'm just worried about how people are gonna use it. Maybe we take a step back here, reevaluate, get solid on everything.

REPLY

B—
Don't second-guess your instincts.
We have already done the beta test.
Or rather, we will do it soon . . .
and I was already able to view the results.
I used the Prototype and accessed our records one year from now,
and am attaching the Beta Test Report.
As you can see . . . the beta will be a success.
Some hiccups of course, but it's part of our path to market.
We can even use this data to help determine which subjects we pick,
to be maximally confident in how it will go.
We are bulletproof on this.

—A

Note: Attached report on Beta Test has been REDACTED.

REPLY

Hey man that's great news. I'm down to proceed. One question though: Isn't that the type of circular info-gathering you warned about? That we're trying to avoid? And also, if we're going to use this data, do we want to maybe filter out the users who are problematic?

REPLY

B—

Drastic times, drastic measures.

We can't change any variables, or we risk completely changing the outcome,

and the users have been anonymized in our data set (referred to only by numbers, not by names).

The ones that we choose will be the ones we are "meant" to choose.

Trust the process.

Also, fire Carrie already, will you?

Leila won't come out and say it but I will.

—A

REPLY

Bro I can't fire Carrie, she'll sue. Leave my shit alone and focus on your job.

Which is gonna be getting beta units ready for a test. Cool? We're doing this.

EMAIL — JULY 30, 2021

From: Paolo Ventrini
To: Ben Boyce, Adhvan Chaudry

Listen Boys, the investors and I are going along with your strategy of bringing a consumer product to market. We are going along with your resistance to merging or selling with a larger conglomerate. But we cannot support a roll-out strategy this reckless. We need time to secure retail partnerships, demonstrate the soundness of our tech, get the lawsuit off our plate, and develop our supply-chain plan.

In other words, we need to slow down, take a step back, postpone any sort of public-facing beta test, and push back our release date.

TWITTER THREAD

@HEYBENBOYCE

The Future 1.0—a fully-functional TIME MACHINE that can see into the future—will be AVAILABLE TO THE PUBLIC on 1/1/2022. #TheFutureIsComing

@HEYBENBOYCE

Put it in your calendars! Price and specs coming soon, but know—it will be priced as a viable CONSUMER PRODUCT for EVERYONE! #TheFutureIsComing

@HEYBENBOYCE

Haters and doubters beware—revolutionary tech comin your way! #TheFutureIsComing

EMAIL REPLY

From: Ben Boyce
To: Paolo Ventrini, Adhvan Chaudry, Carrie Chan

Yo Paolo, appreciate your concern and all, but tell the investors to get on board, the Future train is on the MOVE!

Ben

CHAPTER 16

EMAIL—AUGUST 5, 2021

From: The Future Admin
To: (undisclosed recipients)

Dear User,

Congratulations! You have been selected as a Beta Tester for The Future 1.0. Your usage period of 60 days will be remotely monitored, as a way to troubleshoot the effectiveness of the product.

SECURITY

As you are no doubt aware from the selection process you have been through, security is of tantamount importance. Please review the attached NDA. If you wish to have a lawyer review it as well, there is a separate NDA your lawyer will need to sign first (inform your lawyer that yes, this is in addition to normal attorney-client provisions). The provisions of this NDA we would highlight are—

  - No one should know that you are a Beta Tester. This includes significant others, family members, friends, coworkers, etc.

  - You may not share any information with anyone that you may have only credibly obtained through using the Beta Machine.

- You may not publicly discuss usage of the Beta Machine, or publicly disseminate any information obtained therein.

- You are required to protect the physical security of the Beta Machine. If you have been selected, then your home has already been inspected for reasonable security, but be advised you are not permitted under any circumstances to relocate the Beta Machine.

USAGE

Please review the attached Beta Tester Agreement in detail. We would highlight the following salient points, which are nonnegotiable:

- All of your usage will be monitored.

- You may not engage in financial speculation based on information obtained through the Beta Machine.

- You consent to usage parameters that may be changed, without prior notice, during the course of the Beta Testing period.

We look forward to having you on board the Beta Team!

Ben Boyce
CEO of The Future

EMAIL—AUGUST 12, 2021

From: Adhvan Chaudry
To: Ben Boyce

B—
One of the Beta Testers killed himself.
Apparently, he had recently been diagnosed with ALS.
Within 30 minutes of taking his unit home, he Googled himself, using the Beta unit.

The outcome: similar to the Nikolai situation.

First thing that came up was his own obituary.

Probably he was trying to see his expected longevity, given the disease . . .

but it was his fate to cut it short.

This is terrible.

—A

REPLY

Are you fucking SERIOUS? Did we not see this coming in the Report that you looked up on the Prototype? This seems like exactly the type of thing we should have known about.

REPLY

B—

This incident was not in the report,

and the users (in the data set we have) are all anonymized.

I'm wondering if this is going off the rails.

Either (A) the technology is becoming problematic

or (B) The Beta Report I viewed did not include this anomaly.

Do we need to shut this down?

—A

REPLY

Hey man, relax, no need to shut it down. We're on top of it. Whether you meant to or not, what you're suggesting is actually a good idea, on multiple levels. Meaning, maybe this happened/was always going to happen, but was not "meant" to be included in the Beta Report, bc it was never supposed to be part of the Beta Test.

We had plenty of backup applicants who were ready to step in. Since it was a same-day incident, we swapped out User 53, so now have somebody else in his place. I've got a team moving the Beta Unit over there already.

REPLY

B—

Are you kidding me?

I was not suggesting anything, certainly not that we just swap out a deceased Beta Tester.

This has to be part of the study.

—A

REPLY

Listen dude, I know it's really sad what happened there, and we're not just gonna forget about this. But we weren't about to get any good data from that user anymore, and we need good data. Plus, let's be honest, this is probably a situation like what happened with Nikolai. A suicidal, problematic individual, who was unfortunately gravitating toward our tech, likely because of his suicidal ideation.

EXCERPT FROM CONGRESSIONAL HEARING — DECEMBER 1, 2021

REP. MARSHA CALLOWAY (R-IN): Mr. Boyce, you say that you have a firm handle on this technology. But the incidents surrounding the beta were very troubling.

BOYCE: Overall, the beta test was a huge success. We weren't trying to cover anything up. The swap-in that we did, I acknowledge, we should've been more transparent. But scientifically, it was reasonable. We did it entirely to try to get as much good data as we possibly could. The trials were prohibitively expensive.

REP. MARSHA CALLOWAY (R-IN): The suicide was a troubling event, but it wasn't the only problem. Reports indicate that approximately eighteen of your one hundred beta users violated the agreement they signed and attempted to speculatively profit from its usage.

BOYCE: With all due respect, yes, but that also indicates a fundamental flaw with the design of the beta process. A problem which will be solved, obviously, by just making the technology available to everyone.

REP. MARSHA CALLOWAY (R-IN): That hardly seems obvious to me.

BOYCE: Look—imagine it's, like, the 1800s. And there's a railroad strike, and shipments of apples from California are gonna be held up. That means apple stocks are gonna tank the next day, right? Now, if there's ten guys who get that information, who have access to telegram technology—they sell their stocks, right? They have an unfair advantage, while the rest of us get screwed on our apple stock, because we don't have access to the same info. *But,* let's say everyone has that information technology. The newspapers have it, and they print it on the front page. Then we've got a level playing field.

The beta test—that shows us what happens if ten people know something nobody else does. It's human nature, they act on it. And that's what will happen if you restrict this technology. But open it to the whole world, we all have access to the same info.

REP. MARSHA CALLOWAY (R-IN): Then why even create it? If everyone will have access to the same information.

BOYCE: If you have to ask that question . . . I don't even really know how to talk to you. All I can say is, I'm sure you weren't an early adopter of the iPhone. I bet you were looking over your friend's shoulder saying, Why would I even want my email on my phone? But I bet your iPhone was the first thing you looked at this morning.

REP. MARSHA CALLOWAY (R-IN): Mr. Boyce, I would advise you to watch your tone when addressing members of this committee. We will be considering legislation in the coming weeks which could make your product illegal in this country.

BOYCE: Oh, that's a great plan. Then, only every other country in the world will have access to the most important info tech revolution since the Internet. Really forward-thinking.

REP. MARSHA CALLOWAY (R-IN): I would like to propose a motion to consider Mr. Boyce in Contempt of Congress, and to—

BOYCE: Wait, wait, wait. I'm sorry, OK? Senator Calloway, I apologize, I am simply *passionate* about my product.

REP. MARSHA CALLOWAY (R-IN): Tread lightly, then, Mr. Boyce. And I would like to point out one more thing. Which is that, before you talk about your position as so self-evidently undeniable, maybe you should consider why your own co-founder no longer seemed to agree with it.

BOYCE: Well . . . there were mitigating factors, in terms of my co-founder. At that time. He was starting to become . . . less than maximally reliable, in certain ways, with respect to his mental health.

REP. MARSHA CALLOWAY (R-IN): That wasn't the only problem with the beta test though, was it?

BOYCE: . . . Yes, we did encounter a security issue.

EMAIL—SEPTEMBER 2, 2021

From: Alice Muncy
To: Ben Boyce, Adhvan Chaudry

Mr. Boyce and Mr. Chaudry—
Hi, this is Beta Tester 19. I tried calling the support line at first, but then I thought based on your orientation talk and given the nature of my problem that you wouldn't actually want me to discuss with anyone else yet, so I'm writing to you and hoping you can call me back please when you get this.

It appears that my Beta Unit has been stolen.

REPLY

From: Ben Boyce

Alice—good move reaching out, thank you, sorry I've been in meetings back-to-back. Please sit tight we will be there in person in less than an hour. DO NOT contact police or discuss w any other TF personnel.

EMAIL

From: Ben Boyce
To: Adhvan Chaudry

Hey man, where you been all day? Dealing with some serious shit on this missing Beta Unit. I went out to her spot in person with Kevin from Security, didn't take anyone else, and Kevin is cool he can keep a lid on this. He thinks our exposure is limited and we can keep this under wraps.

Question on my mind is—how did someone find out the name and info on one of our Testers? Thought we

were all buttoned up here. And maybe an even better question, coming up YET AGAIN, is this—why did we not see
this coming?

REPLY

B—

The only reason I can think of for why we didn't see this
coming is because of the successful cover-up.

The one that we have not done yet, but inevitably will do.

Unless you want to explore the possibility that doing so is
morally wrong.

Unless you want to consciously try to break us from this
path.

—A

REPLY

I don't think it's wrong, it's just good business. And it's
not a cover-up, it's damage control.

Look, I'm all over it. Kevin connected me with Watermark, they're this private investigation/security firm that
specializes in corporate cases like this, expensive af but
honestly the shit they can do is pretty fucking legit.
They're helping track down the Beta Unit and also getting
into keeping it quiet, data management, all that.

Also, based on their rec, we're going to pull the plug on
the Beta Test a little early. I mean, we're Day 28, so 30 is
right around the corner, and it's credible to say 30 was always the goal. Should have all remaining units back and
accounted for within 3 days.

My question for you is—what's our exposure here? We've got a Prototype that's in the wind now, no clue where it is, what does that mean for us?

REPLY

B—

I see three distinct possibilities . . .

Which I will enumerate in increasing order of We-Are-Fuckedness.

1) The burglary was random. In that case it is highly un-likely the thief will ever figure out how to operate the transtemporal functionality, and we're essentially in the clear. W.A.F. score: 1.

2) The burglary was targeted for personal gain. Someone is now using it to get rich in the stock market, win the lot-tery, etc. This will likely, eventually, be found out and blow back on us. W.A.F score: 4.

3) The burglary was targeted for corporate gain. If that is the case, it was no doubt undertaken by some party that intends to reverse-engineer the Beta Unit and build one of their own. W.A.F. score: 8.

In terms of options, there aren't many.

—A

REPLY

Hey man, we're on it. Kevin says the Watermark guys are the best in their business and they're leaving no stone un-turned here, it should just be a matter of time before we get to the bottom of this.

REPLY

B—

I'm sure they have plenty of experience tracking down stolen time machines.

In the meantime, I have a new wrinkle to make you aware of.

Check out the attached, which I pulled from the Prototype this morning—

Quoted Text:

((THE FUTURE LAUNCHES STRONG IN U.S.

After months of hype and rampant speculation, The Future stores around the country opened on New Year's Day to lines around the block and strong sales. Insiders were expecting solid numbers, since over 40,000 people had pre-ordered the Future 1 units online, which were available Sunday for pickup and shipping. Since the company reported estimates that another 50,000 units had sold in its 21 locations, it's clear that expectations have been met or exceeded.))

In case it's not clear . . .

That is from the same article we shared with the investors.

But the sales figures are slightly lower.

And the number of stores has dropped by one.

In other words—for the first time—we have discrepancies.

—A

REPLY

Hey man, discrepancies of one store and a couple thousand units don't seem like that big a deal in the grand scheme of things, and in light of what we're dealing with here. Namely a STOLEN UNIT, and the prospect that our entire business could unravel.

REPLY

B—
Our business is selling machines that see the future, accurately and infallibly.
If they don't do that anymore . . .
if these Discrepancies persist, possibly even increase . . .
we might as well be in the horoscope business.

—A

EXCERPT FROM CONGRESSIONAL HEARING—DECEMBER 1, 2021

SEN. DANA BOUCHER (D-NV): Mr. Boyce, what is the next question I'm going to ask you?

BOYCE: Uh . . . No idea.

SEN. DANA BOUCHER (D-NV): But this is a hearing of public record. Surely, in an effort to prepare for it, you would have been able to access the transcript of our questions, and of your own testimony.

BOYCE: Yes.

SEN. DANA BOUCHER (D-NV): Then let me ask you a direct question, and I would remind you that you are under oath here. Did you obtain and view a copy of the transcript of this hearing?

BOYCE: . . . I did.

(AUDIBLE MURMURING)

SEN. DANA BOUCHER (D-NV): So. You should be able to answer, what am I going to ask you next?

BOYCE: I am not able to recall at this time.

SEN. DANA BOUCHER (D-NV): How about this, then: is your colleague, Mr. Chaudry, going to join us at any point today?

BOYCE: I am not certain.

SEN. DANA BOUCHER (D-NV): A detail like that would have to be salient in your recollection of those materials. Is Mr. Chaudry going to be here?

BOYCE: Look, the way I saw it . . . Adhi *did* show up. From the beginning. I read a version of this testimony that he was in. And . . . honestly, what's happening today . . . it's not supposed to happen like this.

SEN. DANA BOUCHER (D-NV): "Not supposed to"? Interesting. So then you admit, here and now, that your technology is not as infallible as you previously represented?

BOYCE: I will acknowledge, there have been, only recently, certain . . . Discrepancies, we call them. And, so far as we can tell, they originated during the beta period.

SEN. DANA BOUCHER (D-NV): Meaning you think the beta tests may have caused them?

BOYCE: We think the *theft* may have caused them. Which is why, since then, and moving forward . . . we have elected to drastically step up our security measures. I can assure you, the situation is under control.

SEN. GREG WALDEN (D-OR): The senator's time is complete, moving on to—

SEN. DANA BOUCHER (D-NV): Mr. Boyce, in what way is the situation even remotely under control, when—

SEN. GREG WALDEN (D-OR): Senator Boucher, if you will yield the floor, we will—

SEN. DANA BOUCHER (D-NV): Mr. Chairman, if I may be permitted one final remark? Thank you. Mr. Boyce, it is clear that you have *nothing* under control. You have a missing co-founder, a machine that doesn't work, and a glimpse into a horribly dark future that you are refusing to share, even though it theoretically impacts us all. If you want this legislative body to view you and your technology as anything other than a dangerous threat, you need to open up your books, your company, everything, and let us see what is behind the curtain.

SEN. GREG WALDEN (D-OR): The senator's time is *finished*. Mr. Boyce, any final reply?

BOYCE: . . . I have no comment at this time.

CHAPTER 17

EMAIL—OCTOBER 2, 2021

From: Adhvan Chaudry
To: Ben Boyce

B—
I have been deep-diving on the Prototype this morning . . .
and have found MANY more Discrepancies.
New developments in the future that were not observed
even last week.
Perhaps the most frightening being these articles . . .

U.S. Launches Ground, Air Campaign in Ukraine

U.S. Launches Pre-Emptive Strike Against Russian Forces
in Ukraine

Intel from "The Future" Device Drove Pre-Emptive
Ukraine Strike

Russian Standoff in Ukraine Could Escalate

U.S. Cites "Future Human Rights Abuses" as Justification
for Pre-Emptive Strike

China Accuses U.S. of Escalating Conflict, Cites "The Future" Intel

War on the Peninsula Looms

I'm attaching the linked articles.
Please take the time to read them all.
This is NEW. This is not something we've seen before.
We need to figure out how to handle this . . .

—A

REPLY

Hey man, you need to cool it on this. Step away from the Prototype and get some air. We always knew that our tech would get tangled up with international politics. We made a conscious decision not to know too much. And we made a firm POLICY not to download (and certainly not to SHARE) any data about future global events, which, if it leaked, could be hugely problematic.

Kevin and I huddled up about everything that's going on and decided we need to implement some new security protocols. A memo is going out tomorrow about the particulars, but thought I'd loop you in early.

Basically we're locking down use of the device so it's only gonna be usable as it relates directly to pressing matters relevant to the future of the company, therefore will only be accessible to the two of us (me and Kevin). I figure you won't mind too much, you haven't even been using it lately.

REPLY

B—

First off—who the fuck is Kevin?

And how is it even conceivable that he is spearheading a policy that locks me out from accessing my own invention?

Why would you maintain usage rights while I'm locked out?

—A

REPLY

Listen dude, this is a drastic-times, drastic-temporary-measures type of situation. Don't worry about it too much. And Kevin Martindale, for the record, is a former member of a three-letter agency, with a pristine record of national service, and now he's a highly recommended private security expert. If you were involved in day-to-day operations in the least, you would know this.

In case you're not savvy to what this means, our tech got straight-up STOLEN! Also honestly it bums me out you're calling it your invention when I think it's undeniable this tech wouldn't exist without both of our contribution.

Now, where are we on the 2.0? Time to get back to it. THAT is the solution to the problem you're talking about. The real problem. The problem of our POWERLESSNESS. And if there's anyone who can crack it, it's YOU.

EXCERPT FROM CONGRESSIONAL HEARING — DECEMBER 1, 2021

SEN. DIANA JACKSON (D-MI): Mr. Boyce, what was "the 2.0"?

BOYCE: The what?

SEN. DIANA JACKSON (D-MI): There are rumors, substantiated by several former employees, who allege that your company has invested significant resources in research for a new technological project referred to internally only as "the 2.0."

BOYCE: Yes, well, that was for a project, in its infancy, that we are not interested in discussing publicly at this time, for trade-secret reasons.

SEN. DIANA JACKSON (D-MI): If you would like this legislative body to look favorably on your endeavor, as concerns our forthcoming legislation, you might want to rethink your position on that.

BOYCE: Right. Well . . . our first device is the 1.0, which lets users look forward in time by one year. We imagine that we will reach market saturation for that product eventually . . . and as such, we want to be able to follow up with a new product. The 2.0. Which, naturally, will let users see forward in the future by a two-year time horizon.

SEN. DIANA JACKSON (D-MI): I thought you previously stated that you were not able to build a machine with that functionality.

BOYCE: Yes, well . . . not yet. We're still in development. But we're confident, in time, that we'll—

SEN. DIANA JACKSON (D-MI): Some have speculated that the one-year limit may not be technological, but . . . historical. That there will be cataclysmic global events which disrupt the world on such a scale that . . . well, maybe we can't see the world two years from now because there won't *be* a world to see.

BOYCE: No, no, we have absolutely no evidence to support that. And, as soon as we have a working model with two-year functionality, we will be able to put those overblown rumors to rest. It's just like, the way computers and phones get faster every year . . . this is our equivalent, letting you look two years ahead, instead of one. And, you can imagine, down the line . . . we might have the 3.0. And the 4.0. Et cetera. You can imagine what those will do.

SEN. DIANA JACKSON (D-MI): So your plan is to get people hooked on the future, and then just spoon out a little more at a time, so people are always paying top dollar to get a little further out ahead of the next guy.

BOYCE: That's a cynical way to put it, but yes. We intend to deliver better and better information services with each new iteration.

SEN. DIANA JACKSON (D-MI): So the 2.0 has nothing to do with the possibility of actually sending a person back in time?

BOYCE: I wish. But Adhi made it abundantly clear to me, that was all just sci-fi nonsense.

SEN. DIANA JACKSON (D-MI): So you never even entertained the possibility of attempting to build such a device?

BOYCE: Never.

INTERNAL MEMO FROM THE FUTURE SERVERS

NEW PRODUCT RESEARCH REPORT

"The Future 2.0"

ADHVAN CHAUDRY

Theoretical Objective: Physical transtemporal regression—that is, time travel, in the manner of an individual physically leaving the present timeframe, and moving into another (previous) timeframe.

Theoretical Possibility: As outlined by the theory of general relativity, it is conceivably possible to travel to an earlier point in time (though never to a later one). This is achieved, on the simplest level, by an individual departing from one point so rapidly (faster than light speed) that they arrive at their destination earlier than the moment at which they departed.

Of course, based on the same Einsteinian principles, it is not feasible to imagine accelerating a physical object (i.e., a rocket in space) to a speed at or beyond light speed, simply due to the firm limit of the constant c.

However, our 1.0 technology is built on the principle of Bell's theorem, which shows how quantum-level *information* can be transmitted instantaneously, in defiance of this limit.

Therefore, *if* a physical object (i.e., a person) could be converted from physical mass into information, the information could conceivably be transmitted in the same quantum-computing manner we have utilized with the 1.0 Prototype.

Translating mass into data may sound counterintuitive, but less so in the theoretical framework of string theory, which views all point-like particles as one-dimensional "strings"—that is, energy with a specific vibration. That vibration determines the mass, charge, and position of the corresponding particle in physical space. So it is conceivable that, with the proper arrangement, said data (and therefore, said particles) could be transmitted to an earlier point in time.

To use a broad analogy: this could be thought of as akin to a fax machine, which translates a physical object through visual/optical data into a signal, transmits the signal at a distance, and then "prints" the object back into physical form on the other end.

Of course, this requires a fax machine on both ends—it is not possible to transmit a fax to a location without a fax machine. Similarly, a "2.0" device would need a destination for the transmitted subject to "land" in, which means that the machine could never transmit anyone/anything to an earlier point in time than when the device was first built.

Theoretical Limitation: The primary limitation comes in the fact that translating a given particle/string into pure information (so it could be transmitted to an earlier point) can be achieved only with infinite energy density, on par with a black hole.

The Difference from 1.0 Technology: The existing technology we've created allows information to loop to an earlier point in time, which means that the timeline remains unaltered by its usage.

However, a technology that transmits a physical presence (esp. a human presence) would potentially enable a deliberate alteration of events, and a splitting of the timelines, creating two (or more) parallel realities. This concept is understandable mainly in terms of multiverse theory (e.g., Hugh Everett's Multiple-Worlds Interpretation of quantum physics paradoxes).

That said, such possible alteration of the timeline is by no means a certainty. It is possible that, if this technology *will* be invented someday, then it already *has* been invented, and time-travelers are already among us. Experimental investigation would be required to determine which fundamental framework of reality corresponds to truth.

Existential Limitations: It is not clear that transporting a body to an earlier time would protect the mind contained therein. Even setting aside notions like "the soul," it is possible that a brain perfectly transported through time would nonetheless fail to preserve the consciousness contained within it.

Moreover, even if the transmission were successful, the transported individual would be unable to return to his present, and would permanently be stranded in the past. He would effectively become one of two bodies in the timeframe, raising problematic ontological questions:

Could both "individuals" survive and coexist?

Would the "traveler" have agency and free will in the new timeline?

If so, would he theoretically have the ability to change the past?

CHAPTER 18

EMAIL — OCTOBER 4, 2021

From: Adhvan Chaudry
To: Leila Keener-Boyce

L—
Could you do me a favor?
Check out this email that I pulled from the Prototype?
(Which, apparently, I'm going to write six months from now).

Quoted Text:

((B—
Everything is looking legit on the manufacturing specs.
The pricing guide numbers are just as they should be.
Hope you and Leila are doing well.

—A))

Does this honestly sound like me?

—A

REPLY

Hey A,

I don't really understand your question. But you write emails in a pretty distinct way, and this is definitely in that style.

Looking at it again, I guess . . . you don't usually call me Leila. And I guess that saying this to Ben is a little weird, in light of what happened. But hopefully that just means he's not going to find out, and we're all going to go back to everything being normal. Right?

REPLY

L—

I can literally never imagine a universe where I'd say "legit."

And everything back to normal . . . maybe.

But I'd never say something so disingenuous.

I'm not going to try to convince you to blow up your life, but I'm never going to pretend everything is fine.

I love you.

—A

REPLY

Hey A,

Come on, we talked about this. You know how I feel. But it breaks my heart and rips me up to even see those words. It's up to you how you want to manage your friendship with Ben from here on out, but I just don't see what's gained by not at least trying to be nice. If we're going to keep this quiet, let's really keep it quiet, right? And with respect to the email, I don't really even understand what you're getting at . . .

REPLY

L—
What if someone in the future is spoofing my emails?
Ben has currently locked me out of using the Prototype . . .
so I've been looking through the correspondence I have in my records,
and I've noticed it's pretty fucking sparse.
Like, I'm only sending a couple brief emails a day.
All very similar, and don't say much.
Made me start to wonder:
what if the messages in my account are written by someone else?
All so that when I look ahead, it seems like I'm there,
it seems like I'm alive and happily working away,
even if I'm not.

—A

REPLY

Hey A,
OK, I hear where you're going with this, and I just want to say, let's not overreact. Keep in mind, you've been here before, even if it's been a few years now. Last time, you thought that it was the other people in your department. Now you think it's your coworkers. This is a pattern.

I get it, you're under a lot of stress. It's easy when a lot is being asked of your brain to want to stay sharp and then maybe you don't take your meds at normal times. I'm gonna come over and we're going to just sit down and talk so we can nip this in the bud and be healthy, happy, and calm. We all love you and you're going to be OK.

REPLY

L—
Et tu?

—A

MENLO PARK MENTAL HEALTH CLINIC

Intake Session Notes—Mar 7, 2019
Patient: Adhvan Chaudry
Intake Counselor: Dr. Ana Dawoud

PRECIPITATING EVENTS FOR HOSPITALIZATION:

Campus police were alerted that Patient was suffering from psychotic episode, after Patient's phone conversation with a friend earlier in the night.

Officers found Patient bleeding on the lawn in front of Stanford University Student Services Building. Patient had destroyed several windows by hand, and left arm was severely cut from punching through glass. Patient was at risk for lethal exsanguination if he had not been discovered, but he nonetheless attempted to evade officers. Following medical hospitalization, Patient was arrested for destruction of property and resisting arrest.

DIAGNOSIS HISTORY:

Patient has been assessed for Bipolar Personality Disorder since age 17. Intake assessment affirms BPD as appropriate diagnosis, along with indications of comorbid Social Anxiety Disorder and Generalized Anxiety Disorder.

Patient has also been assessed for substance abuse issues (age 17) but reports he was only using cannabis to treat his anxiety, and has not had any substance abuse issues since beginning pharma treatment for his diagnoses.

MEDICATION HISTORY:

Patient has been medicated with lithium, antipsychotics (Zyprexa, Risperdal), anticonvulsants (Depakote), SSRIs (Lexapro, Paxil, Zoloft) and benzodiazepines (Xanax, Ativan, Valium). At time of episode, Patient's most recent treatment therapy included Risperdal, Paxil, Ativan. Patient reports he had discontinued regular use of all but the Ativan for the past 3 to 4 months, blaming side effects of sluggishness, diminishment of full mental capacity, impotence.

TREATMENT HISTORY:

Patient has received inpatient psychiatric treatment 2x (age 17, age 21) and has been consistently treated on an outpatient basis.

PATIENT DESCRIPTION:

Patient is mid-20s PhD candidate in Computer Science graduate program. Physically fit. No reported housing issues. Social member of his community. Limited romantic and sexual history (more later).

SESSION NOTES:

At time of assessment, Patient was lethargic, depressive, and filled with shame. Patient had been treated with antipsychotics and precipitating manic state had subsided.

Nature of Patient's manic states: grandiosity combined with paranoid delusion. At peak states of agitation, Patient believes himself to be only individual capable of solving major global crises. During these episodes, he also believes the course for which he worked as a TA was a theatrical production entirely for the purpose of tricking him, testing him, or monitoring him (varies). Patient believed peers and colleagues were in on an elaborate deception targeting the contents of his mind.

Over course of last 2–3 weeks, Patient had come to believe that the federal government was spying on him through his university. Incident at Student Services building resulted from belief that the University was monitoring his thoughts through radio devices concealed therein.

Patient also reports romantic fixation on a female friend who is married to a close male friend of Patient (incidentally, same male friend who notified Campus Police of Patient's episode, and likely saved his life). Patient believes female friend to be the only person he is capable of loving, while Patient's male friend is the only person in the world who loves him. This overblown self-dramatization of personal life is consistent with BPD.

Patient reports strong desire to improve his mental health, and acknowledges role of discontinuing medication in this episode. Patient acknowledges history of suicidal ideation but reports none currently.

RECOMMENDATION:

48-hr inpatient hold for ongoing assessment and monitoring, followed by intensive outpatient therapy (group sessions, individual talk therapy, psychiatrist-guided pharma protocol).

EXCERPT FROM CONGRESSIONAL HEARING — DECEMBER 1, 2021

REP. ALEJANDRO CORTES (D-NM): Mr. Boyce, were you aware of the mental-health history of your co-founder?

BOYCE: Aware? Of course. I was actively involved in it from college onward. When he had his breakdown in grad school, I was the one who helped get him into treatment, and helped him avoid going to jail. I was there for him all the way.

REP. ALEJANDRO CORTES (D-NM): Were you ever concerned about his ability to responsibly participate in managing the company?

BOYCE: Managing was really my job. That's why we made a good team. Adhi's a genius, but you leave him to his own devices, he's gonna get lost.

REP. ALEJANDRO CORTES (D-NM): Is it possible that might explain his absence today?

BOYCE: Possibly. I dunno. He's high-functioning, so, the episodes, you never really see them coming until it's too late. And when all this started going down—when he started getting a little bit paranoid and pulling away, I wasn't paying as much attention maybe, because I was dealing with other issues.

MEDIUM.COM POST, LATER PICKED UP BY *HUFFPOST*— OCTOBER 12, 2021

THE FUTURE IS NOT FEMALE
By Carrie Chan

Unless you've been hiding under a rock, you know that The Future is on track to become *the* tech story of the decade. Their technology is being widely heralded as a communications revolution that will empower people equally to take charge of their future.

"Equally"? Riiiight. Don't believe the hype.

I was working at The Future until just recently, in what I considered to be the enviable position of Chief Marketing Officer. I enjoyed the title, and the startup-with-cash-to-burn salary. But the time came when I had no choice but to leave, due to a culture of sexism, secrecy, and boys' club power dynamics that I could not bring myself to remain a part of.

Before going any further, I have to be honest about part of my time at The Future that I'm not proud of. For six months on and off, CEO Ben Boyce and I engaged in a relationship that crossed lines of what is professionally appropriate. On at least one occasion, the relationship became physical.

Now, I know, "crossed lines" and "became physical" are frustratingly vague, but trust that I'll dish in more depth soon. For now, I've got lawsuits to worry about.

The real point I want to make is about how emotionally difficult this hostile work environment became. It was *impossible* to maintain healthy boundaries in a situation where every interaction was infused with an unspoken expectation that I would play the role of the "cool girl"—unfazed by raunchy conversation and leering looks.

On top of that, the situation got a whole lot worse when Ben brought his wife to work at the company (where she is still employed). Ben would flirt with me one minute, then switch it off as soon as she approached. He was clearly playing mind games and obviously enjoyed the power dynamic.

Meanwhile, he teased the possibility that "our future" together was very promising (as he'd seen through his little device), which I knew was an insinuation intended to entice me toward a romantic relationship. Anyone who has dated in the Valley (or probably any other major city) knows this is classic fuckboy behavior (yeah, married men can be fuckboys too).

Now, the heart of this is not simply the all-too-familiar story of an illicit office romance. It is the story of a technological wonder, being controlled by men, and used to exploit women.

I asked Ben, on multiple occasions, for permission to use The Future's Prototype device. After all, Ben and his co-founder, Adhvan, regularly used it, and it was slated for imminent commercial release to the public. And I knew it could be invaluable for me in doing my job.

But Ben refused every single time—except for in the one instance when it would directly benefit him, and help him cover up his misconduct.

In fact, Ben seemed to enjoy refusing to grant me access to his precious Prototype. He would tease me with hints of what he might know. On occasion, he implied that he would provide infallible stock tips in exchange for sexual favors (yeah, "just the tip" jokes, try not to barf in your mouth).

The problem here is not limited to this company, or this technology. It is a systemic oppression of women by men, using the leverage of technology and the wealth of this industry.

If we want our future to be different from what I saw at The Future, we need to stand up to this company—to boycott their upcoming product launch until we see real, actionable change in the way women are treated there, and throughout Silicon Valley.

TEXT MESSAGE EXCHANGE

LEILA KEENER-BOYCE
October 12, 2021 1:52 PM

Honest question here: how much more of this am I going to be asked to put up with? Because my tolerance is stretched to the breaking point, and I need you to at least be clear about what I'm up against.

BEN BOYCE

Babe this chick is off her rocker. The only reason this is happening is I made it CLEAR to her that I'm not interested and happily married.

Happily, right.

Hey first you were mad bc you thought I was gonna end up with her Now you know that's not gonna happen and you're still pissed

Are you trying to convince me that I don't have the right to be upset about my husband being accused of sexual harassment?

Look I'm really sorry. I fucked up. I owe it to you to deal with this. We will, I promise. But the work part has to happen first The press are asking if I'm gonna resign. This could cost us everything.

I'm at the office working on a public statement.

You can help me, or not.

As far as we're concerned, this is definitely
not "over." But I also don't want you to botch
this or embarrass me any more than you already
have. So yes, I will be there in 20 minutes,
and you don't do anything without running it
through me.

PRESS RELEASE STATEMENT FROM BEN BOYCE

I am shocked and disappointed by the accusations from our former employee that were published online today, in a piece that
blindsided our company.

First, as a happily married man, I must address the allegations
and insinuations. Ms. Chan was flirtatious toward me since the
first time I met her. I attempted to keep our interactions professional nonetheless. At one company event, I did, unfortunately,
during a lapse of judgment connected with excessive drinking,
share an inappropriate moment with her. But it was never a sexual
relationship, and I am deeply sorry for how I hurt my wife through
my poor judgment, which I will never do again.

Second, regarding our company culture, I am appalled by Ms.
Chan's reckless and unfounded allegations. As a Black entrepreneur, I, and my Indian American co-founder, Adhvan Chaudry,
are aware of what it means to belong to a marginalized group, and
to try to distinguish yourself in the predominantly white culture
of Silicon Valley.

At The Future, we treat women with utmost respect. Hopefully, there is no more clear indication of that than the fact that my
wife, Leila Keener-Boyce—as proud and strong a feminist as you
are likely to find—chose to leave her previous law firm to work
here. We will continue to try to grow and find new and better ways
to elevate our female colleagues, but we will not stand idly by and
accept reckless accusations.

The Future is, by its nature, a democratic technology. We have chosen to build our device, and will soon roll it out, in a way that benefits the greatest number of people possible. The Future is an equalizer and champion of the oppressed. Historical inequalities and injustice, including the marginalization of women, will be challenged and eventually erased by the technology we are building for YOU.

TEXT MESSAGE EXCHANGE

LEILA KEENER-BOYCE
October 12, 2021 7:25 PM

ADHVAN CHAUDRY
Dark times, Lei.
Calling this woman's story into question.

Come on, think about it from my perspective.
All I have to go on is what Ben tells me.
Given that my marriage and my livelihood are
both staked to this company, maybe you could
cut me a little fucking slack here.

I just want you to be your best self.
The you that college-you would be proud of.

I did the best I could with the information I had.

You could've asked me.

Are you saying you knew about this?

Of course I knew.
WTF. Why didn't you talk to me sooner?

Wasn't my place.
But if you asked, I would never lie to you.

OK then. Was it really just a kiss?
Far as you know.

Yes.

Well, more of a sloppy make-out, but yes,
that's all I saw.

Wait you're telling me you actually saw this happen?
At the 4th of July party?

Yes. After you left.
Everybody was quite drunk.
Not that that's an excuse.
Why do you think me and Ben had that fight?

I can think of several good reasons actually.

Fair enough.

I asked him about it repeatedly, he told me it
was about money.

Can you imagine me hitting him over $?

I can't really imagine you hitting anyone at all.
I hope you don't think you were defending my
honor or some macho nonsense.

I was just mad at him.
Sorry I didn't tell you sooner
Didn't feel like the right thing to do.

Because he's your friend?

Something like that.

I'm your friend too, you know.

Yes but I wanted you to be more.
Which is why I couldn't tell you.

Ugh. You didn't think that maybe knowing the
truth about that would've spared me some of
the guilt about what happened between us?
I've been losing sleep over this.

I couldn't let it be part of your decision-making process.

Well, mission accomplished I guess. But now
I've got other decisions to make, like whether
or not I should leave.

Ben, or The Future?

Both. And to be honest, the main reason
I'm feeling conflicted is that my dad would
love to be right. About both. And that's perhaps
the only thing that could make this worse.
So. Should I stay or should I go now?

It's a real dilemma.

Can't you just tell me what I'm actually going to do?
I know you've seen more than you've told me.

I can tell you that you will be fine.

Come on. Please.

If I tell you, my telling you will be entangled with the
choice.
Better if you don't know.

If that's how you honestly feel about it, then why do
you want to put a machine into the world that pretty
much does exactly that?

I'm starting to wonder that myself.

CHAPTER 19

DOD INTERNAL MEMO

Internally Circulated 10/6/2021

Publicly Released 9/15/2022

Downloaded Through Prototype 11/3/2021

Department of Defense
1000 Pentagon Rd.
Washington, DC 20301-1000

Memorandum to
Secretaries of the Military Departments
Chairman of the Joint Chiefs of Staff
Undersecretary of Defense
Chiefs of the Military Services
General Counsel to the DoD

SUBJECT: SECURITY THREATS FROM EMERGING CIVILIAN TECHNOLOGY

The civilian technology firm The Future has developed a consumer product that (per their claims) enables the user to access the Internet in the future. Their stated intention is to launch the product for sale in the United States on 1/1/2022. This memorandum summarizes potential security threats posed by this technology.

    1) Foreign Military Powers

International governments which have access to this technology will be able to foresee future troop deployments and military tactics of the U.S. Armed Forces, which could be used by them for strategic advantage.

2) International Terrorists

Terror groups including (but not limited to) radical jihadis could use The Future technology to plan attacks for maximum damage, or could use foreknowledge as a recruiting tool (especially toward populations with lower educational and technological access).

3) Foreign Intelligence Services

Hostile uses of the technology include gathering information about our planned intelligence operations, future satellite data gathering, digital spy craft and deception, etc.

4) Weapons Technology Advances

The Future device/services could be used to transmit/intercept/relay underlying plans for upcoming missile, firearm, and cyber-weapons systems, into the present moment, creating technological leaps for our enemies.

Recommendation: The DoD moves to recognize this firm and its technology as a Threat to National Security (TNS), and advises immediate legal intervention to compel them to cease and desist until proper regulatory procedures can be put in place.

EMAIL — NOVEMBER 4, 2021

From: Ben Boyce
To: Leila Keener-Boyce

Hey babe, I know things are a bit weird right now, but something came up I'd like your help on. Kevin and I were using the Prototype to review some things coming down the pipeline, and we got our hands on this DoD memo.

It was written last month, but it will be publicly available (I think through a leak) late next year. Sharing with you bc it seems like we should try to get ahead of this. And given that we are experiencing certain Discrepancies now, not sure what will happen with this . . .

REPLY

Got it. Wonderful. I was just thinking, fighting off this Google lawsuit on behalf of my unfaithful husband isn't giving me enough to do, I could really use a legal battle with the Department of Defense. So yeah, let me get right on this.

And hey, I might be able to strategize on this effectively if you would share any additional info about what's coming down the pipeline. But I know that's not gonna happen. So I have to field this blindly.

REPLY

Hey babe, I hear you on all of those frustrations. That said, I'm not clear on what it means in terms of whether or not you're going to address this, or if I should engage someone else on staff to do it.

EMAIL—NOVEMBER 8, 2021

From: Leila Keener-Boyce
To: (undisclosed recipients)

To the Secretary of Defense and DoD Staff:
As Chief Legal Officer for The Future, I am writing to you pre-preemptively in regard to the DoD Memo "Security Threats from Emerging Civilian Technology."

Underlying all this, I believe, is a fundamental misunderstanding about the nature of our technology, and the way it will affect the world once it is deployed uniformly (meaning, with equal access to all, which obviates any strategic advantages or security threats).

I am reaching out in the hope that we can avoid costly and drawn-out legal action. We have not violated any laws, and our company does not fall under the jurisdiction of the Defense Federal Acquisition Regulation Supplement, and therefore is not subject to the scrutiny of your Department.

Sincerely,

Leila Keener-Boyce
Chief Legal Officer
The Future

REPLY

Ms. Keener-Boyce,

Thank you for your message. I am inclined to ask how you got your hands on this Memo, which is security-graded Confidential, but that is not the most pressing issue on my mind.

I think we may be able to broker an understanding. I would love to have a closed-door sit-down with you and the co-founders Boyce and Chaudry. Please relay my request to them, and if they are amenable, then my office will arrange travel to D.C. posthaste.

Sincerely,
Michael P. Stenhoff
Secretary of Defense

FWD

From: Leila Keener-Boyce
To: Ben Boyce, Adhvan Chaudry

Hey guys, looks like the DoD wants to meet with all of us. I suspect that means all three at once, and that attending this is mandatory. The DoD has pretty much no authority over consumer products, but there is some precedent for them to designate our company a threat to national security, which would effectively allow the FBI and DOJ in the front door.

I know it's a difficult time, but can we all set aside our differences enough to go and convince the military that our computers aren't going to blow up the world?

REPLY

From: Ben Boyce
To: Leila Keener-Boyce, Adhvan Chaudry

Yeah I can handle that.

REPLY

From: Adhvan Chaudry
To: Ben Boyce, Leila Keener-Boyce

L—
I write this reply with full expectation that it is being read by the Federal Government.
If I say no, I suspect that I will be summoned to the meeting with chloroform and a white van anyway.
So yes I'll be there.

—A

REPLY

From: Adhvan Chaudry
To: Ben Boyce

B—

Re: Lei's comment about "blow up the world" . . .

I'm guessing you have not shared with her the articles I pulled from the Prototype re: Russia, Ukraine, etc.

You know, the ones where our tech actually does set the stage for WWIII.

We should likely do so before walking into this mtg.

—A

REPLY

Hey man, I hear you, but I don't think we should tell Lei. What's gained by it? We gotta just take the 5th on all this, talk about the tech more generally, and her knowing only implicates her too.

We seem to be in a new situation here. The initial predictions are no longer all holding. That means we can't take all that as gospel. This DoD meeting—there's no reason we have to give them anything, it might be a chance for us to see what we can get.

EMAIL

From: Paolo Ventrini
To: Ben Boyce, Adhvan Chaudry

Boys, I hear from a little birdie that you have been summoned to a meeting at the Pentagon. I feel it is important that I attend to represent the investors' interests here, as it is likely that whatever consequences are brought up will affect the bottom line of the company. Please do not create another Google-type situation.

Paolo

REPLY

From: Adhvan Chaudry
To: Paolo Ventrini, Ben Boyce

P—
The Pentagon does not issue +1's,
so we could not invite you even if we wanted to.
Take it up with the Secretary of Defense.

—A

REPLY

From: Ben Boyce
To: Adhvan Chaudry

"The Pentagon does not issue +1's" lmfao thank you for brightening my day. Also what is Paolo pissed about, we're still growing and still making these dickweeds money hand over fist.

REPLY

B—
Appreciate the olive branch,
but laughing your ass off at my email is not a substitute

for trusting me with our technology.

I'll see you at the Pentagon.

—A

TWITTER POSTINGS — NOV 9, 2021

@HEYBENBOYCE

Just got out of closed-door meeting with Department of Defense officials about The Future. They want to exclusively acquire rights to The Future technology. #TheFutureIsYours

@HEYBENBOYCE

We will not be bought by the MILITARY-INDUSTRIAL COMPLEX! #TheFutureIsYours

@HEYBENBOYCE

They are threatening to label us a threat to national security. Why? Bc this technology is POWERFUL. #TheFutureIsYours

@HEYBENBOYCE

Your govt does not want you to have any control over your future. #TheFutureIsYours

@HEYBENBOYCE

Fight the Power! The Future is coming soon! #TheFutureIs Yours

TEXT MESSAGE EXCHANGE

ADHVAN CHAUDRY

November 9, 2021 7:25 PM

Do you really think Ben tweeting like Trump is the best way to handle this?

LEILA KEENER-BOYCE

Of course not. But he's certainly not listening to me.
And he no longer has a cute Communications girl
telling him what to do. So, cat's out of the bag.
Besides, didn't you see all of this coming?

I did not.
We are off the map now.
I no longer know any more about the future
than anyone else.

Is that why you were so quiet in the meeting?

One reason maybe.
Just listening. And thinking.
It's clear I can't count on Ben to do much of either.

Haha those were never his strong suit.
It was good to see you today, even if the
context was strange.

The context has always been strange, for me.
I'm glad that now we're at least on the same
strange page.
But yes.
It was good to see you too.

EMAIL — NOVEMBER 9, 2021

From: Orville Crane
To: Adhvan Chaudry

Mr. Chaudry,
Writing to introduce myself as a real fan of your work.

As you can imagine, the DoD was greatly annoyed by
your co-founder's response to that closed-door meeting. I
must acknowledge, the generals set the agenda there, and

we the scientists trusted them to proceed with some measure of respect for the incredible work you've done. Won't make that mistake again.

In light of the fallout from that meeting, we hope you'll view us at DARPA not as "the government" per se. We thought we might make a more direct appeal to you, for a more specific reason.

We know that you have pursued what you label the "2.0" version of your technology for some time now. We also know that you have abandoned it as theoretically impossible, due to the necessity of a supplemental technology—that is, teleportation, as you put it—and the necessity of inordinate amounts of energy.

Now, I cannot say anything here that is classified, but what is *declassified* is that one of the technologies that we at DARPA started working on as early as the mid-'60s was, to put it indelicately, *teleportation*. And that while teleportation may sound like sci-fi, we were exploring the very real possibilities for how mass could be translated into information, and sent instantaneously across great distances. That project made some progress but was abandoned in the wake of the MKUltra kerfuffle over at the CIA.

However, you are no doubt aware of the 2007 Barrett et al. paper "Deterministic Quantum Teleportation of Atomic Qubits." And you could probably make guesses about how that may have affected (perhaps even revived) DARPA interest in the teleportation project. Meanwhile, if you looked at the last decade's reports on defense spending and DARPA funding in particular, versus the recent published/implemented output, you'd likely think either (A) we are a huge black hole for taxpayer money, or (B) we have been cooking up something *really fucking cool* over here.

Well, jury's still out on the tax-dollar black-hole thing, but I would just like to say . . . why don't you come down to the DARPA lab before you head back to California. I'd like to show you something *really fucking cool.*

Orville Crane
Chief Special Projects Director
Defense Advanced Research Projects Agency

REPLY

O—
I'm interested.
To be clear, does this invitation extend to Ben too?

—A

REPLY

Mr. Chaudry—
This invitation is to you personally and you alone, and we would prefer that you not even discuss it with anyone else. Nondisclosure is of utmost priority with our organization.

If you have qualms about coming without your co-founder, I will absolutely respect that. But based on his behavior on social media in the wake of our meeting, we do not feel that he is reliable when it comes to national security. The choice is yours. And as you weigh it for yourself, I would simply encourage you to consider: if the opportunity were presented to him, and not to you, what would he do?

I hope we'll see you soon,

Orville Crane
Chief Special Projects Director
Defense Advanced Research Projects Agency

REPLY

O—
I'll be there.

—A

CHAPTER 20

THE BLACK HOLE: ANONYMOUS MUSINGS OF A
SCI-FI SUPERFAN

"Fuck Doctor Who"

I discovered *Doctor Who* in middle school,

during the unmatched reign of David Tennant.

I dreamed that one day he'd come and sweep me away in the TAR-DIS.

For the uninitiated, Doctor Who is a Time Lord—

an immortal alien who keeps taking on new bodies (hence the new actors).

In every iteration, he is joined on his adventures by new Companions,

who get to leave home and follow him through time and space.

As a kid with no friends, I was captivated by the prospect of being a Companion,

of meeting the brilliant and powerful Doctor,

of a friendship that transcended the bounds of my humdrum reality.

But as I grow older, I can see . . . Doctor Who is a narcissistic sociopath.

An immortal who drags mortals into his dangerous galactic escapades.

He demands that they leave their home, friends, and family,
risk everything, and commit wholeheartedly to following him.
But he makes no reciprocal commitment to anyone.
He risks nothing of himself.

The Companions are merely dupes,
fangirls and fanboys who give their everything for a fraction of the
attention of a greater being.
We are meant to watch with renewed delight,
as Doctor Who takes new forms, and finds new Companions.
All he's really doing is chewing through people,
using up their talents and their passions in the service of his own
goals,
his own self-aggrandizement.

Well, fuck that.
Perhaps growing up is reaching the moment when you no longer
yearn to be a Companion,
and are ready to see yourself as the Doctor.

EMAIL — NOVEMBER 12, 2021

From: Adhvan Chaudry
To: Leila Keener-Boyce

L—

If I ran away . . . would you come with me?

Suppose it was somewhere (maybe somewhen) that we'd never be found.

Suppose I had a way to start over.

Really, genuinely start over.

Would you?

—A

REPLY

Hey A, I don't know what you're talking about. There is no starting over. Not for us, not for anyone. I'm sorry, that is just reality.

Listen, I care about you. And I love the dreamer inside of you. But sometimes maybe it takes you out of your own life. Sometimes maybe the tug of what could be stops you from acknowledging and enjoying what actually IS. Here and now, right in front of you.

You have, literally, your dream job. You have friendship and respect and success. I'm not saying life is perfect or the world is all fine and dandy, but maybe it's time to start facing reality and making things better, instead of constantly looking for a way out?

Lei

EMAIL — NOVEMBER 13, 2021

From: Ben Boyce
To: Adhvan Chaudry

Hey, you gonna be back in the office today? We're going into production in a few weeks and there are still some kinks we need to work out in the operational interface. Evelyn is afraid that there might be a way to basically jail-break the device . . . I told her that was impossible but I didn't really know enough to explain why. Can you talk to her?

EMAIL

From: Ben Boyce
To: Adhvan Chaudry

Hey I heard you weren't even back from DC yet, and that you were taking another meeting. Is that true? If so, we need to discuss this right away.

EMAIL

From: Ben Boyce
To: Adhvan Chaudry

Dude you can't just ignore me like this. I let you get away with not coming in and not picking up your phone but you gotta at least reply to messages. Hit me back ASAP.

EMAIL

From: Ben Boyce
To: Adhvan Chaudry

Hey man, this is your last chance I'm seriously consider-ing drastic action here. You are a leader at this company

and this is a crucial moment. We are UNDER ATTACK
from all fucking sides! We are at risk of missing our
LAUNCH. We are facing a lawsuit that is big enough to
SWALLOW US ten times over.

REPLY

B—
Wanted to let you know . . .
I am stepping down from my position as CTO,
and forfeiting my salary for the rest of the year.
I am no longer part of The Future.

—A

REPLY

Ummm wtf are you talking about? This is your company
too, this is not a job you can just QUIT! Come in and
TALK TO ME!

REPLY ON THE SAME THREAD

Don't just ignore me. You really think you're gonna be
better off on your own?! You think you could've done
something like this without me? Do you even realize, the
job you got at Google out of grad school, that was ME
putting you forward for that! And THIS job obviously you
never would've had if I hadn't raised the money. And then
I stuck my neck out to keep you on the Board five months
ago. So literally your entire career, every dollar you made,

I have been involved with, and now you're walking away, seriously?! I dunno what's going on in your head but if you care about me, our friendship, our company at all, you gotta stick around and see this through.

EMAIL

From: Adhvan Chaudry
To: Prisha Chaudry

Mom—
Wanted to let you know, I've decided to leave my job, which means leaving the company I have built.
I am embarking on a new venture, and for the first time in ages, truly stepping into the unknown.
I am walking away from a sizable payout, but I see no alternative.
As a result, I may not be able to continue sending you money.
I'm sorry for any disappointment I may have caused. Now, or in the past.

—A

REPLY

Adhvan thank yI the mesage I am sure to leave your company is right by you or you would not. Ther369pprox.369 ntmentsapointment I am very proud you are smart and work hard maybe now you are time to find a nice girl. On Sunday I will make daal you can come over please in time for the Internet account is not correct. Life is funny you never know what happens but better to not be alone.

EMAIL — NOVEMBER 15, 2021

From: Adhvan Chaudry
To: (undisclosed recipients)

Colleagues—

In a short span, we have created something truly amazing here.

But when I reflect on what we've done, and where we're headed,

I am reminded of Robert Oppenheimer, father of the atomic bomb.

Upon witnessing the first detonation

which "burned with the fire of a million suns"

he spoke one sentence, quoting Krishna in the *Bhagavad Gita*:

"Now I am become Death, the destroyer of worlds."

It was, first and foremost, an expression of Oppenheimer's fear of the power of the weapon he had created.

I share that fear with respect to the technology of The Future.

I fear that we have become Death, destroyer of worlds.

But in our case, it may have an even more apt meaning.

The Hindu belief system has a non-linear understanding of time.

All events—past, present, and future—are inevitable and real, all at once.

The "destroyer of worlds" is not a bomb.

Or a god.

It is *time*.

What I've seen of where this technology is taking us has shaken me.

I do not intend to abdicate my responsibility in creating this, but I cannot continue to be part of building it.

I need to do something to stop it.

I need to take action to make the world better, in the here and now,

instead of staring helplessly into a future we cannot avoid.

I thank you all for your tireless work these past eight months.

I know you'll be in capable hands under the guidance of Evelyn, an exceptional engineer who is more than equal to the task of filling my shoes.

I wish you all the best of luck moving forward.

—A

TEXT MESSAGE EXCHANGE

BEN BOYCE

November 15, 2021 2:14 PM

You see Adhi's res letter?

LEILA KEENER-BOYCE

Yes. You didn't see this coming?

Out of the fucking blue
I mean obviously things haven't been easy
between us
But this is crazy
What can we do about this?

The first step will be finding a way to spin this.
News will get out soon, and we need to make a
public statement so it doesn't sound quite as bad.
Equally important will be an internal communication.
The troops are restless already and this won't help.

I'm not worried about internal perception.

> You should be. It's what sank Facebook, as
> much as anything. At least have your Comms
> girl draft an email.
> I assume it's another girl you've put in that
> position.

I don't have time to engage with that.

> Of course.

This Adhi deal is not just a problem
This is a total betrayal
He is deliberately fucking us
He knows I wouldn't want to put Evelyn in
his position but now I have to
Mf just punched a hole in our deck and sailed
off in a lifeboat
We need to figure out how to bury him

> Bury him?
> You do realize he is sick, right?
> He is not in his right mind.

I honestly dgaf anymore.
Breach of contract? Negligence?

> You are still fending off a lawsuit from Google.
> Do you really want to sue your co-founder now?

Yes.

> Well, I'm not going to be part of that.
> If you sue Adhi, I'm out.

EMAIL—NOVEMBER 16, 2021

From: Ben Boyce
To: (undisclosed recipients)

Hey Team,

I know many of us (myself included) were totally disarmed by Adhi's decision to leave the company. The news was deeply troubling to me, because Adhi was not only my partner but my friend.

At this point, I have to talk about something I never wanted to talk about publicly. But I have a responsibility to you all, and to the truth. Adhi suffers from significant mental-health issues, particularly bipolar with manic episodes. He has for many years. He had a manic episode two years ago which nearly got him put in jail and kicked out of Stanford—and would have, if I hadn't intervened on his behalf.

Adhi's decision, and the paranoid delusions that led up to it, are the product of a mind that is not well. Let us remember that before we question the work that we are engaged in doing here. We will be wishing Adhi a speedy recovery as we move forward.

For those who have expressed doubts about the future of the technology in his absence, have no fear. Our new Chief Technology Officer Evelyn Andrada has been working in the quantum-computing field for over a decade, and has already proven herself as an invaluable team member, who now takes on the mantle of leading us into an exciting new chapter.

The Future is a company with a vision for the world—one that could revolutionize human thought and communication, one that could pave the way to solving global warming and ending international conflict! Any who cannot embrace that vision are welcome to leave, as Adhvan

left. We wish no ill will, we merely march onward into a
brave new world that we know we will shape forever.

Thank you,
Ben Boyce

EMAIL

From: Ben Boyce
To: Kevin Martindale

Kevin, we've got a big problem with this Adhi situation.
Need to figure out where he is, what he's doing, and why
he actually left. Prob gathering material for a lawsuit but
also just basic intel. Is this a situation where Watermark
could be helpful? What's our ballpark price on something
like this?

REPLY

Hey Boss Man. Absolutely 100% the right call. Watermark has investigative services we can engage on this. I
budgeted it out assuming a 30-day period, ballpark we're
looking at 80K, obviously will extend if we need to go
longer. Don't worry, I'm all over this.

EMAIL

From: Thomas Keener
To: Leila Keener-Boyce

Leila,
It is a sad day when I have to talk to my own daughter in
this format, which I hate, so I will try to be brief.
    Your position with The Future is untenable. With the
now-well-publicized departure of one of your founders,
the company is melting down from the inside. Your board

now has cause for emergency removal of Ben. Our lawsuit is about to become a fish-in-a-barrel situation. We're just hoping to get in and get value before the SEC eviscerates your company.

As your father, I am reaching out to say, please, for the sake of our family, cut your losses. You and Ben can still exit this situation with a modicum of dignity, and a more-than-healthy sum of money. It is your duty, not only as his legal counsel but as his wife, to talk him down from his pride, and talk some sense into him.

Sincerely,
Dad/Thom

REPLY

Hi Dad,
You taught me to never give up, which I imagine you are regretting right about now.

Ben is not perfect, by any means. But when it comes to his ambition and pride and commitment to his business, I cannot pretend to be the least bit surprised by any of it.

You, on the other hand, have spent your life professing that your work is in service of your family. But in this situation, you have actively sought out a conflict between the two—and as it escalates, your choice is clear. You are choosing work, and leveraging our relationship to help you win.

I think it is only fair to let you know . . . I have seen the future. As a result, I know I'm not going to lose this one. I honestly could tell you the point-by-point, blow-by-blow of the settlement we're eventually going to get to . . . but that would take the fun out of getting there.

Love,
Leila

CHAPTER 21

EMAIL—NOVEMBER 16, 2021

From: Evelyn Andrada
To: Ben Boyce

Mr. Boyce,

Not sure if you've been reviewing the technical reports I've been submitting but felt I should call your attention to a few particularly salient problems.

After Adhvan identified the first Discrepancy two months ago, we created a system of Discrepancy Testing using a sample of 2,200 data points, all gathered from the earliest days of using the technology.

The general trend is simple: the number of Discrepancies is rising. Perhaps even more alarming, there are some data points that did not come back as Discrepancies one month ago, but come back as Discrepancies now. Which means that either our technology is failing at increasing rates, or the future is "changing."

We are hoping that you will schedule a time to meet with our team to discuss the implications of these findings, as well as potential strategies for mitigating them.

Evelyn Andrada
Chief Technology Officer
The Future

REPLY

Evelyn, I gave you Adhi's job in the hope that you would do what Adhi did: take care of the technology so I don't have to worry about it. I'm sure there's bound to be some hiccups, any tech company is going to have that. Just get it as good as you can get it so that we can go into production, which we need to do. I'm traveling tomorrow and will be gone for a week and a half securing retail spaces.

I know you looked up to Adhi as a mentor, but I just want you to know . . . he was not really all that special. He was a smart guy who stumbled onto a big idea. Making it work can be achieved by any other smart guy (or girl like yourself). I believe in you!

REPLY

Mr. Boyce,
While I appreciate your vote of confidence in my intelligence and abilities, I need to add a couple things.

First, Adhvan actually IS special. I understand that he made the decision to leave and is not coming back, but he may be seen, one day, as a once-in-a-generation genius, on the order of Nikola Tesla. I say this merely to make you aware of the scope of the undertaking our team is now left with, trying to carry this work to the finish line.

Second, I had hoped to explain this in person, but I feel it is important to make you aware of the nature of some of the Discrepancies that are arising, which is alarming in itself.

For example: The Prototype initially predicted that the Warriors would win the NBA Finals in 2022. This prediction was affirmed one month ago. However, currently when you search for "NBA Finals Winner 2022," you get articles announcing that the NBA season was postponed and delayed due to security threats. Further searches on the matter trace the problem to a singular event (see attached article) which was definitely NOT part of the future two months ago.

Please review the attached, and let me know when we can meet to discuss, since I think our policy of nondisclosure is starting to become ethically untenable.

ATTACHED NEWS ARTICLE—DATED SEPTEMBER 16, 2022

DEADLY EXPLOSION AT MADISON SQUARE GARDEN

Halfway through the Knicks–Cavaliers game last night, a pipe bomb detonated near the press box of Madison Square Garden. First responders report that two individuals were killed, and several more wounded. Authorities have not yet released the identities of the victims.

In the ensuing chaos, fans fled the arena in terror. Fire crews and paramedics were on the scene within minutes of the explosion, and the work of sifting through the rubble continues.

FBI sources report that they have not apprehended any suspects, or identified any persons of interest. They are currently reviewing surveillance footage in an attempt to trace the origin of the package. It is believed that the bomb was placed inside the arena prior to the game, and detonated remotely.

While no specific suspects have yet emerged, the anti-tech activist group COTA (Citizens Opposing the Technological Apocalypse) is already claiming responsibility. Amy Herzog, head of the FBI's Cyberterror Task Force, was not surprised. "COTA have denounced violence in the past, and said they only want to achieve their goals through strategic hacking. But this latest attack is a clear escalation of their tactics."

Herzog said that recent chatter in fringe online forums like 4Chan indicates significant dissent within COTA, and it is possible that divisions may have split the informal organization into multiple factions. "But let me be clear," Herzog added. "This attack is terrorism, plain and simple, and COTA will be investigated and prosecuted accordingly."

The motivation behind the attack appears to be Madison Square Garden's decision to implement The Future technology inside the stadium. A feature called "Instant Preplay" was recently installed in the arena, which uses the Jumbotron screen overhead to show highlights from upcoming plays, often in dramatic slow-mo. League officials have hoped the approach could revitalize the sports-viewing experience.

The system was adopted in response to declining attendance and viewership throughout the year, ever since the technology came into widespread usage. Now that game outcomes are available in advance, fans have been leaving in droves. The league has tried a variety of measures, including a data blackout, but with no luck so far.

Many fans have seen "Instant Preplay" as yet another industry caving to pressure to accommodate the new technology, and selling out the sports-viewing experience in the process.

Last week's attacks on Wall Street and other financial-sector targets were similarly motivated, and it appears that COTA is broadening the scope of their campaign of disruption. Yet the group's members remain anonymous, and no individuals connected to any of the attacks have been identified.

As of press time, the league has announced that it will cancel upcoming games at all venues around the country, until an adequate review of security procedures has been made.

Meanwhile, The Future is facing harsh criticism, since the event itself was not apparently predicted by its technology. CEO Ben Boyce issued a statement, saying, "We at The Future are tremendously saddened by this atrocity, and our thoughts and prayers are with the victims and their families. We will conduct a comprehensive review, and continue to work to deliver a reliable product and service."

The company remains in the spotlight, as mounting regulatory pressure could come to a head in the coming weeks. Many are calling for Boyce to step down from his role as CEO, but so far he has not publicly commented on his plans.

REPLY

Keep this to yourself for now. I'm sure there is a solution to be figured out. I will be back in office ASAP (cutting off the last three cities of my trip) and we will discuss in person.

EMAIL — NOVEMBER 24, 2021

From: Kevin Martindale
To: Ben Boyce

Hey Boss Man, check out the attached report from PI detail on Chaudry . . .

Attachment:

WATERMARK INVESTIGATIVE SERVICES

Targeted-Individual Surveillance Report #1073

Disclaimer: All information gathered herein was acquired by licensed Private Investigators in accordance with state and city laws regarding the conduct thereof (*California Private Investigator Act* and *District of Columbia Municipal Regulations Chap. 17*).

Subject: Adhvan Chaudry

Daily routine 11/17–11/21:
Staying in deluxe suite at Hilton Hotel in Arlington, wakes up approx 6 AM
Continental breakfast in hotel lobby
Travels via Lyft from hotel to DARPA Headquarters outside Arlington

Passes through security checkpoint approx 730 AM

Outside monitorable range during time in DARPA HQ

Does not appear to leave building during work time

Cell phone records suggest Subject does not use cell phone inside DARPA HQ (research suggests this is not an absolute policy, only certain Top-Secret areas in building restrict cell phone use)

Takes Lyft home from DARPA HQ between 6 and 9 PM

Dinner meals via room service or DoorDash; no meal publicly shared with any other individual during observation period

Hotel time spent inside room or reading in hotel lobby. Reading included paperback copies of *Tao Te Ching* and *Bhagavad Gita*. Lights out in hotel room approx 11 PM.

11/22: Subject followed normal schedule thru continental breakfast, Lyft ride to DARPA HQ. Proceeded through security checkpoint 745 AM.

Subject was not observed departing from DARPA HQ (surveillance team remained onsite until building was completely closed except for night maintenance crew, approx 1130 PM).

Subject was not observed in hotel. Room lights were not illuminated.

Hotel staff confirmed subject had not checked out; however, cleaning staff verified that Subject did not appear to have returned.

24-hr continued stakeout of DARPA HQ and hotel did not account for Subject.

Subject whereabouts currently unknown.

REPLY

Hey Kevin, wtf am I supposed to do with this? For starters, how about what is he actually *doing* at DARPA? Is he applying for a new job, or is he SELLING THEM OUR TECH????

And—whereabouts unknown? Maybe it should just say we got our dicks in our hands? I thought these guys were some elite spy motherfuckers, but obviously they got MADE by a computer programmer who normally doesn't notice toilet paper stuck to his fucking shoes.

REPLY

Listen Boss Man, I know you're not happy, but I can assure you, these guys are total pros. Look what's going on here. DARPA is not fucking around, this is military-level shit. If Chaudry is truly providing state-secret tech info, they could have put a full NSA counterintel detail in place. Yes they may have made our guys, they might have Chaudry at a black site now, some safehouse, hell he could even still be holed up inside the DARPA Lab if they really wanna make sure nobody sees him. I will start working former contacts to get any info I can.

REPLY

Adhi just posted on Instagram, from the Stanford Dish. He is BACK in Palo Alto. Which means either he's in two places at once, or he slipped right past your PI clowns and made it all the way home across the country, and then posted a pic of himself HIKING just as a way to TAUNT US bc he KNOWS I had him followed, and he is rubbing it in my fucking FACE.

CHAPTER 22

SUBPOENA — NOVEMBER 24, 2021

By Authority of the House of Representatives
of the Congress of the United States of America

To: The Honorable Mr. Benjamin Boyce and Mr. Adhvan Chaudry

You are hereby commanded to be and appear before: The Select Committee on Existential Technological Threats to our Democracy

Of the House of Representatives of the United States, on December 1, 2021, at 9:00 AM EST, in the Chamber of the House

To TESTIFY on matters of inquiry committed to said committee; and you are not to depart without leave of said committee.

Furthermore you are required to PRODUCE AND SUBMIT all records in unredacted form related to the research, development, and production of relevant technologies.

Such materials are to be submitted to this legislative body no later than November 29, 2021.

Any refusal to adhere to stipulations of this Subpoena shall be treated as grounds for a charge of Contempt of Congress, and appropriate legal action shall be taken.

Sincerely,

Senator Greg Walden

EMAIL

From: Ben Boyce
To: Leila Keener-Boyce

Hey Princess, I just got the subpoena. I know you warned me but it still felt like a gut punch. Seems like the timing is specifically designed to fuck us here. We go into production (with an initial order of 500,000 units) on 12/1, so we can roll out and open stores on 1/1. Which means we are fully on the hook here for almost $100M.

Also, have you heard from Adhi? We can't find him, and he's gonna have to poke his head out of his hole to go to this hearing.

REPLY

Princess again, huh? Nice, slid that right in.

Yes the timing is obviously strategic. It's not a good sign. They want you over a barrel here, not to accommodate you. They're hoping that you will push back your production date.

As CLO, I need to advise you of the risk here. They absolutely could legislate restrictions on your tech before they shut down at the end of the year, which would mean your stores (and your product) are illegal the day they open.

And no, I have not heard anything from Adhi, which, it's clear, is very much what he prefers.

REPLY

Hey Princess (yep, doubling down on that) I hear you but I don't know if backing down is our best path. Does that just weaken our position?

We've been seeing more and more deviation from the future that we initially predicted . . . which, ya know, should be theoretically IMPOSSIBLE. And we still don't even know WHY.

I'm not sure who I can trust around here anymore. So I'm asking you not as my CLO but as my WIFE, the person whose judgment I respect and admire more than anyone in the world . . . what should I do here?

REPLY

Flattery isn't gonna save the day. But it does get you a few points.

So I'll be straight with you here. If this were some app or phone or, hell, ordinary consumer technology, I would say absolutely, pull the plug on the production schedule, reassess, and move forward with humility and contrition.

But it's clear, this technology is either a total game-changer for the world, or it's nothing at all. And it's obvious from reading just a little bit online, people do want this technology. A bill absolutely will come up, seeking to make your device illegal. But lawmakers have to know that if they legislate against us they are gonna alienate their constituents left and right (literally).

So I would recommend moving forward with production . . . but that means you are going to bet everything on how your appearance goes before the committee. And honestly, the wild card in that equation, as we both know, is Adhi.

REPLY

I love you so much. I'm all in. Thank you, thank you, thank you.

EMAIL—NOVEMBER 28, 2021

From: Ben Boyce
To: Adhvan Chaudry

Hey man, hope you're having a good Thanksgiving break. I don't really know where you are, out hiking or still back in DC, who even knows . . . But I imagine you got the subpoena one way or another.

Thought this might be the right time to reach out and re-open communication. I mean, I know it hasn't been that long, and I had figured I'd give shit more time to settle before I hit you up, but ya know . . . this damn subpoena came along and moved up the timeline.

On a practical level, we're gonna be sitting down together this week in front of motherfuckin Congress, telling our story. It's gonna be real awkward if we're not even on speaking terms anymore.

On a personal level, I can cop to the fact that I've been not exactly the easiest dude to work with. I know we've both done things and said things we're not proud of. I'm down to come to this in the spirit of forgiveness, and also to take responsibility for my part in all of it.

Let me know bro.

Ben

REPLY

B—

Yes, it is clear to me that we cannot remain silent forever.

I concede that I may have been a bit out of sorts when I quit.

Let us meet in the spirit of reconciliation.

How about if we get together at the Dish tomorrow night, say 11?

Beers?

Stars should be visible.

—A

REPLY

Hey man, huge relief to hear from you, and sounding like yourself once again. Yeah by all means, I would love nothing more than beers at the Dish. I'll brush up on my constellations, haha. See ya there.

EXCERPT FROM CONGRESSIONAL HEARING — DECEMBER 1, 2021

SEN. DAVID HOLMES (D-NY): So let us be clear on the sequence of events. Mr. Chaudry quit the company, very suddenly, following your first trip out to D.C. Without giving much of a reason. For a week, you didn't hear from him. Then he popped up again, because you were going to testify before this committee . . . and you met with him the following evening, around Stanford.

BOYCE: Yeah, that's right. At the Dish. It's this big satellite dish near the campus, there's a little hiking trail there. We used to meet up there sometimes and just hang and shoot the shit. It was freezing that night, but I figured he picked it for emotional reasons. It had meaning for us.

SEN. DAVID HOLMES (D-NY): I see. And what time did you meet there?

BOYCE: Eleven o'clock. It was late, but Adhi is a night owl, and he likes being able to see the stars.

SEN. DAVID HOLMES (D-NY): How would you characterize the nature of the meeting between you?

BOYCE: Well, at first . . . it was hard. I got there, and for a minute, neither of us knew what to say. We talked about videogames at first. Honestly, I was trying to figure out if this was even worthwhile, or if I should just bounce.

And then, Adhi apologized. Which was maybe a first ever, between us. He said he regretted leaving me out in the cold. Said he was sorry he hadn't been a better friend. And it was like, I hadn't realized until that moment how much I had my guard up. How *tight* I was wound up. And how hard I was working to be smart and ahead of the curve and not the one that was wrong.

But once he said he was sorry, it was almost like this dam broke, and it was OK for me to say I was sorry too. We talked about everything that had been so tough for so many months, and how we never had any clue what we were really signing up for. We laughed about it—about how two cocky little assholes like us could become billionaires. And we got kinda philosophical about it all. He said this thing about how the universe is funny because you know it's all chaos and physics, but when you look back it always feels like there's some plan that's been leading you up to the moment you're at. It felt like we were on the same page. At the end, we hugged it out.

SEN. DAVID HOLMES (D-NY): Did he give you a reason for his abrupt departure from the company?

BOYCE: He said he got invited to some secret government thing, but he couldn't say more. Which was vague, but I could tell he didn't wanna go further. I mean, I did ask him if he shared any of our tech with them, but he kind of dodged the question, and I could tell it wasn't time to get into that. I said it could all be water under the bridge, if he'd just come back. I assumed he was gonna be in the office the next day. But he never showed.

EMAIL — NOVEMBER 30, 2021

From: Ben Boyce
To: Adhvan Chaudry

Hey dude thanks for meeting up last night. That was great. Seriously, I hate to admit it, but I fucking missed you.

Anyway, I was just checking in to see when you thought you'd be back in the office. I don't wanna rush you but also you'll be like goddamn Superman here whenever you're feeling up for it. And if we have a chance to spend a day getting on the same page before we fly to DC that would be great.

EMAIL — NOVEMBER 30, 2021

From: Ben Boyce
To: Adhvan Chaudry

Hey bud I haven't heard, so I wanted to make sure you're at least OK and got home no prob. I'm sure you can understand in context how I'd be a little worried. If you're not up for office time, it's all good, I'd just like to talk some more before DC.

EMAIL — NOVEMBER 30, 2021

From: Ben Boyce
To: Adhvan Chaudry

OK man I need to head to the airport soon, it's DC time. So a lot of people are worried about you now. The police have been notified and might be coming by to do what's called a wellness check. If you're home, just be cool, this is all pretty normal stuff.

EMAIL—DECEMBER 1, 2021

From: Ben Boyce
To: Adhvan Chaudry

A? Where are you man? You OK? Am I gonna see you there today?

EXCERPT FROM CONGRESSIONAL HEARING—DECEMBER 1, 2021

SEN. DAVID HOLMES (D-NY): So, returning to the night you met with him—is there anyone besides you that knew of, or could confirm, your meeting with him at 11 PM that evening?

BOYCE: Ummmm . . . My wife, our CLO, Leila. She was aware of it.

SEN. DAVID HOLMES (D-NY): And she saw you depart for the meeting, and return later?

BOYCE: Well . . . no. She, uh . . . I've been staying at an apartment that I rented, closer to the office. We've had some personal stuff we're going through, and so we're not in the same place. But I told her I was doing it.

SEN. DAVID HOLMES (D-NY): Mr. Boyce, at the exact time you have said you met with Mr. Chaudry, 11 PM—Mr. Chaudry was in another location. He was at the offices of The Future. Apparently he was the only one there. He signed in, used multiple computer terminals, and gained access to, as you call it, the Prototype.

BOYCE: That's . . . not possible. I was with him.

SEN. DAVID HOLMES (D-NY): It appears not. While the committee was in session, I personally received video evidence and security log records, which show, very clearly, that on the night in question, Mr. Chaudry was at the offices of The Future from 11:03 PM to 12:46 AM.

BOYCE: I mean . . . no way. I'll have to review that. There must be a mistake here. Who'd you get that from?

SEN. DAVID HOLMES (D-NY): An anonymous source. Undoubtedly, someone at your company. Tell me, Mr. Boyce, would you have access to see this security information—to detect if Mr. Chaudry had been entering the premises and accessing computer terminals?

BOYCE: I have access, yes. But I was not aware of any of that. Meaning, I wasn't viewing any security footage or access data that night. Like I said, I was with Adhi. At the Dish.

SEN. DAVID HOLMES (D-NY): Sources have informed me that during the time we have been present in this hearing, the Palo Alto Police Department were dispatched to uphold our subpoena when Mr. Chaudry failed to appear before Congress. I have just received a report that a team of officers entered his home in Palo Alto, where they did not locate his person. But they did find signs of a struggle, including blood.

BOYCE: I genuinely . . . May I ask the reason for this line of questioning?

SEN. GREG WALDEN (D-OR): Yes, Senator Holmes, we seem to be deviating from the scope of this inquiry.

SEN. DAVID HOLMES (D-NY): Mr. Boyce, did you say in a text message, after learning of Mr. Chaudry's decision to leave the company, that you wanted to "bury" him?

BOYCE: I meant legally. I was angry at that time, and I was talking about suing him. With good reason, really, he was abandoning our company, out of nowhere!

SEN. DAVID HOLMES (D-NY): In the event of Mr. Chaudry's death, what happens to his shares?

BOYCE: I don't get them, if that's what you're suggesting. They would be sold, and probably his mother would get rich. But it seems premature to suggest that he's, uh . . .

SEN. GREG WALDEN (D-OR): Senator Holmes, this is not a criminal investigation. And any subsequent criminal investigation could be compromised by attempting to interrogate Mr. Boyce in this public setting.

SEN. DAVID HOLMES (D-NY): Pardon me, Mr. Chairman, I'll try to keep my questions relevant to the technology and the company, but the issues in play are overlapping.

Mr. Boyce, we've established that your co-founder was approached by a government agency about acquiring use of the technology. Did you perceive such acquisition as a threat to your company, and by extension your personal wealth?

BOYCE: Like I said, I don't even know what had been worked out there, so . . .

SEN. DAVID HOLMES (D-NY): You contracted a PI service of questionable legality to follow and spy on your co-founder, yet you ask us to believe that when he simply avoided a question that could completely undermine the value of your company, you took his evasion in stride and did not press him any further?

BOYCE: I mean . . . I trusted him. He's my friend.

SEN. DAVID HOLMES (D-NY): Death threats and spies, is that what friendship looks like to you? Perhaps in Silicon Valley, but for me and my constituents, those values are hardly—

SEN. GREG WALDEN (D-OR): Senator Holmes, I will not tolerate grandstanding at this hearing. If you do not have any further *questions* to ask—

BOYCE: This is insane. And what you're insinuating here . . .

SEN. DAVID HOLMES (D-NY): I am not insinuating anything. I am merely pointing out the fact that your co-founder was jeopardizing the prospects of your company, which means that you would clearly stand to profit from his death. And your past conduct as CEO does not exactly inspire confidence in your innocence.

SEN. GREG WALDEN (D-OR): All right, Senator Holmes, your time is concluded, you will now yield the floor, or face Contempt charges yourself.

BOYCE: Sir, if I could just say one more—

SEN. GREG WALDEN (D-OR): You have said quite enough, Mr. Boyce, and in fact I would advise you to *stop* talking, for your own sake if nothing else. It appears that the police will now be taking a closer look into matters related to the fate of your co-founder, and you should retain counsel before speaking any further on the matter.

At this point, our hearing is concluded. I believe that the nature of your character, and the danger posed by your technology, have both been made clear to the members of this committee. We thank you for your time, and will take these matters into consideration as we make decisions about how this technology is to be regulated.

CHAPTER 23

ARTICLE — THEECONOMIST.COM — DECEMBER 12, 2021

THE END OF THE FUTURE?

In September, tech startup The Future was celebrating life as the youngest-ever unicorn—that is, the company that grew fastest to a valuation exceeding a billion dollars. They did it in eight months, eclipsing the previous 11-month record held by electric-scooter company Bird.

Today, speculation is rampant about whether The Future will even survive to the rollout of their first product and the opening of their first store.

Last week witnessed a dramatic, live-streamed congressional hearing, where co-founders Ben Boyce and Adhvan Chaudry were summoned before the House of Representatives to speak to the presumed safety of their technology. No doubt, the plan was to clear their name, reassure the public, and ensure the seated congresspeople that they too would get a cut of the coming windfall.

Instead, one disaster mounted on another. CEO Boyce was the only one of the two to show up, and he struggled to explain his own company's technology—and the mind-bending implications of how it might change the world. His combative tone alienated his inquisitors, who regarded him increasingly as a hostile witness.

By the end of the hearing, in a truly bizarre twist, Sen. David Holmes (D-NY) had insinuated that Boyce may have murdered his co-founder, who is now officially regarded as a missing person. Boyce is currently under criminal suspicion, in addition to the legal cloud he faces from an SEC investigation and a massive lawsuit from Google.

Sources report that the prestigious VCs who floated the company to its stratospheric valuation have started to sell off like rats fleeing a ship. The company's very first investor, Paolo Ventrini, is alleged to have liquidated his stake, as have two other board members.

Meanwhile, less well-established investors have swooped in, sensing a fire sale and a chance to gain control of the company's technology—assuming it is not soon revealed to be all smoke and mirrors. If Boyce is going to keep his company afloat, he'll have to not only clear his name but pull a rabbit out of his hat with a successful product launch.

TEXT MESSAGE EXCHANGE

BEN BOYCE
December 14, 2021 9:16 PM

Hey Princess will you please just talk to me.
Why are you not even answering my calls?
Seriously even if you quit, you are still my wife.
December 16, 2021 3:07 PM

I came by the house today, wtf?
You gotta tell me where you are.
Please.
December 16, 2021 5:15 PM

LEILA KEENER-BOYCE

Listen, I don't feel safe talking in person.
If you want to discuss anything we can talk
like this.

You don't feel safe?

Please tell me you don't believe all this Adhi

shit.

Why would I hurt him?

> Honestly, most of our conversations the last
> three months are about reasons you would
> want to hurt Adhi.

Babe that is so wrong.

He is my friend.

I got mad at him, but you would be too!

> And then he just happened to disappear?

YES!

December 16, 2021 7:11 PM

Hello?

Princess are you there?

> I'm not talking to you until I talk to Adhi.

EMAIL — DECEMBER 16, 2021

From: Ben Boyce
To: Kevin Martindale

Hey Kevin, this whole Adhi situation needs to be our number-one priority. I need you to find him ASAP and figure out WTF is going on.

REPLY

Copy that, Boss Man, I'm on it.

EMAIL — DECEMBER 17, 2021

From: Evelyn Andrada
To: Ben Boyce

We have entered a strange new period with the technology. The rate of Discrepancy continued to rise up through yesterday, when it became difficult to evaluate further. Starting around 5 PM, we are experiencing at least a partial blackout; that is, a total inability to get a return signal when we attempt to query through the Prototype.

Initially thought we might be facing a new manner of error with our tech, until we reviewed some of the last downloads that came in, which included this news article (published one year from today):

Quoted Text:

((GLOBAL ATTACKS TARGET INTERNET INFRASTRUCTURE

December 17, 2022

Panic consumed the globe today, as reports rolled out about a series of 16 different attacks, which struck major infrastructure targets in nine different countries.

According to Gwen Pallieri, the FBI task force leader spearheading the U.S. investigation, "These reprehensible attacks were coordinated, deliberate, and conducted with military precision. We are treating this as a clear and present danger to American freedom and safety."

Pallieri's briefing alleged that the teams of terrorists responsible for the attacks wielded high-caliber weapons and detonated large-grade explosives. Attackers took hostages, and in some cases, employed violence against security forces at the facilities. In total, four security personnel were killed and many others wounded, while the attackers caused significant damage to the physical infrastructure that enables global Internet service.

Many of the attacks wiped out website-hosting server farms—warehouses and offices that house thousands of racks of servers. At the Lakeside Technology Center in Chicago, gunmen killed two security personnel before affixing plastic explosives to server towers. The resulting explosions instantly disrupted the commodities market, which has been frozen in response.

The SuperNAP, a highly secure government data center outside Las Vegas, Nev., is the reported site of one of the most brazen and daring attacks. A caravan of white vans rammed through the security station, where a security guard was fatally injured, as 10 to 15 masked attackers made a beeline for the main server facility. Once inside, they detonated a series of homemade explosive devices, which shut down operations at the site indefinitely.

An additional attack, with no casualties reported, was launched against undersea cables on the eastern seaboard, which has disrupted intercontinental telecommunications indefinitely.

As a result of the attacks, vast swaths of the Internet are down and inaccessible, and many sites are only partially operational. It is tentatively estimated that 750 million citizens' Internet access has been disrupted, and many may not be back online for weeks or months.

The fringe group known only as COTA (Citizens Opposing the Technological Apocalypse) issued a public statement taking responsibility for the attacks and warning of more to come. The group has stated that violence is not its aim, but contended that it will employ whatever means are necessary to achieve its goal of altering public policy regarding technology.

Editorial Note: Our publication, joining with most mainstream media, has elected NOT to reprint any of the group's own language, which would only magnify their public voice.

The White House has immediately dispatched military personnel to ramp up security at all desirable technology-related targets. The president is expected to give a televised address later this afternoon, though its ability to reach American citizens is significantly compromised.))

So, it appears that the functionality of our technology has become limited at the moment, due to the fact that the Internet, in the future, is being disrupted on a global scale.

I am wondering if it is now time to start to shift our policy on sharing this information. If we proceed, the product will be on sale in 14 days, and everyone will be able to view it anyway.

Evelyn

REPLY

OK yeah this is an escalation from what we've seen before, but I don't think it helps anything to change our plans. You need to delete this email (and that article) and forget about it. People will have access to the information when they buy the product, not till then, or this could massively scare off potential customers.

In fact, I think it would be best to stop cataloguing Discrepancies. It might be time we make a pivot in the way we frame these issues—and start seeing them as a feature, rather than a bug. The Discrepancies could represent opportunities for change! So this story you're sending me is not necessarily an ironclad pronouncement, but instead, a danger that can be avoided . . . as long as we have a well-supported product.

We are now in production. People will be buying TF1 machines in two weeks. All I need you to focus on is shoring up bugs in anticipation of any software updates we might need.

TEXT MESSAGE EXCHANGE

BEN BOYCE
December 24, 2021 9:55 AM

Are you fucking kidding me.
I just got served divorce papers.
On Christmas Eve.

LEILA KEENER-BOYCE

I am sorry for the timing, that was not
deliberate. And for what it's worth, it's not
official yet. I just knew that was the only way
I would get you to take it seriously.

OK you got my attention.

Evelyn forwarded me the article about terrorist
attacks. This is getting out of hand.

Well, that's another reason to fire her . . .
But not sure what else to say.

Ben, everyone else can see that this
technology is running the world off a cliff.
You need to stop this.

What am I supposed to do?
Pull the plug?
I can't. We are bleeding money.
All these investors will sue us.

It is very possible that you will be sued, but I will
help you through it. You will file for bankruptcy, which
really means that WE will file for bankruptcy.
But that is not the end of the world. We will get
back on our feet. We might have to accept
help from my family, you might even have to
work a real job again. But we will get through it.

Lei, someone else is gonna get the technology.
Google is just gonna end up with it.
Or the fucking military.
And they'll abuse it way worse.

> You are in a position to publicly renounce
> your own technology. You can even share the
> information you've gotten. That will tip the
> legislation and it will be banned
> overnight, guaranteed.

I worked so hard.
It's not fair.

> No, it's not. And I'm proud of the work
> you've done. But it's over.
> You can have your company, or you
> can have me. But not both.
> Your choice.

EMAIL (DRAFT) — DECEMBER 25, 2021

From: Ben Boyce
To: (undisclosed recipients)

Hi Everyone,

First off, Merry Christmas! Or rather, as merry a Christmas as you might be able to have this year, in light of everything going on.

I write this note with a heavy heart. I had considered waiting until next week to send this, but I felt nothing was gained by delaying the truth. I owe you all that much at least.

The time has come to put an end to this company, and the technology we have created. Simply put—I have seen too much to go on any further. It has become clear to me that we will not improve the world, as I once dreamed. We will only make it worse. Much, much worse.

That said, I am so grateful to you all for the incredible sacrifice that you have undertaken. I know that many of you skipped out on larger salaries at bigger firms in favor of stock options here, whose value will now be minimal. I will do whatever I can to help facilitate all of you transitioning to the exciting next phase of your career.

Working with this amazing team, I have witnessed incredible innovation and tenacity. But ultimately, it is the *character* I've seen here, which most affects my decision to

The writing of the above draft was interrupted by receipt of the following incoming email:

EMAIL

From: Kevin Martindale
To: Ben Boyce

Hey Boss, the admin team overrode Chaudry's security and we got access to his accounts, so I've been going through looking for anything that might help us. I found some emails related to a Tumblr account which apparently he has, not sure if you're aware but he's been writing a blog, something about science fiction. He's been putting it up anonymously for like 7 years.

Didn't initially think it was a big deal, but I put an alert on it just to monitor activity, see if any comments might help us. And then, guess who published a NEW entry literally LAST NIGHT? Here's the link . . .

TUMBLR BLOG POST — DECEMBER 24, 2021

THE BLACK HOLE: MUSINGS OF AN ANONYMOUS
SCI-FI SUPERFAN

"Justice for Jacob Marley"

Since I have advocated in this forum for expanding the sci-fi canon
　　to include religious texts and vampire TV shows,
　　I would like to propose, today, a timely addition:
　　A Christmas Carol, by Charles Dickens,
　　which, so far as I can surmise, is the first story about time travel.

We all know the broad strokes—
　　Scrooge, the greedy businessman,
　　is visited by the Ghosts of Christmas Past, Present, and Future,
　　who whisk him forward and backward and sideways in time
　　so he can witness the emotional toll wrought by his bah-humbuggery.

Seeing through time, for Scrooge, is a means of finding redemption.
　　The fact that his soul is saved is all well and good,
　　but one must wonder . . . What about Jacob Marley?
　　His business partner, exiled unto death 7 years earlier,
　　is damned to eternal misery in his life as a ghost,
　　dragging his chains, plagued with unwavering guilt.

But Marley has already seen the error of his ways.
    He is the one who exhorts Scrooge, from the beginning,
    with the wisdom he needs to hear.
    He gets the book's first line (*Marley was dead, to begin with*).
    He is instrumental in bringing about the epiphany of our protagonist,
    who embarks on a holiday of transtemporal self-improvement,
    and then, in the book's final chapter, runs joyfully through London,
    kissing children and loudly proclaiming his salvation.
    But we are left to believe that Marley remains a miserable ghost for-
ever,
    simply because his own transformation did not come soon enough.

Surely if this time-bending story can conjure up a way to save Scrooge,
    then there ought to be some hope of redemption for Jacob.
    But there is none.
    "Weary journeys lie ahead of me," he declares before making his exit,
    burdened by heavy chains, and a heavier heart.
    By the end, Scrooge (and Dickens) have forgotten Marley entirely.
    But I hold out hope he will find forgiveness for the wrongs he
wrought in life
    and he will one day be unburdened of his chains.

EMAIL

From: Ben Boyce
To: Kevin Martindale

Thank you this is good work. It's proof that he's alive. But
it might not be enough to make a difference in court. Dig
in and see if you can find more concrete evidence that he's
the one writing this, ideally where he is and wtf he's up to.

REPLY

You got it, Boss Man.

EMAIL

From: Ben Boyce
To: Evelyn Andrada

Evelyn, I'm honestly sorry for bothering you on the holiday, I know I've asked a lot of you lately. All of this has just been consuming my mind.

I know I told you I didn't want to hear about the attacks, etc. but that was a mistake. I'm wondering now if there's more info I should know, especially anything about the group behind them, any leader, anything you can find. I really do care and would like to see any information you have on this.

REPLY

Ben,

It's no problem. I hate Christmas.

I'm happy to share all the information I have about COTA (Citizens Opposing the Technological Apocalypse). But there's not much to be found, most likely owing to the effective takedown of huge swaths of the Internet. There are various rumors, ranging from false-flag conspiracy stuff, to radical Muslim terrorists (there's nothing to support that), to some fringe Luddite faction, but no conclusive proof.

What there is, however, is a short statement online. People are calling it a "mini manifesto" and since there's very little Internet activity, nobody has yet turned that into #Minifesto. It's signed to an obvious pseudonym, and people think it supports the idea it's an anti-tech radical ("going dark" seems to be the implication). Here it is if you're interested—

Quoted Text:

((Technology has enslaved us long enough.

The time has come to cast off our chains.

We have all become Death, destroyers of worlds.

The time has come to stop.

We have all become self-deluded lackeys of Big Tech.

The time has come to take control of our own destiny.

We demand responsible limits on information technology.

We demand citizen oversight of new innovation.

We demand a comprehensive ban on transtemporal data transmission.

Disruptions will continue, and escalate,

until worldwide change is enacted to our satisfaction.

You have been warned.

The Future is over.

—Dr. Dark))

REPLY

Thank you, Evelyn. People may be puzzled by who wrote that in the future, but it is quite clear to me now.

EMAIL—DECEMBER 25, 2021

From: Ben Boyce
To: (undisclosed recipients)

Hi Everyone,

First off, Merry Christmas! I know that the holiday season is a difficult one for all of us this year, as our company is facing serious challenges right now. Legal, logistical, and existential.

My own co-founder, it seems, has turned on us. There have been unfounded insinuations that I am responsible for his disappearance, but those allegations are utterly FALSE, and will be PROVED false soon enough. As you will all learn, he is alive and well, and he will continue to OPPOSE the technology we are creating.

It saddens me that he is joining the side of fear, the side of people who want to STOP this revolution. But we are not about to BACK DOWN. We are in this for the LONG HAUL. We are gonna FIGHT!

I am so proud of the people and the work I see around here. I know many of you skipped out on larger salaries at bigger firms in favor of stock options here . . . and I PROMISE YOU, those stock options will (one day soon) make you RICH, as long as you stick around.

We are moving ahead with all of our launch targets. The 1.0 will be ON SALE in ONE WEEK. The Future is OURS!

Sincerely,

Ben Boyce
CEO and Chief Visionary
The Future

That is the end.
At least, that is the last data I was around to gather, before I left. But please, keep reading . . .

CONCLUSION

B—

Merry Christmas.

My gift to you is this manuscript,

and with it, a possibility for change.

I have gathered these documents and brought them back to you.

Back in time.

I know how this all sounds, but please, keep going.

You are reading this, I expect, on December 25, 2020,

but I wrote it on Christmas 2021,

and I've traveled back to deliver it one year in the past.

As you read this, there are two versions of me in your timeframe—

the time-hopping me that wrote these words,

and another "me" that is one year younger, blissfully unaware of any of
this.

You are going to wish that version of me a Merry Christmas later today,

but first, you need to hear what I (this version of "I") have to say.

You are probably wondering:

Has Adhi finally lost his mind?

Is this an elaborate hoax, or a product of his latest episode?

I assure you, it is not.

The documents in this manuscript are all real.

They were obtained from a variety of sources, mostly online,

and from the servers of The Future (the company you and I are going to
start in the year to come).

Some of these documents are from further in the past.

You have seen some of them before, or even heard them aloud (the toast from your wedding).

Others, no doubt, are thoroughly baffling to you—

coming not only from the year to come, but from the future beyond that.

I have edited these together in an attempt to give a fair portrait,

not only of what this technology does to the world,

but of how it changes people.

How it changed *us*.

I am delivering this manuscript to you after carrying it back in time,

knowing full well it will be met with healthy skepticism.

I invite you to verify its authenticity any way that you can,

and if you are ready to entertain the possibility that all of this is real . . .

or rather, that it all *will* be real, in the timeline I've come from . . .

then I will explain how it has come to be.

Later today, you are going to text to wish me a merry Christmas.

You are frustrated at work and looking for a way out.

You will ask me about the dissertation I wrote in grad school,

and you will ask me to send it to you to read.

When you do, you'll get excited,

and when you get excited, anything is possible.

So you and I will quickly build a billion-dollar company,

and together we will create a technology that will change the world.

Possibly that will destroy the world.

Certainly that will destroy our friendship.

So I've collated this selection of documents

and brought them to you at great personal risk,

at the expense of never being able to return to my own time—

in order to try to change the future.

First, let me make sense of how.

Having read this far, hopefully you understand the difference between

1.0 technology (information sent back through time)

and 2.0 technology (an individual physically traveling back in time).

1.0 Technology can *see* the future, but that future is unalterable.

2.0 technology is a way to change the past by introducing new matter, new consciousness, and new agency into an earlier point in the time-line.

History can be altered.

That's what I'm here to do.

I was, at one point, genuinely convinced that 2.0 was impossible because it would require nearly infinite energy density.

Turns out, it is quite possible.

All it takes is a Large Hadron Collider.

After you and I met with the DoD in November 2021

(I'm using past tense, because it is past for me, though future for you)

I was invited to a separate meeting at DARPA.

They had been working on 2.0 for years, but failing,

because they had never achieved 1.0.

I worked with their team for a week and helped fill in the gaps.

We succeeded.

We built a working device that could send an individual back in time.

Of course, anyone who went would never be able to return.

It was very possible the device would instantly kill the first person who attempted to use it.

A volunteer was needed, to be the Neil Armstrong of time travel.

I raised my hand.

I had good reasons, and nothing to lose.

I traveled back in time by just three months, to August 2021.

I told the DARPA team that would be a good baseline to verify that the technology worked—

so that in the new, earlier timeframe I could approach them and inform them of our success.

In fact, I had no intention of approaching them.

I was conducting my own inquiry, to see if a 2.0 intervention could actually alter the timeline.

I chose August as my destination, because that was when the Beta Test was under way.

I used this as a control, knowing we had already utilized our Prototype to obtain data on how the Beta Test had gone.

I sought to change that data by stealing one of the Beta Units.

Yes, I was the one who stole the Beta Unit,

while you, and the other me, were both wholly unaware.

I'm sorry for the headache that my burglary caused.

This theft was the reason for the Discrepancies you experienced.

Your present was physically disrupted,

so the "future" our Prototype foretold began to change,

and I proved that altering the timeline was possible.

I had hoped changing the timeline in this way might avert some of the negative consequences I had foreseen.

That we might avoid widespread financial collapse, international conflict,

and a Luddite terrorist backlash.

Instead, I only seemed to make them worse.

Perhaps because a challenge, when presented to you, only steels your determination.

At that point (November 2021) I had gone back in time three months,

and re-lived those three months,

and my attempts to improve the future had failed.

I figured that in order to make an impact, I needed an ally.

So I introduced myself to the other me—

the Adhi you knew (will know) in November 2021.

I explained where I'd come from to the other Adhi,

and he was, understandably, rather freaked out.

But he was also excited.

I have always wanted to change the world,

so of course, the other me was thrilled that he finally had a chance.

Together, we decided to undermine The Future.

We needed to create a problem for the company—a problem for *you*—

so we devised a plan to fake the other Adhi's death

in such a way that you would be under suspicion for it.

Not enough that you would actually be jailed

(the plan was for Adhi to publicly reappear long before then)

but enough for the ensuing scandal to disrupt the company's prospects.

We thought that if you were under active investigation for homicide,

you would not be able to launch the product.

When you and I were summoned to D.C.

the other Adhi remained in Palo Alto,

while I (yes, the time-traveling me) went to the DoD meeting with you.
You were unable to tell the difference.
To be fair, I was only a few months older than the other me,
and the stress of this whole endeavor had prematurely aged us both.
When you returned to the Valley and met with "me" at the Dish,
that was the other Adhi, the one from your timeframe,
and while you were talking with that other me,
I was at the office, procuring the documents that I have compiled here.
Alas, the plot to frame you for murder, once again, only seemed to make
things worse.
You decided to go ahead with the launch of the product
and the future our device foretold grew even darker than before.
At that moment (Christmas Eve of the year to come)
it became apparent that nothing I did in that timeframe would stop you,
or foundationally alter the future.
I realized that if I wanted to make a real difference,
I needed to go further back.
I needed to stop The Future from ever being formed,
and stop the Prototype from being built in the first place.
As soon as you announced your intention to go ahead with the product
launch,
I printed the documents I had collated from the company's servers
and on Christmas 2021, I traveled to the DARPA lab in D.C.
Breaking in was easy, since I'd had access to the research facility before,
and even if I tripped an alarm, I had no need to escape.
I would be going in but not coming out.
I used the Prototype to travel back—
but this time, I went further.
A year, in fact.
Back to . . . today. December 25, 2020.
The day when you first reached out to me about my research paper.
The day when The Future was born.
In the hope that I can dissuade you.
In the hope I can convince you to let that go.
Of course, you probably want to say to me:

Why not go talk to yourself?

Why not go talk to the other Adhi, the one native to this timeline?

But that is exactly what I did before, when I traveled back to August 2021,

and I am not proud of how I behaved.

Or rather, how two of me behaved together.

I am not proud of the fact that I tried to get Leila to run away with me,

and I am not particularly proud of the plan to frame you for my murder.

I have come, at long last, to know myself.

I know that I am plagued by the deep belief that I am fundamentally alone—

that I need to fix everything myself,

regardless of right and wrong and who gets hurt.

I will always choose knowledge and information,

and on some deep, unalterable level, in defiance of evidence to the contrary,

I will always believe that *knowing* will make things better.

I will always leap to the conviction that this time around, I can control it.

Which is why I know that if the other me were given this manuscript,

he would thrill with the excitement of discovery.

He would convince himself that he could do it all differently.

He would probably even convince *me* to join him,

to once again believe, *it will be different this time.*

I have learned that I cannot help myself.

If given the chance, I will always open Pandora's box.

So I am trying to do something different

by leaving the decision to someone else.

My Captain. My Kirk.

I am reaching out, hoping that with you, it can be different.

Hoping you will not choose knowledge. Or success. Or control.

But rather . . . friendship.

You see, you are the only real friend I've ever had.

When you wrote to the Student Disciplinary Committee,

there was nothing to be gained by that except for helping me.

When you emailed to put me forward for the job at Google

(which I only learned about while preparing this manuscript)

and when you tricked Paolo in order to keep me on the Board

(which you, reading this, haven't even done yet)—

all of those incidents are evidence

that I am not, as I have feared, alone.

Of course, at darker moments, my mind rebels,

and tries to convince me that even those kindnesses were a clever fiction;

every one of them, certainly, helped you in some way too.

But I have to believe that all of it was real,

and our friendship was rooted in kindness and truth,

because, if not, the world might as well be damned.

In light of what you have read here,

I think it is undeniable that this technology is a problem.

For you. For me.

For Leila and your marriage.

For the world as a whole.

It is a technology that increases information, but diminishes choice—

and the results for everyone are catastrophic.

I have proved to my own satisfaction that the impossible is possible—

that the past *can* be altered—

and in the process, the future can be changed.

The question that remains is:

Can *we* change?

I couldn't.

But nonetheless I'm asking . . .

Can you?

So now, when I cannot do what is best for myself . . .

I hope you will do what is best for us both.

I hope that you will text me—the other me—later today . . .

and just tell him Merry Christmas.

I hope you'll invite him to meet up at The Dish.

For beers.

For stars.

Because this time around, it's up to you.

The Future is yours.

> Sincerely and eternally your friend,
> —A from the future

ACKNOWLEDGMENTS

Writing a book is far from a solitary endeavor. It is inspired by others before the writing even starts, and is nurtured into existence by the enthusiasm, feedback, and support of a whole community. I feel immensely fortunate to have found myself amid a network of brilliant individuals, who all played a role in translating a lark of an idea into the novel you just read.

First off, many thanks to my agent, Zoe Sandler, whose faith and work has helped me realize my childhood dream of becoming a novelist.

Thanks also to my fantastic editor, Sarah Peed, for her excellent work on the manuscript, and for loving Ben and Adhi nearly as much as I did. And to the rest of the Del Rey team, for getting this out into the world in its absolute best form.

To my family for their eternal support, especially my dad, who taught me to dream about the future.

To my brilliant and creative friends, who became my first readers and encouraging givers of feedback, especially Kevin Oeser, Sarah Schuessler, John Carey, Aqsa Altaf, Ariel Heller, Dave Crabtree, Nicole Wachell, Andrew Gori, and the members of my unfortunately named writers' group, Deez Notes.

I would also like to thank numerous people for their assistance with research into the culture of Silicon Valley, including Jason Rugolo, Ashley Grabill, Nick Dazé, and Hunter Rosenblume, among others.

Thanks also to those who believed in the book, including Ryan Casey for passing it along, and producer power-couple Sev Ohanian and Natalie Qasabian, who provided smart creative feedback. And to filmmaker Aneesh Chaganty, who cared enough about Adhi, and about representation, that he made the story better and helped me evolve as a writer in the process.

Finally, infinite thanks to my wife, Casey, who gently suggested that this story might best be told as a novel instead of a weird online experiment, and whose belief in me made it all possible.

ABOUT THE AUTHOR

Dan Frey is a professional screenwriter and the author of *The Retreat*. He lives in Los Angeles.

ABOUT THE TYPE

This book was set in Sabon, a typeface designed by the well-known German typographer Jan Tschichold (1902–74). Sabon's design is based upon the original letter forms of sixteenth-century French type designer Claude Garamond and was created specifically to be used for three sources: foundry type for hand composition, Linotype, and Monotype. Tschichold named his typeface for the famous Frankfurt typefounder Jacques Sabon (c. 1520–80).